Alys Clare lives in Tonbridge. *The Chatter of the Maidens* is the fourth in a series of medieval mysteries set in and around the Weald of Kent.

THE CHATTER OF THE MAIDENS

The serenity of Hawkenlye Abbey has been disturbed by the arrival of a new nun and her two young sisters. Recently orphaned, Alba has had to leave her convent at Ely to take her grieving sisters far away from their sorrow. However, Abbess Helewise cannot reconcile this selfless gesture with Sister Alba's mean-spirited and turbulent presence. The Abbess's anxieties grow when her old friend Josse d'Acquin is brought to Hawkenlye, half dead from blood poisoning. Then a body is discovered. And one of the sisters goes missing. In order to discover what really lies behind Alba's flight to Hawkenlye, Helewise sets off to visit the Fens . . .

ALYS CLARE

THE CHATTER OF THE MAIDENS

Complete and Unabridged

ULVERSCROFT
Leicester

First published in Great Britain in 2001 by
Hodder and Stoughton, London

First Large Print Edition
published 2003
by arrangement with
Hodder and Stoughton
a division of Hodder Headline, London

The moral right of the author has been asserted

British Library CIP DataClare,

Clare, Alys
The chatter of the maidens.—Large print ed.—
Ulverscroft large print series: mystery
1. d'Acquin, Josse (Fictitious character)—Fiction
2. Helewise, Abbess (Fictitious character)—Fiction
3. England—Social life and customs—*1066–1485*—
Fiction 4. Detective and mystery stories
5. Large type books
I. Title
823.9′14 [F]

ISBN 0–7089–4934–7

Published by
F. A. Thorpe (Publishing)
Anstey, Leicestershire

Set by Words & Graphics Ltd.
Anstey, Leicestershire
Printed and bound in Great Britain by
T. J. International Ltd., Padstow, Cornwall

This book is printed on acid-free paper

for my parents,
with my heartfelt thanks for all their love
and support.

Dies nox et omnia
mihi sunt contraria,
Virginium colloquia
me fay planszer,
oy suvenz suspirer.

(By day, by night,
All conspire against me,
And the chatter of the maidens
Draws forth my tears
And my frequent sighs.)

Carmina Burana:
cantiones profanae
(Author's translation)

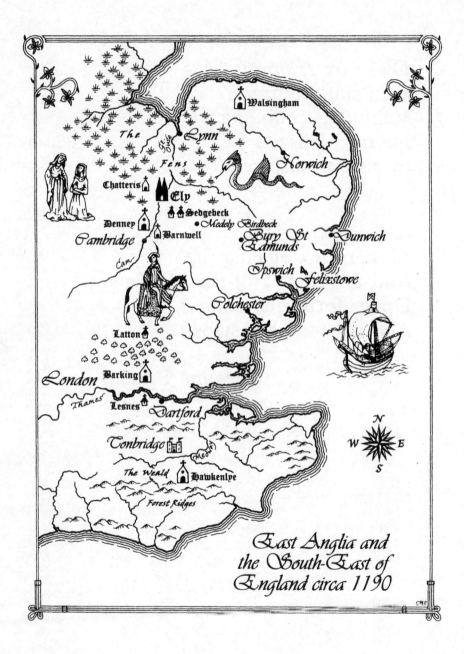

Walsingham

The Fens

Lynn

Norwich

Chatteris

Ely

Sedgebeck

Denney

Medely Birdbeck

Barnwell

Cambridge

Bury St Edmunds

Dunwich

Ipswich

Felixstowe

Colchester

Latton

Barking

London

Thames

Lesnes

Dartford

Tonbridge

Medway

The Weald

Hawkenlye

Forest Ridges

N
W E
S

East Anglia and the South-East of England circa 1190

The fire took hold quickly.

At first, no more than a few whispers of pale smoke issued out of the isolated cottage. Lifted up on the slight breeze, the smoke broke into several tiny plumes, one of which was carried off across the steeply sloping field behind the dwelling. An old horse stood there, half asleep, eyelids drooping. He was disturbed by the smell of smoke, which penetrated even his comatose state; roused to action by the first stirrings of alarm, he shambled off up the slope, only stopping when he reached his favourite shady spot beneath the giant oak tree.

In the small time it had taken for the horse to move away to his place of safety, the fire had grown.

Grown at an alarming rate, as the tiny sparks of flame took hold of the dry material all around, licking along the pieces of straw and brittle hay, eating into the piles of tinder-dry leaves and the handfuls of soft thistledown. Then, the fire's appetite, no longer satisfied by such small offerings, leapt faster than the blink of an eye to the neatly chopped pieces of small kindling.

After that, there was no turning back. Putting out the blaze, even had there been anybody around who wanted or was able to do so, was rapidly becoming an impossible task. The fire had overrun the hearth; what now roared and whooped within the lonely dwelling was like some terribly altered, monstrous form of the quiet, docile domestic fire that usually burned there.

For these giant flames had not been kindled to heat food in a pot or water in a pan. They had been brought into existence for a very different and far darker purpose.

Outside, in the thicket of undergrowth surrounding the little cottage, something moved. A strand of bramble was pushed gently aside, and a stealthy footfall came down gingerly on a stand of nettles. A saw-edged leaf stroked against the back of a hand, and there was a softly muttered oath as the stung flesh was whipped away from the nettle's sharp attack.

The unseen watcher inched forward. Neck craned in the effort to see into the burning cottage without emerging from the hiding-place, the figure soon forgot the small pain of the stung hand as the full power of the fire became evident.

Tension seemed to grip the heavily cloaked figure.

Then, suddenly, there came the sound of a distinct sniff.

Then another. And, as the fleeting hint of the smell of roasting meat grew until it was all but overpowering, the unseen watcher gave a short, unpleasant laugh.

But this was no gleeful expectation of a good dinner. It was not beef, or lamb, or pork that crackled and spat in the roaring flames.

It was human flesh.

The figure had now emerged from hiding, as if well aware that there was no longer any possibility that anybody could be witness to its movements. Creeping slowly forward, one arm raised to protect the face from the fierce heat, the head once more strained to see.

The watcher moved nearer and nearer to the entrance to the cottage. Progress was jerky, as though the desire to see was fighting with the urgent message to flee away from the heat and the pain. The urge to see appeared to be winning: pulling the hood of the cloak right over face and head, leaving the smallest gap for the eyes, the figure inched right up to the gaping hole where the cottage's wooden door had once stood.

For a brief instant, the figure leaned forward and stared into the blazing interior.

Then, relief evident in the sudden lowering of the shoulders as the built-up tension dissipated, the figure turned and walked swiftly away.

★ ★ ★

The fire took a long time to die down.

The flames consumed everything that was combustible within the cottage, and gradually their intensity diminished. As the sun set and evening came on, the brilliant fire faded to a reddish-orange glow. From time to time, another small part of the wooden beams which had once held up the roof would fall into the fire's remains, causing a brief flare-up. And, as the darkness outside grew deeper, a chilly wind blew up, which, for a while, fanned the flames into an echo of their former ferocity.

On the floor of the cottage lay a body. Clad when it had been placed there, now scarcely a trace of any cloth garment remained. The leather boots, too, were ruined, and a heavy buckle, which had once fastened a belt, was now blackened, the belt burned through in places.

The victim lay across what had once been the central hearth. It seemed not to have made any attempt to get away from the fire;

4

helpless to prevent the terrible onslaught of the flames, unable to escape from the conflagration, what had once been human and alive was now blackened and contorted, hair and garments flared to mere remnants, flesh burned from the bones.

As the heat had begun to destroy the corpse, the muscles had stiffened and contracted. And, in a dreadful parody of someone raising their fists to defend themself — as if fists were any use against fire — the body's arms were bent at the elbow and held up in front of the remains of the face.

With a little sigh, a heap of ash and charred wood close to the heart of the dying fire suddenly collapsed in on itself. Even that sound seemed loud, for the night was advanced now and, outside, all was still and silent. Within the burned corpse, however, something continued its work; the fire's energy was still smouldering on, continuing to eat away at bone, fat and marrow.

By first light, there was little left to show of the fire's victim. Most of the bones of the skeleton had detached from each other; all that remained that was instantly recognisable as human was the arch formed by a part of the rib cage.

And the bare, smoke-darkened skull, its empty eye sockets black and staring.

Next to the ribs, something else stuck up out of the floor of the cottage. It was a spike, made of iron, and the end protruding out of the floor had been wrought into a hoop. It had once been hammered into a wall as a tethering-ring for horses.

In the depths of the crevice where the end of the hoop joined the upright section, a fragment of material had escaped the flames. It was tiny, and looked at a glance like the frayed end of a piece of twine.

It was not material. Nor was it twine. It was all that was left of the rope that had bound the victim securely to the spot where he was to die and be cremated.

Part One

Newcomer

1

Josse d'Acquin lay sweating and groaning, wracked with pain and delirious with fever.

His body might have been safe in his bed at New Winnowlands, snug under covers that had been clean when he lay down even if they were now soaked in his sweat, but his mind was not recognising the fact. As far as his brain was aware, he was attempting to climb a harsh rock face, a heavy weight on his bare back and his arm extended below him as he tried to support the weight of a large pig.

The pig, for some reason known only to itself, was periodically lunging upwards, swinging level with Josse and burying its yellow fangs into the hot skin of Josse's upper right arm.

Josse cried out, writhing in the damp bed linen, his aching legs tangling in the twisted sheet. The pig attacked again, fastening its teeth into Josse's arm and letting go with its trotters so that its full and not inconsiderable weight hung entirely from Josse's agonised flesh.

The pig looked at Josse and winked a surprisingly blue eye, and suddenly it began to rain, cold, delicious drops of water that splashed down abundantly, dislodging the grinning pig and bringing blessed, cooling relief for the pain . . .

And Josse's maidservant, Ella, with the air of one talking to herself, said quietly, 'There, there, Master, just you rest easy, now, give that wound a chance to mend' — she bent down to wring out the cloth in the icy water, then replaced it on Josse's arm — ' . . . and, presently, I'll bring you summat to drink and see if you're up to me spooning you some broth.'

Awake and sensible now — or so he thought — Josse watched as the pig trotted away to the far corner of the bedchamber, where it circled a few times like a dog settling in its kennel, then lay down and began to whistle.

'Ella, there's a pig in the corner,' Josse said. Funny, though, his words didn't seem to have come out right. It sounded as if he had been groaning. He tried again. '*Pig*, Ella!' he repeated.

Startled at hearing him speak, she looked up, flashed him a brief, shy smile, then swiftly returned to her wringing and bathing; she was a chronically self-conscious, unconfident woman, and Josse sometimes reflected that he could probably count the number of words she had ever addressed him of her own volition on the fingers of his two hands.

He tried again. Struggling to sit up — which proved unwise as it made his head swim so violently that he thought he would be sick — he waved his uninjured arm in the general direction of the pig. Following his pointing finger with his eyes, he began to say, 'The pig, Ella . . . '

Only to find that it had disappeared.

Ella gently took hold of his left arm and laid it back on the bed, pulling up the covers and arranging them around his chest. He wished she wouldn't, he was far too hot anyway, without being tucked up like a sickly child.

'I'll be back directly,' she assured him in a voice hardly above a whisper, then picked up her cloth and bowl and backed away from the bed and towards the door as if he were royalty.

Josse lay and listened to her heavy tread as she hurried down the narrow stair that led down to the hall. He heard her shout out to Will to inform him that he wasn't to let on to the Master — silly woman, did she imagine that having a sore arm meant Josse had gone deaf, too? — but she was that worried, she feared Sir Josse was nigh on ready to expire of the fever . . .

'Fever,' he murmured aloud. 'Fever.'

It was actually quite a relief to know that he had a severe fever. Fevers brought delirium, didn't they? And sweats, and dizziness that made you want to throw up, and weird dreams, and visions of imaginary pigs in the bedchamber.

Fever. *That* was all right, then.

For a short and rather dreadful time, Josse had been afraid he was going mad.

$$\star \quad \star \quad \star$$

When he next woke, he judged it to be a little before dawn; there was a pearly quality to the darkness, which, if it couldn't exactly be called light, seemed to suggest that the coming of the day wasn't far off.

Josse lay and thought about dawns he had witnessed. But it demanded too much concentration in his weakened state; instead, he let his mind drift.

He realised that he felt different; the world had lost that strange, unreal quality that it had had for the past . . . the past how long? Was it days, or was it weeks? For the life of him, Josse couldn't decide.

I hurt my arm, he recalled. It had been hurt before — I was cut with a sword — and then it got better. I was treated, very expertly . . .

Thinking about that brought a pain of another sort. A pain in his heart, in his memory. He abandoned those particular recollections.

The wound had been mending well, he thought instead. Or so I believed. I went out riding — did I? Is that right? Aye. Riding. With . . . He frowned, trying to remember his friend's name. Man with a wolfhound, wanted me to ride out with him, see the beast go through its paces . . . And I took that ditch, down at the bottom of my own orchard, and old Horace spooked at something and very nearly threw me, except that I managed to hold on. But the jolting and wrenching tore into that cut of mine. And something must have happened to it, some foul air must have got at the open wound, because it went bad.

As full recollection returned — it was to prove only temporary — Josse remembered that the friend with the wolfhound was his neighbour, Brice, and that the pain in his infected cut had been so terrible, so unrelenting, that he had begged Will to lop the arm off and be done with it.

Remembering how bad the agony had been was not a good thing at all, Josse was quickly realising. Whatever reason there had been for the pain's having abated somewhat now no

13

longer applied; with the speed of an incoming tide on a flat shore, it came racing back.

And, as if that were not enough, accompanying it was a sudden heat in his blood that felt like being on fire.

Trying to call out whilst gritting his teeth, Josse yelled for Will. Or Ella. Or anyone . . .

★ ★ ★

Brice of Rotherbridge, who owned the manor adjoining Winnowlands, had felt quite strongly about being roused from his bed before it was entirely light. Stomping down the hall to enquire of his man the reason for the summons, he had been informed that Josse d'Acquin's Will was outside, at his wits' end over his master's sickness, not knowing where to turn or what to do, and . . .

Brice had waited to hear no more. Flinging on his cloak, forcing his feet into his boots, he had been mounted on his horse, out of his own courtyard and riding into Josse's in a shorter time than he would have thought possible.

Creeping into Josse's bedchamber — it soon became apparent that there was no need for stealth, because Josse was not only awake but crying out with pain — Brice was horrified at the state of his friend.

He leaned over the bed — it smelt of sweat and sickness — and put a hand on Josse's forehead. 'He's burning up!' he cried, turning to look at Will, then at Ella. 'How long has he been like this?'

Ella, sensing an accusation, buried her face in her apron and would not reply, but Will stood his ground. Squaring his shoulders, he said, 'It were that day you went hunting together, sir. The Master nearly took a fall, and it tore open that cut in his arm, and — '

'Yes, yes, yes, I *know* that, I was there!' Brice interrupted. 'I meant how long has he had this fever?' Anger rising suddenly, he shouted, 'Don't you understand about fevers, either of you? Your master may be *dying*, and there you stand, useless as a pair of gargoyles and marginally more ugly!'

At this, Ella burst into tears and ran from the room. With one anxious glance after her, Will turned back to face Brice and said, 'There's no call for that, Sir Brice. Ella, she's been wearing herself to a shadow, caring for Master, day, night, all the time. And it's a'cause we don't know what we should rightly do that I came to ask you.' He was glaring back at Brice as ferociously as Brice was glaring at him; it was as a very obvious afterthought that he added, 'Sir.'

Brice's anger had gone as quickly as it had

come. A hand on Will's shoulder, he said, 'I am sorry, Will. Please attribute my rudeness to anxiety. Apologise to Ella for me, too, please.' Will gave a brief nod of acknowledgement. 'Now,' — Brice turned back to Josse — 'what are we to do?'

Close beside him, Will whispered, 'We've sent for the priest, an' all.'

'Father Anselm? Great glory, Will, do you expect your master to *die*?'

'Ssshhh!' Will hissed, although Josse seemed to be too far lost in his own world of pain to hear. 'No, Sir Brice, indeed I do not, leastways, not if there's anything me and Ella can do to prevent it. No, truth is, I do hear tell that the priest has some knowledge of healing, well, more'n me and Ella have.'

Brice was frowning. 'Likely the good Father will hurry your master's passage into the next world rather than heal him,' he muttered. 'He's a blood letter, Will. Believes a good bleeding is the cure for everything from an overheated imagination to a dose of the pox.'

'I'm sorry, sir, I only thought — ' Will began.

Again, Brice dropped a reassuring touch on Will's shoulder. 'You did what you thought best, Will, and no man can be asked to do more. No, I know what we must do for our Sir Josse here.' He smiled briefly as the solution came to him. 'Will, have you a cart long enough to let a tall man lie down comfortably? And a steady horse to pull it?'

'Aye, Sir Brice, that we have.'

'Then, please, go and prepare it. Put in pillows and blankets, whatever you think, and water for drinking and for bathing the patient's burning skin.'

Puzzlement on his face, Will said, 'How far are we going, sir? To what place?'

And, as Brice told him, a smile began to light up Will's face too.

★   ★   ★

Josse, coming fleetingly out of his delirium, was surprised to see three men standing round his bed. Will he would have expected to see — Will and Ella had been unstinting in their care of him — but what was Brice doing?

And, even more unexpected, why was he receiving a call from Father Anselm?

' . . . must *insist* that I be allowed to treat him as I see fit,' the priest was saying in his precise way, thrusting a bowl of what looked horribly like leeches in Brice's face.

'Like you treated old Sir Alard's servant a few years back? Bled him till he was white as the driven snow?' Brice yelled.

'It was necessary,' Father Anselm protested, 'as indeed it is now!'

'Alard's man wouldn't agree with you,' Brice shouted back, 'even if he could, from beyond the grave!' As Josse watched, he gave a nod to Will and, approaching Josse's left as Will went round to his right, added to the priest, 'However, if you really do want to be of assistance, you can help us carry him downstairs to that cart out in the courtyard, and . . .'

But just then, as Will and Brice began to lift him, Josse's attention was distracted. Because, gentle as his manservant and his friend undoubtedly were, the least movement was excruciating for Josse.

And being lifted, manoeuvred out of bed, across the room, down the stairs and out to the waiting cart involved rather a lot more than the least movement.

As they edged their way round the bend in the stairs, Josse passed out.

★ ★ ★

He came round to find himself looking up into a clear, spring sky, with the sun warm on his face and a skylark singing its heart out somewhere nearby.

He was in a cart and, beside him, Will was

dozing, eyes closed, arms folded across his broad chest. Between Will's knees stood a pail of water; aware all at once of how desperately thirsty he was, Josse tried to call out.

By the time Will woke up and heard, Josse's desperation had grown so much that, humiliatingly, he felt like weeping; Will, tutting at his own carelessness and referring to himself by names not heard in polite society, gave him cup after cup of cool water, sponging his face and neck for good measure.

When Josse had been settled back down again, thirst slaked, it occurred to him to wonder where they were headed.

'Will?'

Instantly Will stiffened to attention. 'Master?'

'Will, where are we going?'

A beaming smile lit Will's face. 'Why, Master, we're going to the nuns. It were Sir Brice suggested it, and for the life of me I can't think why me and Ella didn't come up with it ourselves.'

'The nuns,' Josse repeated, thinking happily of shady cloisters, capable, attentive hands, clean, crisp linen and herby-smelling medicaments. 'The nuns of Hawkenlye Abbey.'

'Aye,' Will said, nodding for emphasis. 'That infirmarer sister, what's her name — ?'

'Sister Euphemia,' Josse supplied.

'Aye, her,' Will agreed. 'We're off to see her, sir.' And, with a firm confidence which Josse entirely shared, Will added, '*She'll* put you right in no time.'

2

Helewise, Abbess of Hawkenlye, knelt in the Abbey church, concentrating fiercely on her prayers.

She was praying humbly for the charity to feel love for each and every one of her sisters, even — especially — the least lovable. She was also beseeching God for at least a few days of fine weather, which would stop Sister Tiphaine's constant lament about her non-thriving herb plants. Beneath those two specific requests was an ongoing plea for either an extra pair of hands for herself — which would actually be a rare miracle — or, more realistically, for God's help in making her better at delegation.

It was April, and, so far, the year — 1192 — had been a hectic one for the Abbess of Hawkenlye. In February, there had been that disturbing business with the runaway, Joanna de Courtenay; the excitement of those weeks was still quite a talking point among the nuns at recreation. Then there was the worry over the King, still absent on crusade in the Holy Land. It was all very devout and laudable, Helewise reflected, for a king to do his duty before God with such wholehearted enthusiasm.

But what of King Richard's duty to his realm?

Her mind wandering away from her prayers, Helewise thought of the last time that King Richard's mother, Queen Eleanor, had paid a visit to Hawkenlye. As ever, the lady had been in a hurry, and — also as ever — Helewise and her nuns had tried to make the two brief days, all that Queen Eleanor had been able to spare, as restful and as tranquil as possible.

'Abbess, you and your nuns spoil me,' Eleanor had told Helewise on the first evening when, after a splendid supper brought up to a specially-prepared cell of the guest accommodation, Helewise had tapped on the door and brought in a warmed stone wrapped in cloth for the Queen's cold feet, and a jug of hot, spiced wine to help her sleep.

'It is our great pleasure to be able to do so,' Helewise had assured her.

The wine had made both women relax. As she often did, Eleanor had confided some of her anxieties to Helewise. And, almost as much a joy to Helewise, the Queen had invited Helewise to share some of her own troubles.

The Queen had perceived — to Helewise's mixed relief and regret — that the Abbess was gravely overworked. She had also perceived that it was not in Helewise's nature to ask for help, and she had not exactly offered any.

What she had said was that Helewise must herself effect some changes in the administrative arrangements for the Abbey.

'It is merely a matter of accustoming oneself to a new way of looking at the matter,' she had said firmly. 'You, Helewise, see yourself as the hub of the wheel. Everything that happens in the Abbey is your responsibility and relates to you. Yes?'

'I — well, yes. But that is what my appointment as Abbess means, surely?'

'Naturally. However, imagine, if you will, not a spoked wheel but a triangle, sitting on its base with its point at the top. Are you imagining it?' Helewise nodded. 'Now, draw several lines across the triangle, noting how the lines are narrow at the top and broader towards the base. Yes?'

'Yes.'

'Good. Now, you are the topmost point. The top line, which is the narrowest, is for your immediate subordinates; there are only a few of them, four or five, perhaps. The next line is for *their* subordinates — more of them, do you see? — and the line below for *theirs*, and so on and so forth.'

'I see.'

'Now, according to this model,' the Queen had continued as if Helewise hadn't spoken, 'the only matters that will permeate all the way up to you are those which nobody subordinate to you has been able to deal with.' She had shot Helewise a swift assessing glance. 'Of course, the success or failure of the concept depends on your refraining from leaping in to offer your help and advice before it is asked for and where it is not necessary . . . '

Now, still on her knees before the altar, Helewise suppressed a smile. The Queen, God bless and save her, apparently saw into Helewise's heart with clear eyes. The difficulties that the Abbess was having with this business of delegation were proof of that, without a doubt.

Helewise returned her full attention to God and completed her prayers. Soon the rest of the community would enter the church; it must be almost time for Tierce. After which, Helewise promised herself, she would summon two — or even three — of those subordinates of hers and thrash out the problem of Sister Alba.

★ ★ ★

Some time later, Helewise sat at the large oak table in her room and stared across it at Sister Euphemia, Sister Basilia and Sister Edith. The three nuns were talking among themselves. In fact, Helewise decided, *talking* was not right; they were arguing.

The subject of the discussion was the new nun, Sister Alba. She was in the unusual position of being a professed nun who had left her previous convent and now sought admission at Hawkenlye. In her care were her two younger sisters, Meriel and Berthe. Meriel was sixteen, Berthe fourteen; Alba was considerably older.

To begin with, Helewise had been impressed with the strong sense of responsibility for her family that Sister Alba seemed to be demonstrating. She had, it appeared, torn herself out of a religious community somewhere in East Anglia — a community in which, according to Alba, she had been extremely content and fulfilled — because her little sisters needed her. The parents of the three sisters had recently died, within a week of each other of some violent sickness, and the two younger girls were both overwhelmed with grief and terrified that the sickness would claim them as well.

The parents had not owned the smallholding which they worked, and, according to Alba, her two sisters had been abruptly rendered homeless. She had therefore taken the difficult decision to leave the convent where she had been so happily settled, take Meriel and Berthe under her wing and remove them well away from the scene of their suffering.

She had brought them to Hawkenlye because she had heard tell of the miraculous Shrine of Our Lady down in Hawkenlye Vale, where the holy water was freely given to the sick in mind and body, and which was fast becoming a major pilgrimage site. She had said to Helewise on seeking admittance — and Helewise had detected a certain degree of calculated flattery — that 'they say you have great compassion for the distressed, the sick and the needy, Abbess. And that you never turn away those who come with pure heart and honest intention'.

Helewise had taken them in.

Alba, as a professed nun, had been accepted as a full member of the community, with the provision that she must join the novices rather than the fully vowed for the first six months, to give her a chance to adapt to Hawkenlye's ways. Meriel and Berthe, both of whom, Alba said, were intent on taking the veil as postulants just as soon as they could, were, for the time being and while their distress abated, to be found work as lay members of the community.

That, then, was Sister Alba's background.

Surely, Helewise thought, going over it yet again, there was nothing suspicious about it? Alba had acted with responsibility and sense, hadn't she? Wouldn't anyone have done much the same, in her position?

Yes, it was all very praiseworthy, all very plausible.

And yet . . .

Sister Euphemia had raised her voice to pour scorn on some comment of Sister Edith's, intruding on Helewise's quiet thoughts; the Abbess made herself cease her worrying and listen to the conversation going on before her. But, far from reassuring her, it only served to exacerbate her anxiety.

Oh, dear, she thought after a few moments. Such strong feelings! And who am I to berate them for their emotion, when I have to admit that I feel exactly the same?

She let the three women proceed with their debate, listening attentively and keeping her peace, prepared to act on any sensible suggestion which any of them might make. Queen Eleanor, she reflected briefly, would have been proud of her. After one or two uncertain glances in her direction — was it *that* unusual, Helewise wondered, for them to experience their Abbess sitting quietly and

27

just listening? — the three women appeared to accept her silence and throw themselves into their discussion.

'I had Sister Alba working for me in the infirmary for *three weeks*,' Sister Euphemia said. 'I gave her tuition — as much as I ever give a newcomer — and I made allowances for a very natural squeamishness. They all have that when first they come to me, and I can cope with fainting and vomiting when a girl is new to the blood and that.' Sister Edith gave a visible shudder. 'What I can't cope with,' Sister Euphemia went on, ignoring it, 'is a lack of kindness. A lack of compassion.'

'And Sister Alba, you find, lacks those qualities?' Sister Basilia asked.

'Aye, Sister, she does,' Sister Euphemia said firmly. 'Like I said, it's only to be expected that a girl will blanch a bit, first time she has to dress a suppurating sore, or bandage the bloody stump of an amputation, or hold the bowl while I lance an abscess. And even *I* had to go outside and be sick, back in my early nursing days, when my superior got me to clear up the bed and backside of an old man with the flux, well, it *was* a particularly bad attack, there was masses of blood in the — '

'Yes, quite, no need for you to elaborate,' Sister Edith put in swiftly.

'Humph,' Sister Euphemia grunted, glaring at Sister Edith. Then, as if recalling the point she had been making, she went on: 'See, the thing is not to let the *patient* notice you're upset by the condition of their poor suffering body. That's what I teach all my nurses, that they must learn to cope with their own reaction, that they must never, ever let it show. And *that's* where this new Sister Alba won't obey.'

'Perhaps she cannot obey!' Sister Edith protested. 'Not all of us are blessed with your gifts, Sister Euphemia. I for one do not feel that I could contain my revulsion over — well, over some of the poor unfortunates whom you tend.' Another shudder shook her slim frame, and she put a pale, long-fingered hand delicately to her mouth, as if to hold back her words. Or worse.

Sister Euphemia was scowling at her. 'You'd have to get over your delicate little ways, Sister, if you were ever ordered to do nursing work,' she said shortly.

Sister Edith looked aghast. 'Oh, but I — '

'That's hardly likely,' Sister Basilia interrupted, 'since Sister Edith is such a good teacher.' Sister Edith flashed her a grateful look. 'And now, Sister,' — she addressed Sister Edith — 'what of your experiences with Sister Alba?'

Sister Edith closed her eyes and pursed up her mouth, as if to aid concentration. Her hands lay folded in her lap; Sister Edith hardly ever adopted the custom of all the other nuns, of tucking her hands away in the opposite sleeves of her habit when they were not engaged in a manual task. They were very pretty hands, the skin pale and smooth, the shape elegant, with long fingers ending in perfect, shell-like nails. Now Sister Edith raised them and, very slowly and carefully, pressed them together and held them under the point of her small and delicate chin.

Sister Euphemia gave a faint snort.

After quite a few moments, Sister Edith — who had apparently decided to judge Sister Euphemia's snort as unladylike and therefore to be treated as if it had never happened — opened her eyes, lowered her hands and said, 'Sister Alba came to join me a week ago, and so my remarks must be treated as but a preliminary assessment. However, I must confess that she has not settled at all well with us.' Her dark brows descended in a brief frown, but the dour expression was not allowed to linger for long on her smooth, unlined face. 'She appears impatient with the girls, especially the youngest ones. Equally, she exhibits a lack of sympathy for the aims of our little school. She seems to have no understanding of the particular sufferings and needs of the orphans and foundlings in our care. And I did hear her say that — Oh, but I mustn't!'

'Sister, we are here with the purpose of discussing the difficulties which Sister Alba seems to be having in adapting to our community,' Sister Euphemia reminded her. 'This isn't a bathhouse gossip session; we need to hear anything that may be relevant.'

With a martyred expression, as if to say, very well, but it's not *my* choice to repeat this, Sister Edith said, 'I heard Sister Alba speak to one of the — you know. One of *those* girls.'

'One of the reformatory children?' Sister Basilia asked. Reformatory children was the expression used for the babies of fallen women, abandoned by their mothers at birth when the women, despite the nuns' entreaties, went back to the outside world. And their former manner of making a living.

'Yes,' Sister Edith agreed. 'Sister Alba was actually rather hurtful. Admittedly, the child was playing her up rather, but then she's only five. Anyway, she — Sister Alba — suggested that it was hardly worth her while to teach anything to the daughter of a whore — excuse me, but it was the word she used — when, in all likelihood, the girl would go

31

the same way as her mother.'

'No!' Sister Basilia exclaimed. And Sister Euphemia was looking at Sister Edith with a new, more respectful expression, as if her horror at what Sister Alba had said to an innocent child had shown her in a new and better light.

'In summary,' Sister Edith concluded, when it seemed that nobody was going to comment further, 'I have to say that I do not believe Sister Alba has any vocation for teaching.'

Sister Basilia looked worried. 'No aptitude for nursing, nor for teaching,' she said. 'And I shall only endorse what you both have said when I relate my own experiences. Sister Alba, I'm afraid to say, does not like hard work. Or, at least, not the sort of hard work we perform in the refectory and the kitchens. She volunteered to work as cellarer — she said she knew all about provisioning, and would be very careful over selecting and locking away the wine — and when I said we already had a very capable cellarer in Sister Goodeth, and, in any case, it was not an office usually filled by a newcomer, she looked most upset.'

'So what *did* she do?' Sister Euphemia asked.

Sister Basilia smiled faintly. 'I put her to

pot scrubbing. But I don't think she did very much, I think Sister Anne covered for her.'

'Kind of Sister Anne,' Sister Euphemia remarked.

'Sister Anne is a follower, not a leader,' Sister Basilia said gently. 'She tends to give in before a stronger personality, and do what she's told.'

Helewise, although listening intently, had been gazing into the distance. It was only when she refocused on the trio in front of her that she realised they were all looking at her.

'Thank you, Sisters,' she said. 'You have all done your best with Sister Alba, and I do appreciate your efforts. I will now think on what you have reported, and decide what to do next.'

There was an awkward silence, during which Helewise noticed the three other nuns glance at each other.

'Abbess, may we speak frankly?' Sister Euphemia said.

Helewise suppressed a smile. 'Of course.' You usually do, she might have added.

'We — you — ' The infirmarer cleared her throat and began again. 'Abbess, what the three of us are thinking is that it's not right, you having to be bothered with all this, not given everything else you have to do.

33

Sister Basilia here was remembering that, before, when old Sister Mary was still alive, she was Mistress of Novices, but, what with us not having floods of new nuns any more, the office has sort of been absorbed by the rest of us. Particularly you. And we were wondering, why not appoint someone, and fill the office again?'

For an instant, Helewise wondered crossly if Euphemia had been talking to Queen Eleanor. But no, that was unworthy. And, anyway, they had a point.

'Had you thought of a likely person?' she asked, trying to sound encouraging and not as if she had just had to bite down on her irritation.

Again, the three nuns glanced at one another. Then Sister Basilia said, 'We wondered about Sister Amphelisia.'

Sister Amphelisia. Sufficiently young to retain an empathy with postulants and novices, yet with enough years of convent life behind her to give her dignity and authority. At present, working with the learned and distant Sister Bernadine on maintaining and copying the Abbey's small collection of holy manuscripts. And, as Helewise well knew, not particularly happy in her work.

Sister Amphelisia as Mistress of Novices?

Why not?

Helewise composed her reply before uttering it. 'Sisters,' she said eventually, 'you have clearly given this matter careful and diligent thought, and I am grateful.' She took a deep breath, observing that it still cost her a great effort to hand over authority to another, and concluding from it that she was far too full of pride. She would have to have a long and, no doubt, painful and humiliating session with Father Gilbert, who would doubtless impose heavy penance. For the good of her soul, naturally, and for the furtherance of her growth in the religious life.

Oh, dear.

Where was she?

'I will speak to Sister Amphelisia,' she said, standing up to let the Sisters know that the meeting was over.

Sisters Euphemia, Basilia and Edith bowed, then made their way out of Helewise's room. She listened to their retreating footsteps as they set off along the cloister, waiting to see if they would make any audible comments about what had just happened.

They didn't.

Adding the sin of curiosity — very well, nosiness — to the growing list to mutter into the merciless ear of Father Gilbert, Helewise wearily straightened her back and began to think out how best to raise the matter of her appointment with the potential new Mistress of Novices.

3

The Abbess was emerging from the church in the middle of the following morning when a slight commotion from the gates alerted her to the fact that the Abbey had a visitor.

Sister Martha, who had flung down her pitchfork and gone hurrying across from the stables, was holding the head of a docile-looking horse while the porteress, Sister Ursel, was standing beside the cart which the horse was pulling. Both nuns were exclaiming loudly, and exchanging remarks with a strangely familiar-looking man sitting at the front of the cart and holding the reins.

Before Helewise had time to puzzle out who the man was, another figure leapt down from the back of the cart and, with Sister Ursel trotting along behind him trying to catch hold of his sleeve — 'That's the Abbess! You mustn't go accosting her, she's very busy!' — made his way to Helewise.

'Greetings to you, Abbess,' he said with a sketchy bow. 'Forgive my lack of ceremony, but Sir Josse lies in the cart, gravely sick with the fever, and we, that is, Sir Brice and me, we — '

But Helewise was already running towards the cart.

The man on the front — yes, of course, he was Sir Brice of Rotherbridge, Josse's neighbouring landowner — jumped down as she hurried towards him, catching her as she stumbled. 'Abbess, we need the skills of your infirmarer,' he said quietly, his face close to hers.

'What is the matter with him?' she demanded, panting, heart in her mouth. Then, realising belatedly that she was hardly behaving in a dignified and abbess-like manner, she straightened up, pulled a little away from Sir Brice and said more calmly, 'Sister Euphemia will attend to him as soon as she is able. Sir Brice, will you and — ' She glanced questioningly at the other man.

'Will,' Brice said.

'Please will you carry Sir Josse into the infirmary?' She pointed out the door. 'Sister Martha, Sister Ursel, perhaps you could help . . . ?'

She stood back and watched as, with great care, Will and Brice edged Josse's tall, sturdy body out of the cart, supporting him under each shoulder while Sister Martha, strongly-muscled herself, hurried to hold him under the hips. Sister Ursel took hold of his feet, and, moving with exaggerated care, the four of them set out towards the infirmary. Overtaking them, refusing to allow herself even a peep at Josse's face, Helewise went to alert Sister Euphemia.

The next few minutes were a trial for them all. Sister Euphemia was calm in the midst of the furore, despite having to think of three things at once; in addition to Josse, she was supervising the delivery of a badly-positioned baby and administering a pain-killing sedative to a man who was about to have his gangrenous left hand removed.

She made room for Josse at the far end of the infirmary, in an area which, although its position gave him privacy, meant that his four bearers had to carry him the length of the long ward. Despite their best efforts, between them they managed to upset a pail of water, knock over a small table containing herbal potions and crack Josse's head against the doorframe. The last accident caused their patient finally to break his silence; the howl of pain that emerged from him made Helewise's blood go cold.

With a barely perceptible gesture, Sister Euphemia had summoned two of her nurses. And as, with polite but firm insistence, they made their way past Helewise, Brice and Will, the Abbess and the two men found themselves excluded from Josse's bedside.

The infirmarer caught her eye; Sister Euphemia briefly turned down her mouth in an anxious expression. Oh, dear Lord, Helewise thought. I am very afraid that this is as serious as I feared.

Then Sister Euphemia turned back to her patient. As Sister Beata and Sister Judith began their first task — stripping the patient of his shirt and removing the bloodstained dressing on his arm — Helewise had a brief glimpse of Josse's face.

I cannot bear to see him like this, she thought.

Then, putting aside her personal feelings and assuming once more the mantle of Abbess of Hawkenlye — rarely could she recall a moment when it had been so hard — she said to Brice, 'Please, come with me. I will order something to eat for you and Will, and, if you wish it, we offer you the Abbey's hospitality while we see if he is going to — that is, until there is word of Sir Josse's condition.'

Brice and Will, she noted, looked as stunned as she felt. They seemed to be waiting for her to make the first move away from the bedside and out of the infirmary; with a brief bow to Brice, she led them off, back down the ward and out into the bright sunshine outside.

The long wait was easier for Helewise than for the two men. She was in her own environment, and she had the daily round of duties to occupy her mind, preventing it from dwelling constantly on that white-faced, agonised figure in the infirmary.

She also had the vast solace of prayer. The hour for Sext had come and gone, and it was almost time for Nones, and still there was no word from the infirmary save only, 'He lives'.

On her way to the Abbey church, Helewise caught sight of Brice and Will. They were sitting on a stone seat by the gate. Brice was tracing patterns in the ground with a stick, Will sat with folded arms staring straight in front of him.

She went over to them. They stood up as she approached and, impetuously holding out her hands to them, she said, 'Will you not come to pray with us? When we have said the Office, we shall be asking God that He look kindly on Sir Josse, and that He lessen his pain.'

'I will come, thank you, Abbess,' Brice said.

Will stood mutely, staring at the ground; Helewise thought she saw him briefly shake his head.

But later, when some small movement

caused her to turn round and look down from her position near the altar towards the entrance to the church, she noticed that Will had crept in and was kneeling by himself, just inside the great door.

Somehow, to have Josse's devoted manservant adding his pleas to those who prayed so hard for Josse seemed, to Helewise, oddly comforting.

★   ★   ★

It was at dusk that Sister Euphemia finally came to Helewise with definite news.

Helewise was in her room; as the infirmarer came in and made her reverence, Helewise wondered if she should summon Brice and Will.

As if Sister Euphemia read her mind — it quite often happened between them — she said as she straightened up, 'I'll tell you first, Abbess, if you will allow it. Then may I ask that you tell the others, Sir Brice and what's-his-name?'

'Of course,' Helewise said. Euphemia was, she realised, totally exhausted; it would be far less exacting for her to explain everything to just one person than to three. 'Please, Sister, come and sit here, in my chair.'

Sister Euphemia looked quite shocked at

42

the suggestion. 'Indeed I will not, Abbess!' She squared her shoulders. 'Thank you all the same,' she added.

'How is he?' Helewise asked quietly.

Sister Euphemia nodded. 'He will live. And, with God's help, I believe that we have saved his arm. He's strong, very strong, else he'd have been dead by now. That servant of his has been doing his best, but I suspect that he and his woman haven't any real skill. Probably knew to keep his master drinking, and to sponge that fearful wound occasionally — and I must admit, the dressing was fairly fresh and neatly applied — but I wouldn't imagine either of them knew of any specific for a violently rising fever.'

'But you do,' Helewise said, deliberately making it a statement; she could not bear there to be any doubt.

'I do,' Euphemia agreed. 'Sister Anne and Sister Judith got down to cleaning and dressing the arm, soon as you left us, and I got Sister Tiphaine to help me with the strongest medicine we could think of. Thank the good Lord, it's spring, and the plants we needed are green and potent.' She paused, frowning, as if going over in her head what she had done and wondering if she had forgotten anything. 'Anyway, seems we did right. The fever's broken and is receding.'

'God be praised,' Helewise said softly.

'Amen.' Euphemia was still frowning.

'Sister?' Helewise prompted. 'What is it?'

Sister Euphemia shook her head, as if to drive away whatever thought was bothering her. 'Nothing, leastways, nothing very relevant.' She smiled briefly at Helewise. 'Don't you fret, Abbess dear. Like I said, he isn't going to die, I'm as sure of that as I can be. I don't think the good Lord is impatient to call him home just yet awhile.'

'I was only — ' Helewise began. But she couldn't think how to continue. Anyway, was there any point in denying, to the observant and perceptive Euphemia of all people, the special place that Josse occupied in her heart?

Euphemia gave her another smile, one that brimmed with kindness and understanding. 'Me, I'm puzzling over why a man with a severe wound in his arm should take it into his head to go riding his great horse at large obstacles, that's all.' She sighed. 'Didn't we *tell* him he was lucky to keep the arm, when the wound was first inflicted? Did we really need to say, make sure you don't put it to the test until it's fully healed?' She shook her head, tutting under her breath at the ways of men.

'Apparently we did,' Helewise said. 'He's a man of action, Sister. It must have been hard for him, having to sit around like an invalid.'

The infirmarer gave her a shrewd look. 'Especially when there were things on his mind,' she said. 'Things he was brooding over. A man of action, like you say, would look on a good gallop and a few challenging ditches to jump as a good way of taking himself out of himself. Yes?'

Helewise nodded. She, too, remembered how dejected Josse had seemed, back in the early spring. Joanna de Courtenay might have worked her magic to save his arm, but there were other legacies of that brief time in February which were not so readily healed.

But it was wiser, she thought, not to speak further of things best forgotten.

'Was the whole dreadful cut infected?' she asked Sister Euphemia. 'Will healing be as long and as painful a matter as I fear it may be?'

'Indeed, no,' the infirmarer said. 'That girl knew what she was doing, and the muscles and sinews have mended well. No, like I said, only one end of the wound — where it bit the deepest — was proving stubborn. And when the silly man went off hunting, he must have wrenched the arm and disturbed the scab. He let it get dirty, and some ill humour entered his blood. The result you saw this morning. Fever burning like hellfire and a bowlful of foul pus.'

'Oh,' Helewise said weakly. Euphemia, for all her great strengths and skills, did have a tendency to forget that everyone she addressed wasn't as accustomed to the seamier side of nursing as she and her nuns were.

'Abbess, dear, you've gone quite pale!' the infirmarer was exclaiming. 'Just you stay there and I'll fetch you a restorative — '

'Thank you, Sister, but there is no need.' Helewise took a couple of deep breaths, and the light-headed feeling slowly passed. She met Sister Euphemia's worried eyes. 'May I see him?'

'If you wish to, then of course,' Sister Euphemia replied, sounding as if it were a surprise to have her superior ask permission. 'Only I must warn you, he's very deeply asleep. You don't get a mere light doze, with poppy and mandrake,' she added, half under her breath.

With a swift, silent prayer that she be able to keep her reaction and her emotions under control, Helewise accompanied Sister Euphemia over to the infirmary.

★ ★ ★

Josse lay as if dead, so deeply asleep that he did not so much as twitch.

Sister Euphemia bent down to put her

hand on to his forehead. 'Still hot, but not as bad as he was,' she said.

'The improvement continues?' Helewise whispered.

'Aye.' The infirmarer smiled briefly. 'No need to whisper, Abbess. Right now, he wouldn't hear a battle cry.'

There was a strong smell on the air. Quite pleasant, but with elements oddly at variance . . . Helewise sniffed, trying to identify it.

'We're putting poultices on his arm.' The infirmarer lifted a soft piece of cloth draped across Josse's shoulders to demonstrate. 'See, Abbess? Cabbage leaf to draw out the poison, lavender and self-heal to cleanse, crushed garlic to combat the yellow humours in the discharge.'

Lavender and garlic, Helewise thought. Not exactly an everyday combination of smells.

' . . . prefer it if we'd had lavender flowers, and a few more self-heal leaves,' the infirmarer was saying, 'but Sister Tiphaine's stock of fresh plants is still small, what with the poor weather and all, and, of course, lavender won't be in flower for a while yet.'

The two women stood looking down at Josse for some moments in silence. Then the infirmarer said, with a slight and uncharacteristic tentativeness, 'You reckon he's looking better, Abbess?'

Helewise could have kicked herself. This excellent woman, her skilled and prized infirmarer, had been working herself to a standstill all day, and Helewise hadn't given her a word of thanks or appreciation!

She turned to Sister Euphemia. 'Indeed I do, Sister. And forgive me that I did not say so without prompting.' She hesitated, wondering if to go on. Bearing in mind their relative positions in the community, she should really strive always to maintain her distance, even from the most senior of her nuns. But, on the other hand, there was nobody near to overhear. And Euphemia, as she well knew, was a woman to appreciate and honour a confidence . . .

'Sir Josse is a valued friend and ally of our community,' she went on eventually, making up her mind. 'We should all miss him grievously, were any harm to come to him.' She took a deep breath. She was just starting to say the words, 'especially me' when Sister Euphemia touched her sleeve.

'I know, Abbess,' she said quietly.

And, for the first time in all that long day, Helewise felt tears in her eyes. Strange, she thought, turning away so that her coif hid her face, how often we manage to maintain our composure all the while we are tense and waiting for some dreaded outcome, only to break down afterwards, when it's all over and the worst hasn't happened.

Especially when some good soul says a few kindly words.

Sister Euphemia was being very tactful and bending down to test the poultice. Helewise took advantage of the moment, and wiped away her tears.

'Will you leave your patient — indeed, all of your patients — and come with me to Vespers?' she asked Sister Euphemia presently. The infirmarer was one of a handful of nuns who, when their duties necessitated it, were permitted to be absent from church for the canonical hours.

'That I will,' Sister Euphemia said. With one last look at Josse, she moved away from the bedside. 'There are others who will watch while I am away, and I need to make my thanks.'

'As do we all,' Helewise agreed.

Sometimes, she reflected as the two of them left the infirmary and crossed to the church, joining in the file of all the other members of their community heading for their evening prayers, it was easy to forget.

To overlook the fact that the infirmarer, the nurses, all of them were but instruments. And that, no matter how skilled the hands, healing — not only for Josse but for all those poor souls in the infirmary who had survived to the end of another day — did not come from anywhere but from God.

With her heart light with the relief of Josse's first step on the long road to recovery, Helewise humbly bowed her head before God's goodness and went in through the church door.

4

For the next week, Sister Euphemia battled against the infection in Josse's wounded arm. Although his fever never again rose to a burning heat that threatened his life, the encroaching inflammation in the wound refused to give up.

Brice and Will returned to their respective homes, apparently only partially swayed by the infirmarer's assurance that Sir Josse would live. Will, his face intent, said to the Abbess as he left, 'Pray for him, Abbess. The good Lord'll listen to you.'

And she did. All the sisters prayed, the nursing nuns tried potion after potion, and still the battle was not won. Sister Euphemia, knowing full well what the loss of his right arm meant for a fighting man, nevertheless prepared herself for what began to seem the inevitable.

Then, after a mysterious absence that led to her doing penance for three missed devotions, Sister Tiphaine appeared one evening in the infirmary, a small earthenware pot clutched in her hand.

'Try this,' she said, thrusting the pot at the infirmarer.

'What is it?' Sister Euphemia had removed the cloth cover and was sniffing the contents of the pot. 'Hmm. Smells quite pleasant.'

'Something we haven't yet tried.' Sister Tiphaine seemed reluctant to meet her Sister's eyes.

'All well and good,' Sister Euphemia said, 'but what *is* it?'

'Secret remedy.' Sister Tiphaine gave her a swift grin. 'They do say some of the magic goes, if the secret's revealed.'

'Sister, really, we — ' the infirmarer began. Then she made herself stop, instead thanking Sister Tiphaine with a brief bow and promising to try the new potion on her patient without delay.

It was ever Sister Tiphaine's way, she thought a little while later, watching the sleeping Josse as if the potion would announce its efficacy straight away. She knows her herbs; there is no doubting that; but sometimes, such an air of mystery hangs about her that one would almost suspect she keeps one foot in the pagan past. Magic, she said. The secret potion possesses magic, which would be lessened by revealing its constituents.

Stop acting like a superstitious peasant and remember who you are! Sister Euphemia's conscience rebuked her firmly. Bowing her head, she crossed herself and offered up to God a brief but sincere apology for wondering, even for an instant, if her strange herbalist Sister's words could possibly have any validity . . .

★ ★ ★

And soon, whether because of the Sisters' prayers, the herbalist's potion, the infirmarer's devoted care, Josse's own fortitude, or a combination of all four, the infection began to retreat.

★ ★ ★

Waking up one afternoon from a pleasant doze, Josse opened his eyes to see an unfamiliar face looming over him. A pair of bright eyes stared unblinkingly at him; fringed with spiky, dark lashes, they were the misty, slightly purplish blue of early bluebells . . .

The girl whose pretty face they adorned was dressed in a simple gown of an indeterminate buff shade; her head was uncovered, and her thick dark hair sprang up in wild curls which, it appeared, had resisted the girl's attempt to restrain them in a fillet.

Her youth — she could not have been

more than about thirteen or fourteen — and her style of dress indicated that she was not one of the Sisters; even postulants at Hawkenlye wore black and covered their heads. And, Josse thought, amused, no postulant he had ever encountered had that amount of naughtiness and high spirits in her expression.

He said, 'Who are you?'

The girl gasped. 'Oh! You spoke!'

'Aye,' he agreed. 'Did they tell you I was stricken dumb?'

'No, of course not! They said you had been grievously wounded, and were only just beginning to recover, and that I must sit here and watch you, and, when you woke up, I must hurry and tell Sister Euphemia or one of her nuns, so I'd better do so.'

She leapt up from her half-crouch beside his bed, but, just in time, he shot out his left arm and caught a fold of her skirt. 'Don't hurry away,' he said. 'Stay and talk to me.'

'No, I mustn't!' She looked horrified. 'Sister Euphemia was adamant. The very *instant* he wakes, she said. Oh, please, she'll have me shut up and put on bread and water for a week if I disobey!'

There was, he noticed, a sparkle in her eyes as she spoke; he had a swift impression of a girl who obeyed when she felt like it, but who was perfectly prepared to do exactly as she pleased when she didn't, and hang the consequences.

'Very well,' he said, 'off you go, then. But make sure you come back again.' It would actually be no bad thing to see the infirmarer; his sudden lunge to catch at the girl's gown, even though he had used his undamaged arm, had made him feel dizzy, and sent an angry shooting pain from his wound up into his shoulder.

'I will!' the girl was saying as she sped away. He heard her light voice calling as she ran, 'Sister Euphemia! Oh, Sister, he's awake, and he's *talking*!' before the infirmarer's strict tones interrupted her with a carrying, '*Hush*, child!'

★ ★ ★

The girl was as good as her word. Some time later, when Josse had spent a painful time with Sister Euphemia, she came back. Josse's wound, despite the infirmarer's infinitely gentle touch, was still sending out red-hot waves of pain from the re-dressing; he no longer felt quite as much like cheery conversation as he had done earlier.

And the girl, bless her, seemed to notice. Crouching down beside him, she gave him a sympathetic smile. 'Did it hurt *very* much?' she asked softly. Then, as if she knew he didn't really want to talk, went on, 'I fell out of a tree once and cut my shin open on a rock. You could see right down to the *bone*, it was horrid, dead white and sort of shiny. I used to cry out loud when it was time to change the dressing, and my mother gave me — ' She stopped suddenly, and a look of pain crossed the lively face. Leaning closer to Josse, she whispered, 'My mother's dead. She caught the sickness and she died.'

Josse reached out his left hand — awkwardly, since she was on his right side — and, after a moment's hesitation, she took it. 'It is terrible to lose your mother,' he said quietly. 'I am so sorry.'

She wiped tears from her eyes with her free hand. 'My father's dead, too,' she said. 'He wasn't kind like my mother, but I'm sure he loved us in his way. Alba says he did, anyway.' The girl looked suddenly glum, as if the mention of Alba, whoever she was, had depressed her.

'Alba?' Josse prompted.

'My sister. My eldest sister, there's Meriel as well. She's sixteen — Meriel, I mean — she's two years older than me. Alba's *much* older than us. She's a nun.'

'I see,' Josse said, although he wasn't sure

what he did see. 'You still haven't told me your name.'

'Berthe,' said the girl.

The pain in his arm, although lessening, was keeping up a steady throb. Thinking that a bit of a chat might take his mind off it, if he could summon the energy, Josse tried to think how he might encourage his enchanting companion to talk while he listened.

'Berthe,' he repeated. 'Now, I can see that you're not about to take the veil, and — '

'Oh, I am,' she interrupted, surprising him. 'Not till I'm older, Alba says, but we've both got to, Meriel and me. Alba says we must, we've got no home, nowhere to live, now that Father is dead.' She leaned closer and confided, 'He didn't own the farm, you see. It was all right for me and Meriel when he was alive, we looked after him and we didn't mind, really, when he — well, we always had enough to eat and, as Father used to say, we had a roof over our heads and were warm and dry most of the time, which was more than many folks could say. We weren't to complain, Father said, and when he heard me — I mean, we didn't need to complain. He was quite right, I had disobeyed him, and it was his fatherly duty to — And then when Meriel met — I mean, there was — Anyway, we're to be nuns, and there's an end to it.'

She had, Josse thought, told him more by what she had left out than by what she had said. He had the strong impression that there were aspects of her young life that she had been ordered, under pain of some dreadful reprisal, to keep secret. Why else would there have been the abruptly cut-off remarks?

And why, when she had referred to the dead father several times, had there been no further mention of the mother?

Josse tried to plug the gaps and put the picture together. A tenant farmer, would-be master of his own few acres, making do but only just, head held high and woe betide anyone who pitied him. Heavy-handed in his punishments when his family complained, domineering, cowing a gentle wife to silence. Nothing put by, so that, when his daughters were suddenly orphaned, they were left both homeless and penniless.

And so they had come to Hawkenlye, where, without any consideration of whether or not they had a true vocation, they were all to be nuns.

This little thing, with her naughty eyes and her chatter, a nun?

Ah, but —

Josse had forgotten where he was. And, more importantly, which wise soul ruled this

Abbey's comings and goings. Abbess Hele-wise, he thought, with a rush of relief, would never admit a postulant because somebody else said she must. She, with her wise and perceptive eyes, would not force this child — Berthe — to take the veil unless Berthe was quite sure that God had called her, and that she wanted to answer His summons.

'How do Alba and Meriel feel about being nuns?' he asked.

'Meriel doesn't really show what she's feeling, not at present, anyway, but Alba quite likes it,' Berthe said. Ah yes, Josse remembered, Alba was already in Holy Orders. 'Well, as much as Alba ever likes anything.' A faint grin crossed Berthe's face. 'Alba says we are not put on this earth to enjoy ourselves, that we must work, and pray, and fight every moment to overcome original sin.'

'And do you?' Josse didn't think it very likely.

'I don't really think I understand what original sin *is*,' Berthe said, dropping her voice to a whisper, 'but I'm quite sure Alba's right, and we've got to be on our guard against it.' The blue eyes stared intently at Josse. 'Do *you* know?' she asked, still in a whisper.

'Er — ' Josse was not entirely sure that he understood any more than Berthe did. 'Um

— because Adam and Eve sinned,' he said, thinking hard, 'every one of us comes into the world tainted by that sin. Well, the same sin, sort of.' He gave her a weak smile, hoping his paltry explanation would suffice.

Clearly it didn't. 'But what *was* the sin?' Berthe persisted. 'If Adam and Eve did it, then it was years ago, really ages and ages, and surely it's not still lurking around trying to lure us into transgression *now?*'

Lure us into transgression, Josse thought. He didn't imagine that little phrase was Berthe's own. Who, he wondered, had been preaching at her?

'Er — well, we can't really help how we get here,' he stumbled, 'it's nature, and it's the same for all of us, king, knight and poor man, pope and saint. Oh, except the Holy Virgin Mary, because she was the Immaculate Conception.' He was afraid he was entrenching himself more deeply and irrevocably into philosophical argument with every word. 'See?' he concluded hopefully.

Berthe shook her head. 'No. Not at all.' She was frowning. 'What do you mean, how we *get* here? And what's Immaculate Conception? I thought conceiving was when mares and cows are put with the stallion or the bull, when they're going to bear young.'

But Josse, with a surge of relief, had

60

noticed that his end of the infirmary had another visitor. One who, soft-footed, had arrived without his having noticed, and who, from the smile on her face, appeared to have overheard at least part of the conversation.

He grinned at Berthe. 'I am not really the right person to ask,' he said. 'But, as luck would have it, this good lady is. Berthe, have you been presented to Abbess Helewise?'

★　★　★

Helewise had put off her visit to Josse until after Nones. It was not that she didn't want to see him — far from it, she had been impatient to reassure herself that he really was on the way to recovery since first Sister Euphemia had told her of the sudden improvement in his condition.

It was, in fact, because of that impatience that she had forced herself to delay. She had, she was all too aware without her confessor having laboured the point, spent far too much time recently worrying about Josse. Oh, not to the detriment of her attention to her duties — she had made quite sure of that.

But it was, she had been discovering, quite possible to perform one's duties convincingly while one's mind and heart were engaged elsewhere. Even — and she was bitterly ashamed of herself — to recite the Office with her lips while her thoughts lay with that long, still figure in the infirmary.

She had already prayed for God's forgiveness for that surely hurtful sin against His love, even before Father Gilbert had imposed his penance. Forcing herself to wait for almost all of the day before going to see Josse with her own eyes had been her idea; it had cost her far more than anything Father Gilbert had ordered.

Even having reached the infirmary, she did not allow herself to hurry immediately to Josse. Instead, she made sure that other patients received their due, stopping here by the bed of an amputee, there by a man newly recovered from the flux, and making a little detour to the area where two recently-delivered mothers proudly showed her their newborn babies. She also sought out and spoke to the infirmarer and her nurses with, as always, a word or two to each one.

It was hard, infirmary duty. The nursing nuns worked long hours, and refused to allow anybody to pass from this world into the next unless they were quite sure that God's summons was not to be denied. Helewise, well aware that some of the tasks which Sister Euphemia and her nuns performed with horrible regularity would turn her stomach, wanted always to ensure that the infirmary staff knew how much their Abbess appreciated them.

Finally, she allowed her steps to follow the well-trodden path to Josse's bedside.

' . . . What's Immaculate Conception?' a light young voice was demanding. Berthe, Helewise thought, beginning to smile. Oh, dear, Josse seemed to have got himself into rather a pass. And was he really up to discussing the niceties of theological philosophy, convalescent as he was? Resisting the urge to chuckle, Helewise stepped forward.

The relief on Josse's face as he saw her — and instantly dumped his little problem into her lap — suggested she had been right. He wasn't up to it.

Berthe had shot to her feet and was making Helewise a passably graceful bow — 'Thank you, Berthe,' Helewise murmured — and Josse had relaxed, with evident relief, against his pillows.

'Young Berthe has been cheering me up with a nice chat,' Josse said.

'Yes, so I heard,' Helewise replied; the mild irony had been intended only for Josse, and only he gave a brief smile in recognition.

'Abbess, am I allowed to ask *you* about Original Sin and that?' Berthe demanded. 'Josse says — '

'*Sir* Josse,' Helewise corrected.

'Sorry, Sir Josse says you can explain better than he can . . . ?'

Helewise took a breath. 'Original Sin refers to the disobedience of Adam and Eve in the Garden of Eden, a disobedience which, because we are all descended from the first parents, we inherit,' she said. She shot Josse a glance of mock reproof. 'The Virgin Mary may indeed be the one Holy soul born without inheriting this sin, or so our ecclesiastical teachers would say, which is why we refer to our Blessed Virgin as the Immaculate Conception.'

'But — ' persisted the irrepressible Berthe.

'Berthe, dear, this is neither the time nor the place for theological instruction,' Helewise insisted gently.

'I'm sorry, Abbess, only Alba says — '

'I am well aware what Alba says.' The words had emerged more harshly that Helewise had intended; it was unfair to be angry with Berthe because of Alba's shortcomings. 'Off you go, now, Berthe,' she went on, much more kindly. 'Your visit has obviously done Sir Josse good' — Josse nodded enthusiastically — 'but I wish to speak to him now.'

Berthe had flushed with pleasure at the compliment. 'Have I really done you good?'

she enquired, looking from Josse to Helewise and back again.

Helewise's 'Yes' and Josse's 'Aye' sounded together like a chorus.

Berthe's smile spread until it encompassed her whole face. 'Oh, I'm so *glad!*' she exclaimed. Then, impetuously, 'I wish Alba would let me be a nurse instead of a nun, I'd really much rather. Goodbye!'

Helewise watched Josse's eyes following the girl as she hurried away. Then he turned to her.

She knew what he was going to say. As he opened his mouth to speak, she said, 'No, Sir Josse. Before you do me the injustice of even asking, let me assure you that I will not be accepting Berthe as a postulant, not until she herself wants me to.'

Josse gave her a rueful smile. 'Sorry, Abbess.'

'No need for that,' she said shortly. Indeed, she should not be impatient with him; the poor man's recent state of health had surely made him deaf and blind to the subtleties of what had been going on in the community.

Just when she could have done with his wise counsel, too.

She studied him. He was still very pale, but then that was only to be expected; he had been shut away inside for so long, as well as having been so desperately ill. She glanced at the wounded arm. The dressing seemed to be smaller than when she had last visited. Was that a good sign?

He had followed the line of her glance. He, too, was looking down at his arm. 'It is healing, Abbess,' he said. He managed a grin. 'Only hurts now if I try to throw a punch.'

'I am quite sure there is no call for that here,' she said primly. Then, unable to hold back the question any longer: 'Sir Josse, was Berthe confiding in you just now?'

'Before we got going on Original Sin, you mean?' The old humour was back in his eyes.

'Yes.'

He sighed. 'Aye, that she was. Not a happy tale, is it?'

'That's just it! I don't know what the tale is, not really.' She hesitated. Was it right to suggest that a nun had been deliberately misleading her? Not one of her own nuns, perhaps, but, nevertheless, one that Hawkenlye had taken in . . .

Making up her mind — this was Josse, her friend! How many times before had she confided in him and been glad of it? — she said, 'All I know of Sister Alba, Meriel and Berthe is what Alba has told me.' She kept her eyes steadily on Josse's. 'And, although it pains me to say it, I have become increasingly certain that Sister Alba is lying.'

5

If only, Helewise thought later as she sat alone in her room, unburdening myself to Josse could make my anxieties vanish. But that would not only be a miracle, it would also be unjust, since the anxieties are, after all, my concern.

She sighed. It was strange how, once she had begun on her misgivings about Sister Alba, they had appeared to grow, so that she heard herself voicing concerns which, until then, she had hardly known she was worrying about. Sister Alba was prickly, difficult to work with, extremely pious — and hers was a particularly heartless, unloving, unforgiving sort of piety — and, as if that were not enough, she also threw her weight about and bossed any of the other nuns who would allow it.

What really concerned Helewise was that, despite Alba telling her more than once that she had been a fully professed nun for five years, Helewise just could not bring herself to believe it. All nuns were different, naturally, just as all women were different, but there were certain things — speech mannerisms, small daily habits such as always holding a door open for another sister and checking in the refectory that one's neighbours had all they needed — that Alba just never did. Also, although it was a minor detail, there was that rope girdle that the woman wore. It was old and grubby, frayed at the ends, and far thicker, longer and heavier than the ones worn by all the other nuns. Did Alba wear it for the same reason that one might wear a hair shirt? Its weight and its length must surely have made it almost as uncomfortable. But that sort of personal, private penance was not normally performed for others to see; was it just another rather unattractive facet of Alba, that she demanded others witness her perpetual discomfort and praise her for it?

And — although Helewise kept this reservation strictly to herself — she could not, try as she did, detect any real and convincing signs of a vocation in Sister Alba. Helewise berated herself constantly over this — only God knew whom He had called and whom He hadn't, and it was not Helewise's business to demand proof. But Alba showed no love! No charity! And in church when the nuns lost themselves in their joyful, mystical meditations and prayers, which took them so close to the Lord, Alba usually spent her time glaring around from nun to nun, occasionally nodding her head, as if she were mentally reminding herself who had made this or that mistake or error.

And the product of her observation she would, sooner or later, come along to reveal to her Abbess.

Then there were her two young sisters. Berthe — oh, Berthe! Helewise broke away from her depressing thoughts and let a picture of Berthe — happy, laughing — momentarily cheer her. Yes, Berthe was a delight. It would take a sea change to turn her into postulant material, but then why was that necessary? Plenty of people lived good, satisfying, useful lives without taking the veil.

And, as for Meriel, she certainly was not happy. In fact, she gave every indication of being lost in a grief so deep that it appeared to have all but drowned her. Was she grieving for her mother? More than likely, but if so, why was Berthe not similarly afflicted by sorrow? Something Josse had said had stayed in Helewise's mind, because it echoed an observation made by two of the other nuns: he had remarked that Berthe seemed to be in some doubt as to when exactly her mother had died.

Alba had told Helewise originally that the sisters had just lost both parents. But Helewise was almost certain now that that had been a lie; it seemed instead that the mother had fallen victim to some mysterious sickness several years ago, and that it was only the father who had recently joined his late wife in death.

Not that it could be important, Helewise thought; the girls were all orphans, no matter when the two parents died. But why lie about it?

And if Meriel was not mourning her mother, for whom *was* her heart breaking? Not the father, surely — none of the three had been heard to speak of him with affection. They had been in awe of him, obedient to him, afraid of him. But Helewise was quite sure they hadn't loved him.

Oh, dear. She got up from her throne-like chair and began pacing her room. Soon, the movement began to soothe her. As the turmoil of her thoughts eased and, once again, she felt calm, she reflected that, as usual, it had been a help to talk to Josse.

Not that he had said anything much — poor man, he was still so weak, even conversation seemed to tire him — but, as Helewise was leaving him, he had made the most comforting comment she had heard from anybody on the vexed question of Alba and her sisters.

'They are still quite new to this community,' he had said. 'And, although you and most of your nuns probably do not realise it, Hawkenlye can be somewhat daunting to a newcomer.' He had smiled briefly, as if remembering his own introduction to Helewise and her nuns. 'Plus, we must not forget that the girls have just lost their father, *and* their home, either of which alone would be enough to make a person act a little oddly. Give them time, Abbess. See how another month or so here in your community affects them.'

She had left him then. Had had to, in fact, since the infirmarer had been hovering, muttering about people who stayed too long and tired her patient so that he didn't want any supper and was too overwrought for a good night's sleep.

With Josse firmly pictured in her mind's eye, Helewise prayed that he heartily enjoy both his meal and his sleep.

* * *

At the end of April, a sudden warm, dry spell of weather brought a rush of visitors to the Holy Water shrine down in the Vale. The monks who tended the shrine and cared for the pilgrims were kept busy all day and well

71

into the night and, as always happened, soon Brother Firmin requested some reinforcements from the Abbess.

The Abbess, who was well aware that her nuns were just as busy as the monks and the lay brothers in the Vale — and, moreover, that this was a constant state of affairs and not affected by the tide of fair-weather pilgrims — nevertheless did her best to oblige. She begged a nun from the refectory and one from the reformatory, and, since Berthe had no particular duties, asked the girl if she would like to spend a few days helping to look after the visitors. Berthe leapt at the chance.

A short time after Berthe had been despatched with the two nuns, there came a loud knock on the door of Helewise's room. Before she had finished saying 'Come in', the door was thrown open and Sister Alba hurried over the threshold.

'You've sent Berthe to work in the Vale!' she said. Her voice was raised and her face was flushed.

Helewise made herself count to five. 'Sister Alba,' she said quietly, 'you are new to Hawkenlye, and we must make allowances. However, I cannot believe that such an entrance into a superior's presence can have been permitted in your previous community.'

'I haven't time — ' Alba began.

'You will go outside,' Helewise said, ignoring her, 'and come in again. Correctly, this time.'

Face now flaming with suppressed anger, Alba did as she was told. Her second entrance was marginally more courteous; after letting her wait in silence for a few moments, Helewise said, 'Now you may speak.'

'Berthe is working in the Vale,' Alba said, controlling her voice with an obvious effort, 'and she mustn't. That is, it's best if she doesn't. She's — er, it's not right. For her.'

Helewise could hardly believe she was hearing right. 'Berthe has been sent to assist the monks in looking after our visitors,' she said. 'The work is neither hard nor exacting, and Berthe was perfectly happy to go.'

'But — ' Alba seemed to be struggling with some violent emotion; her hands, Helewise noticed, were twisting and pulling at the rope around her waist. Then: 'Please, Abbess, won't you send someone else instead? One of the nuns?'

'Two nuns have already been sent,' Helewise said coldly. 'And, Sister Alba, it is not for you to order what work the nuns are put to.'

Sister Alba's face worked. Then, abruptly

73

changing tack, she demanded, 'What sort of people go to the Vale?'

'People who seek Our Lady's cure, as given in the Holy Water,' Helewise said.

'Local folk? Travellers? Pilgrims?'

'All of those.' Helewise made herself speak levelly.

'Ordinary folk or nobility?'

'Both.'

'Do they come from far afield?'

'Indeed they do. We have a reputation for miracles at Hawkenlye, Sister Alba, as you knew perfectly well when you brought your sisters here.'

Alba brushed that aside. 'Abbess Helewise, I'm begging you — I wouldn't insist if it were not so important, but — '

'Sister Alba, you forget yourself.' Helewise got to her feet and walked round her table to stand before Alba. Where any other nun would have read the signs and at least lowered her head, if not performed a penitential reverence, Alba glared at the Abbess face to face. 'You are dismissed,' Helewise said. 'Go back to your duties, and try to put your sister's whereabouts out of your mind.'

'But — '

'Go,' Helewise said very firmly.

And, with a last ferocious scowl, Alba

turned on her heel and flounced out, banging the heavy door behind her.

★ ★ ★

Helewise was used to her nuns not only obeying her without question, but, when they could manage it, anticipating her commands.

It did not enter her head that Alba would defy her and so, when Sister Martha came to tell her that Alba had gone down to the Vale and had ordered Berthe to come straight back to the Abbey, Helewise thought at first that there must have been some mistake.

There was not.

Berthe, according to Sister Martha, had protested vehemently against her elder sister's heavy handedness, and her shouting had alerted not only Sister Martha, but also Sister Ursel, in the porteress's lodge, and Sister Tiphaine, busy in the herb garden.

'And, Abbess,' Sister Martha had added, wide-eyed with amazement at these extraordinary happenings, 'when the little lassie tried to wrench her arm away and set off back to the Vale, that Sister Alba grabbed her sleeve so roughly that it tore, then smacked her hard across the cheek! Poor Berthe, she'll have a great bruise there come morning!'

'Thank you, Sister Martha.' Helewise

headed for the door, Sister Martha at her heels.

'Seems to me that Sister Alba needs a good talking-to,' Sister Martha panted as she hurried to keep up with Helewise's long strides. 'Seems to me you should — '

'*Thank you*, Sister!' Helewise repeated, rather more forcefully. Goodness, were *all* her nuns going to copy Alba's insubordination?

'Yes, Abbess. Sorry, Abbess,' Sister Martha said contritely.

'That's better,' Helewise murmured. But not loud enough for Sister Martha to hear.

She strode out across the courtyard. It wasn't difficult to locate Alba, she reflected, one had but to follow the sound of the angry, shouting voice.

Quite a crowd had gathered. Sister Euphemia had come hurrying out of the infirmary and, as Helewise joined the throng, she was elbowing her way through towards Alba, calling for a bit of hush, her patients weren't to be disturbed.

Helewise said, 'Silence, please. All of you.'

Her nuns, used to keeping an ear out for their Abbess's quiet but carrying tones, instantly ceased their thrilled, gossipy chatter.

Leaving just the one voice.

' . . . down there showing yourself like some little trollop, flashing those blue eyes

76

and batting your eyelids, flirting with anything between the ages of six and sixty' — suddenly the furious shouting went up a tone — '*showing yourself to anyone that happens to have eyes to see you!*'

'Sister Alba,' Helewise said.

Alba turned and said rudely, 'What?'

There was a collective gasp from the nuns.

'Let go of Berthe.' There was no response. 'At once!'

Something in Helewise's icy voice seemed to penetrate; Alba let go of her sister, and Berthe hastened away from her. Sister Euphemia, who must have noticed the bright pink swelling on Berthe's cheek, put her arm around the sobbing girl and led her away.

Helewise rejected the swift thought she had just had, of humiliating Alba by announcing her punishment out in the open, in front of a dozen avidly listening nuns. With a brief gesture, she beckoned Alba to follow her, turning her back and leading the way to her room.

She was just wondering what she would do were Alba to refuse to follow her when a soft murmur from the nuns suggested that, for once, Alba had decided to obey.

When Helewise and Alba were once more in Helewise's room and the door was firmly closed, Helewise said, 'Sister Alba, you have countermanded one of my orders, hurt your own sister, and seriously disturbed the peace of the community. You leave me no choice but to impose a severe punishment. Have you anything to say?'

It occurred to her that, so far, Alba had given no reason for the desperate measures she had taken to remove Berthe from the Vale. Would she do so now?

No. Lips folded into a tight, unforgiving line, Alba maintained her silence.

'Very well,' Helewise said. 'You will go from here into the church, where you will prostrate yourself in prayer. You will ask God to forgive your sins against your sister and against this community, and you will remain there until the arrival of our confessor. You will then kneel before him, make your confession, and receive whatever penance he sees fit to impose.'

Sister Alba had been listening carefully to the Abbess's pronouncement. Watching her, Helewise had the growing feeling that something was amiss . . . Alba's face had gone from its hectic flush to a deadly pallor.

And, out of nowhere, Helewise suddenly felt a dreadful sense of threat.

Her instinctive awareness was what saved her, for, just as Alba swung a furious fist right at her, Helewise stepped back.

And Alba, off-balance from lunging into empty air instead of into her Abbess's face, fell to her knees.

Instantly Helewise jumped round her, flung open the door and cried, 'Sister Martha! Sister Ursel! Come here!'

They were still standing in the same spot, where they had formed part of the rapt group around Alba and Berthe; faces reflecting their astonishment, they began to walk across to Helewise.

'*Hurry!*' she yelled. Then, catching sight of a party of lay brothers headed by Brother Saul — no doubt word had spread, and they were coming to see the fun — she called out to them. 'Brother Saul! Brother Michael! Here!'

The nuns and the lay brothers arrived together on Helewise's doorstep. Wordlessly she stood aside, gesturing inside to where Alba, now sitting on the floor, had buried her face in her hands.

'Abbess?' Brother Saul said quietly. 'Are you all right?'

'I am perfectly all right, thank you, Brother Saul. Please would you and one of the brothers — Brother Michael, perhaps — escort Sister Alba here to the punishment cell.' There was an instant buzzing sound as several nuns and monks all began whispering in horror. 'Make sure she has water and something in which to wrap herself. Then lock her in.'

The lay brothers did as they were bid. All resistance seemed to have leaked out of Sister Alba; she accompanied them with lowered head and without a word.

There wasn't a word from anybody else, either. What had just happened was too awful to be spoken of. At least, until the shock wore off.

★ ★ ★

The punishment cell at Hawkenlye was a small and windowless room built into the stonework beneath the nuns' dormitory, where it formed part of the undercroft. It was chilly and damp and, once the door was closed and barred, almost totally dark. There was just enough room for someone not above average height to lie down stretched out.

In the near half century of Hawkenlye Abbey's existence, the cell had never before been used.

Helewise's first reaction was fury, that she had been forced to this terrible and drastic response to Sister Alba's intransigence. But, as she knelt before the altar, all alone in the church, soon fury changed to remorse. Oh, dear God, what have I done? I've sent a human being to that awful place! Forgive me, I —

But her fervent, panicky prayer stumbled to a stop.

You had no choice, her conscience said firmly. No nun is permitted to strike another. Sister Alba should really have been sent straight to the punishment cell for her attack on Berthe. When she compounded that by trying to hit her superior, you were left with no alternative.

Helewise felt a sob rise in her throat. She suppressed it. It was, after all, the lot of those in command to impose harsh penalties from time to time. No use weeping about it.

She continued her prayers, slipping into some of the familiar and beloved forms of words that always brought comfort. And, eventually, she felt calm.

As she got up from her knees and left the church, the sole emotion she had left was pity.

★　★　★

She had been anticipating a quiet end to what had been anything but a quiet day. Sister Alba had been provided with food and water, and two of the nuns had wordlessly handed covers from their own beds to Sister Martha, to be given to their Sister in torment. Special prayers had been said at Compline and now, Helewise fervently hoped, there remained nothing further for the community to do but to settle down for the night.

But, as the nuns left the church and headed for their dormitory, they all heard the sound of pounding footsteps from outside the gate, swiftly followed by loud banging and a voice shouting, 'Open up! I need help; a man's been attacked on the road to the Vale! Open *up!*'

Sister Ursel glanced at Helewise, who nodded her permission. As the porteress rushed to unbolt the gates, followed by several more of the nuns, Helewise caught at the sleeve of Sister Martha. 'If you would, Sister, slip out of the rear gate and find Brother Saul. We have more need of him and his companions, I fear.'

The man at the gate had been admitted and, shaking and clearly in shock, he was blurting out his story. There was blood on the front of his tunic.

Helewise approached him. Holding up her hand to quieten him, she said, 'Help is coming. We have summoned some of our lay brothers, who will accompany you back to where this poor man lies and bring him here to the infirmary, where we may tend him.'

'Reckon you'll be too late, Abbess,' the man said. Calmer now, he was looking at Helewise with heavy-lidded, sorrowful eyes. 'Reckon nobody could survive long, not with half their head bashed in.'

Somebody gave a low moan of distress. Belatedly, Helewise ordered the horrified nuns to go to the dormitory. I have only the trials of today, she thought ruefully, to excuse my lapse. Dear Lord, go with them, and protect them as they sleep and dream.

She waited alone for Saul, who arrived very soon afterwards, two other sturdy lay brothers with him. One of them, she noticed with relief, had had the good sense to arm himself with a stout stick.

She saw them on their way, the man who had sounded the alarm walking in their midst. Then, turning to go and join Sister Euphemia in the infirmary, she noticed the lone and forlorn figure of Berthe, coming towards her from the dormitory.

'Berthe.' Helewise put out her hands to greet the girl.

But Berthe shook her head. 'Oh, Abbess, don't be kind to me, not when we're bringing you such troubles!'

'None of which are your fault, Berthe,' Helewise began. 'And, in any case — '

But Berthe was rapidly losing what little control she had left. Flinging herself into Helewise's arms, she sobbed, 'Abbess, oh, dear, Abbess, Meriel's gone missing!'

Part Two

Travellers

6

The dead man had been a visitor at the Holy Water shrine in the Vale. Brother Saul and Brother Firmin had both talked briefly to him, and they had a vague impression that the man had spoken with a strange accent.

That, and the information that he had been well equipped for travelling and unaccompanied, was all that the brothers could add to what was evident from the man's dead body. Which was that he had been around thirty, bearded, with dark hair and a swarthy complexion, sturdily built, of middle height, and well nourished.

One or two of the other pilgrims — pop-eyed with amazement to have the extraordinary thrill of a murder in a place where they had gone for prayer and healing — said that the dead man, who had but recently arrived, had attended some of the services conducted by the brothers, but had hidden himself away at the back, as if he wanted to be unobtrusive.

Nobody knew his name.

But, whoever he was, somebody had badly wanted him dead. He had been attacked from behind, and struck down with a series of blows to the back of the head. There was evidence of severe damage to the skull which, in one place, had collapsed into a distinct indentation. It appeared that further blows had been struck after the man had been felled, since there were deep cuts across his brows.

The body, the surrounding area and the clothing of anybody who had touched the corpse were all heavily stained from the copious amounts of blood that had spattered out like a fountain.

Helewise asked Brother Saul to go through the dead man's belongings. Saul reported that the man's small leather satchel was well made but worn, as if from long use, and that the pilgrim's broad-brimmed hat was decorated with the shell of Santiago di Compostela, and the souvenir badge from the Shrine of Our Lady at Walsingham. His water bottle, made from a gourd, looked quite new.

He had been dressed in a simple tunic and cloak which, like the rest of his garments, were of cheap, undyed fabric. His boots, however, were sturdy and made of good leather.

From the bloodstains on its thick end and from the location where it had been discovered — beside the dead body — it appeared that the man's heavy, iron-tipped walking staff had been employed as the murder weapon.

Helewise sat with Brother Saul and Brother Firmin in the rough shelter where the pilgrims took their meals. Brother Firmin, who headed the fully professed monks in the little community, was clearly distraught and not a great deal of help; Helewise had to arrest the swift wish that he would go away and find something else to do and send her one of his other monks instead. Not that any of them would be a great deal better, she reflected; they were excellent at tending the shrine and seeing to the small needs of their visitors, and their devotion to the Virgin and her Holy Place was remarkable. But when a practical mind and a deft pair of hands were required . . .

Each to his own, the Abbess told herself firmly. God calls us all, but sets each of us on a different path.

'Brother Saul,' she said, meeting the alert eyes of her secret favourite among the lay brothers, 'your summary?'

Brother Saul paused, brows together in a frown of concentration as he gathered his thoughts. Then, with admirable brevity, he said, 'I would judge that the dead man was an habitual and well-travelled pilgrim. The souvenir badges suggest extensive journeys, and both the scrip and the boots show wear. He may have come from far away, he travelled alone, and he liked to keep himself to himself.' Saul paused again. 'We know that he sat here, in this very shelter, for the evening meal, and we surmise that he went for a walk before settling for the night, where he encountered his killer.'

'He *was* deliberately killed?' Helewise asked. 'It cannot have been an accidental death?'

Again, Saul seemed to think carefully about his reply. Then: 'Had the weapon been a stone, then it might just have been possible that he had slipped and bashed his skull against the stone as he fell. But the thick knot at the top of his staff shows blood and hair, and the hair seems to look very like that of the dead man.'

'And it is surely beyond the bounds of possibility for a man to kill himself by falling on his own staff,' Helewise concluded for him.

He nodded. 'Yes. And, Abbess, there are the wounds to the forehead to consider. A fall could scarcely inflict damage to both the back and the front of the head simultaneously.'

'Indeed not. Thank you, Brother Saul.'

It was her turn to think. Beside her,

Brother Firmin was fretting, his hands busy with the end of the cord that he wore knotted around his waist. He was muttering under his breath, and Helewise wished he would stop. Saul, by contrast, sat still as a rock, eyes focused on some spot in the middle distance.

Presently Helewise said, 'Are any other pilgrims absent this morning? Who were here yesterday, I mean?'

'All are present, Abbess,' Brother Firmin said. 'No more new arrivals, for which we must thank the good Lord, since it would only add to our burden to have newcomers in our midst, making everything more complicated.'

'Quite.' Helewise suddenly turned to Saul; something in Brother Firmin's little outburst had reminded her of a question she should have asked already. 'Brother Saul, was there anything about the position of the body to suggest whether the man had been coming to the shrine or going *away* from it?'

Saul must have been thinking the same thing, for instantly he said, 'Going away, I would judge, Abbess. I should say that he was walking along the path when somebody crept up on him from behind — perhaps they were tiptoeing in the grass, so as to be quite silent — and struck him from behind.'

'With his own staff,' she mused.

'Aye.'

She met Saul's eyes. 'Did they wrest it from him to strike him, then?'

Saul shook his head. 'I cannot imagine that was how it was, Abbess. Taking the staff from the dead man would have alerted him to the fact that someone was attacking him, and surely, in that case, the heaviest blows would have fallen on the front of his head. They'd have been face to face, wouldn't they?'

'Yes, they would.' She was thinking hard. 'Then, Brother Saul, can it be that, setting out merely for a stroll, he didn't take his staff, but left it here, by his bedroll? And that someone else crept in to fetch it, then followed the poor man and killed him?'

Brother Saul began to speak, but Brother Firmin overrode him. 'Abbess Helewise, you speak of the Holy Vale as if it were a den of thieves and cut-throats!' he protested. 'Killers stealing staffs and stalking each other? Caving in each other's heads on the path? And now some girl has gone missing, they say? Dear Lord above, but all this *cannot* be true!'

For a tiny instant, Helewise caught a flash of sympathy in Brother Saul's eyes as he looked at her, as if to say, see what we have to put up with?

She made quite sure her expression was bland as she turned to Brother Firmin. 'It is shocking and dreadful, Brother Firmin, I agree. Particularly for you who tend this precious place. However, it is not the first time that we have had violent death here, and I do not suppose it will be the last. For the sake of the dead man and, indeed, for all of us, our duty now is to find out what happened, and, with God's help and if it is within our power, see that the perpetrator is brought to justice.'

'Amen,' Brother Saul murmured.

Brother Firmin crossed himself. Then he said, 'You have Sir Josse d'Acquin in the infirmary, Abbess?' She nodded. The same thought had occurred to her. 'Might I suggest that you talk this over with him?'

Her faint irritation with the old monk vanished as she stared into his earnest, anxious eyes. 'I shall indeed, provided he is strong enough.' She rose to her feet and, courteously, the two brothers did the same. 'Thank you both for your help,' — she nodded to them — 'and I will keep you informed.'

Brother Saul walked with her back up the path from the shrine to the Abbey. Neither of them spoke until he left her at the gate. Then he said quietly, 'It's a nasty business, Abbess Helewise. I shall pray for your success in resolving it quickly.'

It was, she thought as she went into the Abbey, a heartening thing to know that Brother Saul was praying for you.

★　★　★

Josse had reached the stage of convalescence when he was well enough no longer to sleep all day but not sufficiently strong to get out of bed. Not that he hadn't tried to; contravening Sister Euphemia's strict orders, he had made an attempt to walk to the latrine. And, just as she had predicted, had fainted and suffered the ignominy of being carried back to his bed.

He had made it clear that he needed someone to talk to, and, to his delight, the cheerful, bubbly Berthe had become his most frequent visitor. Not only did she keep him informed about the small — and not so small — happenings in the community; she also got him playing the most absurd, childish games. It did him good to hear her laugh, and even more good to laugh with her.

A couple of days ago, she had brought her sister Meriel with her. Studying the elder girl's sad, pale face, Josse had felt a great sympathy for her. He tried to draw her into the conversation, asking her about her work — she was helping Sister Emanuel in the home where elderly nuns and monks were cared for — but the girl was monosyllabic in her answers.

Was *this* sister in accord with Alba's order that they all be nuns? Josse wondered. Was her misery a reaction to what was in store for her? Poor lass, it cut deep, he thought, whatever sorrow she bore.

The girls had left his bedside together, Berthe leaning down to give him a kiss on the cheek — she smelt of fresh air — and Meriel giving him a little bow. But, as they left, Meriel turned and smiled at him. And suddenly he had seen what a beautiful young woman she was.

This morning, he had received no visitors. And there had been some sort of a commotion the previous night — someone had been brought into the infirmary very late, and he had heard snatches of whispered conversation.

Nobody had come to inform *him* what was going on. Nobody seemed to have time for so much as a 'Good morning, Sir Josse, how are you feeling today and what would you like for breakfast?' One of the least communicative of the nursing nuns had brought him a wooden tray of bread and one of the infirmarer's hot, herbal concoctions. It was the one for healing wounds, and it tasted absolutely foul.

All in all, by noon, Josse was feeling

thoroughly disgruntled.

When, a little later, Sister Beata came along to usher in a visitor, he was surprised and delighted to see that it was the Abbess.

'Abbess Helewise, you must have detected my discontent, and been angel enough to respond,' he began, smiling up at her.

But she neither smiled back nor replied in a similar vein; instead, coming to stand close beside him, she said in a low voice, 'Sir Josse, trouble has come to us.' And, briefly and succinctly, she proceeded to tell him all that had happened in the Abbey and the Vale over the past day and night.

His first question, when at last she stopped to draw breath, was, 'Do you think that the two events — the death and the girl's disappearance — are connected?'

'That is what is vexing me most,' the Abbess admitted. 'But all that in truth links the two things is their timing. I fear that to treat them as connected may mislead us.'

'Hmmm.' Josse scratched his head with his left hand. 'The dead man had an odd accent, did somebody say?' The Abbess nodded. 'And the sisters, Alba, Meriel and Berthe, come from some distance away?'

'Indeed. Sister Alba mentioned having been in a community at Ely.'

'Ely,' Josse repeated. 'In the Fenlands of East Anglia.'

'Do men there speak with an odd accent?' the Abbess asked.

Josse shrugged. 'I have no idea. But it seems always true that people speak differently in different areas of a country — I know they do in France — so it is fair to say that yes, probably they do in East Anglia.'

'But it is too little evidence from which to conclude that the dead man and Meriel were known to one another!' the Abbess exclaimed.

'I agree,' Josse said. 'Let us merely keep it in mind.'

The Abbess seemed to be engaged in her own thoughts; for some moments she did not share them with him. He kept his peace, knowing how irritating it could be when somebody interrupted a line of reasoning that was reluctant to resolve itself.

After a time, she raised her head and met his eyes. But what she said took him completely by surprise; in as normal a tone as if she were announcing that it was time for dinner, she said, 'I shall have to go to Ely.'

'What on earth for?' His response was automatic; with a very little amount of thought, he could have answered his own question.

'Because that is where they came from. Where Sister Alba came from, anyway. She was in a convent there.'

'And you know which one?' Josse had no idea how many religious establishments there were in the vicinity of Ely, but he seemed to remember having been told there were several; apparently the geographic setting of the Fens suited those in search of solitude and the contemplative life.

'I shall find out,' the Abbess said with dignity. 'Then I shall be able to ask Sister Alba's former superior all the many questions I have been puzzling over.'

'And that will help you to find Meriel?'

'Not necessarily,' she admitted. 'However, I sorely need to penetrate this screen of secrecy that exists around the girls. They won't tell me the truth; Sister Alba because she has made up her mind not to, and Meriel and Berthe because they are very afraid of something or someone. Of Alba, for all I know.' She gave an exasperated sigh. 'I see only one way out of the dilemma, Sir Josse.'

'Could someone not go for you?' he asked gently. 'It is a very long way and, on your own admission, the Abbey is in a time of trouble. Would you not do more good staying here?'

'Perhaps. But, Sir Josse, I *cannot* send anybody else on such a delicate matter.

Goodness, I should not really be speaking to *you* of this!' She looked faintly shocked at her lapse in convent etiquette.

'I understand,' Josse whispered. 'You are, in effect, doubting the word of a professed nun and, because your mind and your conscience cannot rest until you know the truth, you are going to have to go and check up on the tale you have been told. Yes?'

Dumbly she nodded.

What a problem, he thought, relaxing back on to his pillows. And she was right, he could see that — she could hardly despatch even one of her senior nuns to the superior of another convent to ask, did you have a nun called Alba here, and was she any good? I need to know what she told *you* of her background, because I'm quite sure she told me nothing but a pack of lies.

No. There were some tasks that only the commanding officer could do, and this looked like one of them.

He said, knowing what she would say, 'Will you not wait for a week or so, and allow me to escort you?'

She gave him a smile of great sweetness. 'No, Josse, I won't. For one thing, if I were to agree to that, you would get up and set out before you were ready, and we might well end up back where we started. For another, I don't believe I should wait at all. Meriel is missing, we know her to be in a very depressed state, and — well, the sooner I discover what lies behind this sorry affair, the sooner we may be able to help her. If, that is, we manage to find her,' she added under her breath.

'Now, then, no defeatist talk!' he muttered back. He felt the bonds imposed by his sickness acutely just then, though, and it was hard to put any levity into his voice.

'I shall ask at Alba's convent if they know the whereabouts of the former family home,' the Abbess was saying. 'They ought at least to be able to supply the father's name. I cannot imagine a convent in which a woman arrives with no background and no past.'

'She did not give you her family name when she came here?' Josse asked.

'No, she merely said she had come from another convent. In Ely, as I said. And, before you ask, she provided no details of her sisters' former lives either, other than to say they were recently orphaned.'

'If I can't be of any other help to you,' Josse said — which in itself was a painful admission — 'then may I make some suggestions about your journey? I am a not inexperienced traveller, as you know, and perhaps I may be able to ensure a bit of comfort for you on the road.'

She gave him another smile. 'I was hoping that you would. Please, proceed. I'm listening.'

For some time after that, he went through a list of the preparations he would make for a journey from Kent to Ely. It was, he told her, a good time of year for travelling; the days were lengthening perceptibly, the weather was warm, and a long dry spell meant that the roads would be in a good state. Furthermore, April usually saw the start of the pilgrimage season; although this meant that wayside inns might be busy, that was compensated for by the fact that there was safety in numbers. You were far more likely to reach your destination when the roads were well peopled than as a solitary traveller; then, you were prey to thieves.

But, in any case, she should not, of course, go alone; he was adamant about that. 'Could Brother Saul be spared?' he asked. 'I have always held his sense and his capability in high regard.'

'So have I,' she agreed. 'I shall ask Brother Firmin in such a way that he has no choice but to say yes.'

'You should take one other,' Josse said. 'Another lay brother. It might be best to get

101

Saul to propose someone.' A thought struck him. 'Has the Abbey mounts for three?'

She frowned. 'We have the cob, the pony and the mule,' she said. 'Although the mule is very old and weary. Brother Saul can ride the cob — he often does — and I suppose I could ride the pony.'

'He's only a small pony,' Josse said.

'Yes, but very strong.' She gave him a sidelong glance. 'I hope, Sir Josse, that you are not implying I would be too heavy a burden.'

She was a tall woman, and well built, and that was exactly what he had been implying. 'Er — I — well, of course not, Abbess, it's just that you have a long road to travel, and — '

Her face alight, she interrupted him. 'Oh, what a fool I am! I had forgotten, but we *do* have another horse. A pale chestnut mare, a most beautiful animal, given into our care by — ' Her hand flew to her mouth and she stopped.

But she hadn't needed to say. Josse knew as well as she did who had ridden a pale chestnut mare. Someone whose new life must surely make caring for an elegant, well bred mare almost impossible . . .

'You have Joanna's mare,' he said tonelessly.

'Yes,' the Abbess said quietly. 'She left her with us. We promised to take care of her — she is called Honey, by the way — and we are allowed to ride her in exchange for her keep.'

'I see,' Josse murmured. But he was hardly listening. He was thinking of Joanna. With an effort, he made himself attend once more to the Abbess.

' . . . can't think of a lay brother small enough to ride the pony, which means we shall still be a mount short, unless we take the mule,' she was saying.

'Take Horace,' he said. 'He's at New Winnowlands, but someone can be sent to fetch him. *I'm* not using him,' he added bitterly.

'Horace,' the Abbess breathed. 'Oh, Sir Josse, are you sure? Such a valuable horse, and so *big*!'

'Get Saul to find a man who's a good rider,' Josse said. Suddenly he was weary of talking. Weary of being in pain, weary of being a prisoner in his bed when he wanted to be out in the fresh air, busy with myriad things that would take his mind off his memories.

The Abbess must have understood, for she leaned over him, put a gentle hand on his forehead and said softly, 'We will speak again before I depart; I cannot go until I have sought and obtained permission from the Archbishop. But for now, dear Sir Josse, rest. Sleep, if you can.' She hesitated as if not quite sure whether she should go on. Then, deciding, she whispered, 'You *will* get better. That I know.'

Then she was gone, leaving him wondering sleepily whether she had referred to his wounded arm or his sore heart.

Probably both.

★ ★ ★

He woke later from a fretful dream. Something was worrying him, some connection he should have made and hadn't . . . Something important, to do with the Abbess and her quest . . .

No. It had gone. He went back to sleep, and this time slept so deeply that, when next he woke, whatever it was that had been troubling him had disappeared without trace.

7

Brother Firmin was very reluctant to spare Saul, one of his hardest workers, to accompany the Abbess to Ely, so she had to turn a polite request into an order. The old monk made one or two comments under his breath, which Helewise pretended not to hear. Then, when she was back in her room fuming silently about silly old men who had forgotten there was any other world save the cloister, he confounded her by tapping softly on her door and presenting her, with the sweetest of smiles, with a small phial of the holy water 'to keep Our Lady with you on your travels'.

Brother Saul, on being informed of his unusual mission, was filled with a very obvious delight. His normally sombre face split into a wide grin, over which he appeared to have little control; he wore the same expression constantly for the next few hours, until the first delight wore off.

Helewise went to find him in the stables; he had rounded up the cob — who, for some long-forgotten reason, answered to the name of Baldwin — and was grooming him within an inch of his life.

'Brother Saul, may I interrupt you?' she asked, coming up behind him.

Instantly he stopped what he was doing and gave her a bow. 'I am at your disposal, Abbess. What can I do for you?'

Touched at the devotion in his face, she said, 'Saul, Sir Josse advises me to take *two* of the brothers with me. Now, this raises a couple of questions; one, who do you think would be suitable, and two, would this suitable man be up to riding Sir Josse's horse? That is,' she added, fearing that she had not been very diplomatic, 'unless you would like to ride it?'

Brother Saul was shaking his head emphatically at the very thought. 'Not me, Abbess, thank you all the same. Great hairy thing,' he muttered. Helewise thought, suppressing a smile, that it was just as well she knew he was referring to the horse. 'No, I like old Baldwin here,' he said, giving the cob a friendly slap. His face took on a frown of concentration. Then, clearing again, he exclaimed, 'Brother Augustine! He's the boy we want, Abbess!'

'Brother Augustine?' she repeated. 'I don't believe I know the name ... ' What an admission, she berated herself. I am Abbess here; I should know everyone in my community!

Brother Saul must have read her consternation. 'You might not know the name, Abbess, but I'll warrant you know the boy. Dark hair, dark eyes, foreign look about him, legs from his feet to his armpits, natural touch with animals and crotchety children?'

'*That* is Brother Augustine?' Of course she knew him! Why, she had remarked to Brother Firmin only last week what a help the lad must be when there were babies and toddlers needing to be watched while their parents were at prayer! 'But I thought he was called something else . . . Gus, that was it.'

Saul grinned. 'Aye, we mostly call him Gus. He seems to prefer it.'

She said, 'Tell me about Brother Augustine, Saul, if you will.'

Brother Saul leaned an arm over the cob's back, and, in that relaxed position, began. 'He's been with us six months or thereabouts. Family are tinkers — fairground entertainers, that sort of thing — and Gus, he'd been hearing Our Lord's call for a year or more when they fetched up here. His mother took sick — had a baby that died, and it took it out of her — and they came to the Vale to take the healing waters. Now young Gus loves his mother, anyone with eyes can see that, and he was that thankful when she recovered and began to smile again that he reckoned this was the moment to answer God's call.'

'If he's been here six months,' Helewise said doubtfully, 'then doesn't that mean his novitiate is over, and he's about to take the first of his vows?' It was not a moment to take a novice monk away from the Abbey, she thought.

'He's not a novice,' Saul said. 'Not yet, anyway. He's a lay brother.'

'But — ' Helewise began. If the boy had heard God's call so clearly, then why had he not asked to join the professed monks? It is not for me to ask, she told herself sternly. It is between God and Brother Augustine. Instead, turning her mind to practicalities, she said, 'He rides well, this Gus? Well enough to get Sir Josse's horse safely to Ely and back?'

'Aye, God willing,' Saul replied. 'See, he's got no fear, Abbess. He'll be happy enough sitting up there on old Horace's back, even though the animal's as high as a house. Been in the saddle since he were a little tacker, I'll warrant. Travelling folks, you see.'

'Indeed I do.' Helewise nodded gravely. 'Well, then, Saul, I suggest that, when you've finished polishing Baldwin, you take Brother Augustine over to New Winnowlands and bring Sir Josse's horse back here.'

Saul looked doubtful. 'Will they let me?' he asked nervously.

'Of course they will,' she said. 'They know you, Saul, don't they, Sir Josse's manservant and his woman?'

'Aye, but — '

Touched by his modesty — did he not know he had the most honest face of any man? — she said bracingly, 'No buts, Brother Saul. Go and see Sir Josse, explain your mission, and he will tell you what to say.' She turned to go. 'Oh, and Saul . . . ?'

'Abbess?'

'When you return, would you please groom the chestnut mare, too?'

Saul grinned. Beckoning her, he led her the few paces along to the end stall. Looking over the half-door, Helewise saw Joanna's mare. Her pale coat had been groomed until it gleamed. 'Oh!' Helewise exclaimed, instinctively holding out her hand, 'I had forgotten how beautiful you are!'

The mare came up to her, nuzzling a soft nose in her outstretched palm. The dark eyes studied her, and then the mare tossed her dainty head and gave a gentle whicker.

'Hello to you, too,' Helewise murmured. I am going to ride this lovely horse, she thought, a thrill of excitement coursing through her. For a *very* good reason, I am going on a long journey through springtime England. I know that the fact of my being so delighted at the prospect suggests that I should not be doing it, but really, I have no choice.

The mare had extended her head over the door, and Helewise leaned her face against the warm, smooth-haired flesh of the mare's gracefully arched neck. Forgive me, Lord, she prayed, if I am eager to go out into Your world. It does not mean that I love Hawkenlye any the less, nor that I am weary of my service to You in this place. But I must go.

As she walked back across the courtyard to her room, she resolved to tell Father Gilbert of her joy at the prospect of her journey. No doubt he would find a way to help her cope with it.

★   ★   ★

Her elation was, however, swiftly tempered by the realisation that she must decide what to do about Alba; the woman could hardly be left in the punishment cell indefinitely, and only the Abbess could release her.

She knelt in her room, asking for guidance.

And, after a while, she recalled an occasion when somebody else had had to be penned up at Hawkenlye Abbey. Not a monk, nor a nun, but a sad, mentally sick young man who had committed an unlikely murder. They had put him in an end chamber of the infirmary undercroft, in a dark little room with a lock on the door. Oh, Helewise thought, but, apart from being larger, was that any better than the punishment cell?

There are other rooms down there, she thought, there *must* be. Getting up, she hurried off to look.

She found what she needed. Not the end chamber, at the dark far end of the undercroft, but a larger one near to the entrance. It had a sizeable grille in its stout door; anybody imprisoned within would have at least some daylight.

She went in search of Brother Erse. He was a carpenter and could, she was sure, fit a bolt to the door in the time it took to arrange the chamber for its new prisoner.

★ ★ ★

When the room was ready, equipped with a straw pallet, covers, a jug of water and a drinking cup, Helewise asked Brother Erse to fetch Brother Saul and, with Sister Martha for support, the four went to let Alba out of the punishment cell and take her to her new accommodation.

A night in the tiny, dark cell had calmed

Alba. Blinking in the daylight, she walked obediently between her escorts across to the infirmary; ushered down into her new quarters, she gave a faint smile.

'You will be taken out for a walk in the fresh air twice a day,' Helewise told her, 'provided you behave. Your meals will be brought to you down here. You may have all reasonable comforts and, if you give no trouble, we will allow you a lantern at night.'

Alba would not meet her eyes.

Help me, dear Lord, to reach her! Helewise prayed silently. 'Alba?' she said gently. 'Is there anything you wish to say?'

Alba raised her head. Resentment was evident in her face, but also a grudging appreciation. She opened her mouth and, for a moment, Helewise thought she might be about to speak. But then, with a slight shake of her head, Alba turned away.

⋆ ⋆ ⋆

With a heavy heart, Helewise returned to her room and sent for Berthe.

The girl came quickly, and Helewise was touched to see the clear signs that she had been crying.

'Berthe,' Helewise said, 'I am going on a

112

journey. I must talk to the superior of the convent where Alba was before she came here. Can you tell me where it was?'

There was fear in the girl's face. She shook her head.

'Are you quite sure?' Helewise persisted.

'*Yes*, Abbess! Honestly, I *really* can't tell you that, I don't know it. She never said, and when I asked Father where she had gone and if we could visit her, he said she was dead to us and we must forget her.'

You poor child, Helewise thought, watching as Berthe struggled with renewed tears. 'Never mind,' she said — and how inadequate the words sounded, in the face of the girl's distress — 'it's all right, Berthe, I believe you.'

Berthe was watching her with a strange expression. She looked almost guilty, Helewise thought. Then, after some inner struggle that was painted clearly on her face, the girl said, 'We lived at Medely. That's where my father's farm was.'

'Medely?' Helewise repeated. The name meant nothing.

'Yes! It's quite a small place. And we — ' But then she folded her lips tight shut.

'Berthe?'

'I can't!' she cried. 'Oh, Abbess Helewise, you've been so nice to me and I *want* to help, but I just *can't*!'

113

You are afraid, Helewise thought compassionately. If I pressed you a little harder, I think you might break down and tell me what I need so badly to know. But what would that do to you, child?

No, she thought, I shall just have to do it the hard way.

She dismissed Berthe with a swift blessing — the poor child was surely in sore need of the Lord's blessing — and then summoned Brother Michael, giving him orders to ride down to Tonbridge and report the death of the pilgrim to Sheriff Pelham.

Thinking that at least she wouldn't have to deal with *him*, since, by the time the Sheriff got himself up to Hawkenlye, she would be on her way to Ely, her enthusiasm for her journey began to creep back.

* * *

The Abbess was not the only one eager to be on the road. In the infirmary, Josse lay aching for the party to be gone; only then, or so he hoped, would he be able to have any peace.

He kept envisaging them on the road; the Abbess, her faithful Brother Saul and this lad, Gus. The one who was going to ride Horace. Would they know what to do if anything unexpected happened? Supposing one of the

114

horses pulled up lame, supposing someone took a bad fall, supposing they found the road flooded, or a river crossing place impassable, would they know how to make a detour?

Had *any* of them the first idea of how to *get* to Ely?

The Abbess had visited him frequently over the past two days, serenely answering every objection. But she doesn't really know what it's going to be like, Josse fumed to himself; when did she ever go off into the blue with only a lay brother and a boy to protect her?

Then, early in the morning of the day that the party was to set out, he had a visit from Brother Augustine.

The boy stood in front of him, a friendly expression on his face. He looked, Josse thought, neither nervous nor overawed at this important mission for which he had been selected.

'I thought I should come to see you,' he said without preamble, 'being as how you've been kind enough to let me ride your horse.'

'Good of you,' Josse muttered.

The boy noticed the irony — Josse could tell by the swift response in the dark eyes — but instead of taking offence, he said, 'I know how you feel. You set a store by the Abbess, and you would give anything to be riding off instead of me. But you can't, because nobody here will risk you opening up that cut again. They nearly lost you last time. I just wanted to tell you, Sir Josse d'Acquin, that I know exactly what I'm being entrusted with, and I understand the honour and the responsibility of being asked to go in your place.' The dark eyes were fixed to Josse's, and Josse found the boy's gaze oddly compelling. The boy added softly, 'I would die before I let any harm come to her.'

Strangely, Josse was convinced by the quiet intensity with which the melodramatic words were spoken; he found that he entirely believed the boy's sincerity.

'I hope and pray that it will not come to that,' he said, careful to make his own words sound equally sincere. 'And thank you for coming to see me. I appreciate it.'

'Do you feel better now?' Brother Augustine asked.

Josse knew he was not referring to his physical state. He thought about it. Did he?

'Aye,' he said eventually. He gave the boy a grin; it was the first time he had felt like smiling for some time. 'I already knew that she — the Abbess — had a good and faithful companion in Brother Saul. Now that I have met you, Brother Augustine, I know that she will have two men with her with whom she'll be as safe as if I myself were going with her to Ely.' One of the boy's dark eyebrows went up in faint enquiry. 'Well, almost.'

The boy smiled. His teeth, Josse noticed, were white and strong looking; combined with the boy's tall, well-muscled frame, it seemed to suggest that his childhood on the road had been a healthy one. 'We shall look after her,' he said.

Josse nodded. 'Aye.' He sensed that the boy wanted to be off, but he could not resist a final enquiry. 'Now you do know the way? You're quite sure? Because I can't imagine that either the Abbess or Brother Saul could even guide themselves as far as London, or, even if once they could, they'll have forgotten, and — '

'I know the way,' the boy interrupted. He did not offer anything to back up his statement, but, watching him, Josse didn't think he needed to. The lad gave off an air of quiet confidence that was more impressive than a wealth of breathless assurances.

'Then it remains only for me to wish you God's speed, and a safe return,' Josse said.

'Thank you. We are to attend a special service in the Abbey church, then we set out.' A flash of excitement lit the young face. 'Abbess Helewise says to tell you she will come and say goodbye before we go.'

Josse watched him walk away, long legs covering the ground in smooth strides. Then he closed his eyes to add his own plea to the Lord to take care of the little party and bring them safely home again.

⋆   ⋆   ⋆

For the first few miles on the road, Helewise's pleasure in the sunny morning and the smooth gait of the chestnut mare were overshadowed by her memory of Josse as he said goodbye.

She had almost cried out, 'Oh, very well, we'll postpone the trip for a fortnight, a month, however long it takes you to be fit again! Anything, but don't look at me like that!'

Of course, she had kept her peace. But it had cost her a lot.

Brother Augustine was riding ahead, turning round from time to time to make sure that Horace's sprightly pace was not too fast for the mare and the cob and their riders. Helewise could hear Brother Saul behind her, keeping up a constant flow of softly spoken chatter to the old cob. Both men, she realised with relief, were showing the tact to leave her to her thoughts.

She decided to adopt Saul's tactics, and

118

began talking to the mare; even more important for me to do so than for Saul, she thought, since he and Baldwin are old friends, whereas this lovely mare and I are new to one another.

She began, tentatively and self-consciously at first, to introduce herself to her mount. Honey's ears twitched interestedly. Pleased to have a response, Helewise found it easier to find the words to say and, by the time they were descending the long slope down to Tonbridge and the river Medway crossing, she was chatting to Honey as if they had known one another for years.

★ ★ ★

According to Brother Augustine's reckoning, they covered not far short of twenty miles the first day. But then, he added, the horses were fresh and well rested, the weather was fine and warm, and the road good and firm under their feet. When he proposed that it was time to think about where they were going to stop for the night, Helewise almost urged him to go a little further; however, when she slid off Honey's back to stretch her legs for the final mile or so, she was very glad she hadn't.

It was many years since she had ridden any distance. And, although the mare's saddle

119

was expensively made and comfortable, Helewise's legs and thighs had stiffened up badly. Muscles she had forgotten she had seemed to squeal their protest, and she longed for the chance to rub on some of Sister Euphemia's special mixture. Yes, it would burn like fury, but it worked . . .

'All right, Abbess?' Brother Augustine called back to her.

'Fine!' she said, gritting her teeth and forcing a smile.

'Not far now,' the boy went on. 'There's a small convent I know of, up the road a way. They're generous to travellers, and they know me. They'll be honoured to receive the Abbess of Hawkenlye,' he added gravely.

Oh, dear, Helewise thought. Yes, I must present a suitably dignified demeanour. They have every right to expect that, from an Abbess.

But it wasn't going to be easy to be dignified, when the only way that she could walk was with her legs bowed out wide enough to circle a beer barrel.

8

The journey from Hawkenlye to Ely took a week.

It had been, Helewise thought as, on the morning of the seventh day, they set out from Barnwell Priory northwards into the Fens, an illuminating experience. There had been moments of fear-tinged excitement, such as crossing the river Thames between Dartford and the Essex shore on what had seemed far too small a boat. And, one night, they had been delayed in finding the tiny priory where they were to put up and, on the dark fringes of Epping Forest, Helewise had convinced herself she had heard the lonely, spine-chilling howl of a wolf.

She had noticed quickly that, each night, Brother Augustine chose a religious house for their accommodation. Sometimes this was a wise choice — the Benedictine nuns at Barking treated Helewise and her party as grandly as if they had been visiting royalty, and Helewise had been offered the extraordinary luxury of a *bath* to soothe her aching muscles. On the other hand, there was Latton; tiny, dark, very well hidden away — it was Latton which they were searching for when they had almost become lost in Epping Forest — the prior and his two canons had been able only to offer their guests a share of their own meagre soup and dry bread for the evening meal. Helewise had slept on a damp straw mattress in a corner of the chapter house, and the two lay brothers had slept in the tumbledown stable with the horses.

She had asked Brother Augustine the next morning if there were any option other than staying with monks or nuns. Looking slightly abashed, he replied, 'Well, not really, Abbess.'

'Where used you to put up, when you travelled with your family?' she persisted.

Brother Augustine's tanned face flushed slightly. 'We knew of — places we were welcome.'

'Could we not stay there, in those places?'

The blush was deepening. Brother Augustine hesitated, then, apparently deciding that this awkward conversation would come to an end more quickly if he steeled himself to be forthright, said, 'Abbess, it's different now. Then, we used to pay our way with our skills. A chair mended, a charm against warts or a cure for an aching back, a good tale or two that nobody had heard before, a song and a dance. That sort of thing.'

Intrigued, she ignored his obvious diffidence and said, 'What used you to do, Brother Augustine?'

Looking as if he wished he were anywhere but there, he said, 'I sang.'

'And could you not sing for your supper now?'

Brother Augustine's embarrassment made him lower his head. Then, looking up and catching her eye, suddenly he grinned. 'Not *that* sort of song I couldn't, Abbess.' The grin widened. 'Not in this company, and wearing the habit of a lay brother.'

'Oh!' Of course! Why hadn't she worked that out for herself! 'I see, Brother Augustine.'

No more had been said on the subject of their nightly accommodation.

But as Augustine's quite natural diffidence in the elevated company of his Abbess had abated, a great deal was said on many other subjects. Knowing that Saul would understand, Helewise had spent much of the first couple of days of the journey talking to the young man, trying to draw him out of his reticence.

Remembering what Saul had told her of the boy's devotion to his mother, she had first asked Augustine about his family. The question uppermost in her mind was did he miss them, and the itinerant way of life; after one or two preliminary pleasantries, she asked him.

'I do miss them, my mother and my father and my brothers and sisters,' Augustine replied after a moment's consideration. 'And I can't say as sometimes I don't hanker for the excitement of being on the road — you know, new sights every day, the pleasure of going back a year later to some favourite place and having the same warm welcome.' He paused. 'But I know Ma's well now, and she loves the life she leads. She understood when I explained to her about the Lord, how I heard Him calling to me, and she gave me her blessing over entering Hawkenlye.'

Helewise, riding beside him and watching him closely, noticed that his gaze had shifted, and that he was contemplating something distant. Not wishing to intrude on his thoughts, she said nothing.

After a while, he turned to her and, with a disarming grin, said, 'Sorry, Abbess. I've forgotten what it was you asked.'

Smiling in return, she said, 'Don't worry, Augustine. I think you have already answered me.'

But her curiosity was far from satisfied. As they rode on and the long days passed, she was increasingly impressed by Augustine's ability to find the way; how did he manage it?

Had all those years as a traveller given him some enhanced sense of direction so that, always knowing which way was north, the rest followed automatically? And how did he manage always to find provisions when they needed them and pure water when their gourds were nearly empty?

She asked him, but he seemed not to understand his abilities, nor even to believe they were anything out of the ordinary. When pressed, he merely shrugged and said, 'We could all do it, all of us. I suppose we sort of pick it up from each other.'

In addition, as the lad's confidence grew, he began to entertain his two companions with tales from an apparently inexhaustible supply; here the legend of a giant whose footfall made a pond; there a chilling story of a black dog whose appearance heralded the spectral apparition of his headless master; here a poignant tale of a little boy slaughtered by brigands who, despite having had his throat cut, managed to sweetly sing the 'Ave Maria' until his pathetic little body was discovered.

Augustine was, Helewise noted, a fine storyteller; when he had finished the tale about the little boy, she observed Saul wiping a surreptitious tear from his eye.

The weather stayed fine; there was always

enough to eat and somewhere to shelter for the night. Helewise, riding through the beauties of the countryside in April, wondered if she had ever felt more content. She had to keep reminding herself of her serious purpose; at times, it was very easy to forget all about it.

★   ★   ★

Now, leaving Barnwell with the joyful sound of the Augustinian canons' morning worship still ringing in her ears, Helewise looked around her eagerly at the changing landscape. First, we had the green, wooded hills of Kent, she reflected; few surprises there, she had spent most of her life in Kent and, in her youth and during her married life, had travelled her home county extensively. Then into Essex, where the great tracts of forest of Epping and Waltham had thinned as they went north and, for many miles, had travelled on what, according to Brother Augustine, was an ancient Roman road. Traffic had been heavier then; they had shared the track with carters, parties of merchants, and the occasional pilgrim band.

Augustine had told the Abbess that, once they reached the Fens, the landscape would change. His brief words of preparation had been enlarged on alarmingly by one of the monks at Barnwell who, on hearing that they were bound for Ely, had paled, shaken his head worriedly and tried to dissuade them.

'But you'll have to cross the Fens!' he exclaimed. 'And 'tis a terrible place! Black, oozing mud, dark, dangerous waters hidden under the mists, and there's no folk living there but have webbed feet and the ague. And they do say there's monsters and demons, living on the islands!'

Monsters and demons, she had thought, smiling at the man's superstitious dread. Dangerous waters, indeed. But, as the day's ride continued and they progressed north-wards, she realised that the old man might have been right after all . . .

The sodden soil, for one thing, was indeed so dark as to appear black. And there was water everywhere, perilously concealed, just as the monk had said, by sudden curls and swirls of mists that seemed to come out of nowhere and disappear just as mysteriously. Sometimes there would be a small 'pop!' and then a sudden foul smell, as if some unimaginable subterranean thing had briefly put its dreadful head above the surface and exhaled a mouthful of filthy breath.

There were few signs of human habitation. They passed one or two rough-looking settlements on isolated islands, and from one a large dog came running, barking ferociously until stopped with a hard cuff from a man dressed in what looked like a sack. Augustine waved and called out a friendly 'Good day!' but the man responded with a shake of his large fist.

The track meandered its way around the wetlands, but sometimes, when the sheet of black water seemed to extend endlessly on either side, they would have to proceed along a raised causeway.

Trying to calm her apprehension, Helewise called out to Augustine, 'Who built these raised tracks? Do you know, Augustine?'

He turned in the saddle and said, 'No, Abbess. They do say they were always here.'

Always here. A shiver of atavistic fear ran up the Abbess's spine. Perhaps they were built by demons and monsters . . .

From behind her, Saul said sensibly, 'Maybe it were the same folk that built the old roads. Eh, Gus?'

'Maybe,' he called back. Then, when the causeway had carried them on to the next stretch of wider track, he added, 'My grandfather found a sword, once, not far from here. Somebody told him to put it back where he found it, because it was an offering. To the spirits of the place.'

'An offering,' Helewise breathed. I should not be listening to this pagan talk, her conscience told her firmly. Only she didn't seem to be listening. 'Did he put it back?'

Augustine smiled. 'Not at first. But then he had a dream, in which black hands came snaking up out of the water, sliding round his neck and choking the life out of him. Next morning, he picked up the sword, ran back to the spot where it had lain all those years, and flung it in.'

She felt her heart begin to thump with fear. But then Saul, chuckling, said, 'My, but you tell a fine tale, Gus!' and she thought, with relief, yes. It's only a tale. And the dread went away.

★　★　★

Their progress that day was slow. Helewise thought that, on occasions, they seemed to double back on themselves; however, August-ine was a confident leader, and she did not think she should question his decisions.

They crossed a clearly defined waterway, which Augustine said was Wicken Lode, and, on the far bank, stopped to eat a light meal from their dwindling provisions. Augustine, Helewise noticed, was looking about him as he ate, apparently searching for something.

He exchanged a few words with Saul, then, approaching her, said, 'Abbess, we have to find one of the big causeways that lead up to Ely. There's three of them and, as far as I recall, one's not far from here. But I suggest I go and look, while you and Brother Saul stay here with the horses — I'll be best off on my own two feet.'

There seemed nothing to do but agree.

* * *

He was gone for some time. But he reappeared with such a pleased expression that Helewise and Saul knew without asking that he had been successful.

'I've found it!' he called out, waving both hands for emphasis. 'It's quite near, we shall be over it and arriving at Ely in no time.'

Arriving at Ely. As she mounted the mare and followed Augustine off towards the causeway, Helewise remembered, for the first time that day, what she was doing there. Now that they had almost reached their destination, she would soon have to take over the leadership from Augustine. She would have to find Alba's convent — and, she suddenly realised, how sketchy was the information telling her how to go about *that*! — and then she would have to find a diplomatic way of

130

informing Alba's former superior that her erstwhile nun was now incarcerated in a cell in Kent. Quite a comfortable cell, admittedly, but incarcerated nevertheless.

Help me, oh, Lord, she prayed with silent fervour as, with careful feet, Honey picked a path behind the reassuring bulk of Horace. I cannot do this alone.

They followed the causeway for some miles, and Helewise continued her praying. Then a sudden cry from Augustine made her raise her head.

'Look!' he shouted, pointing in front of him. '*Look!*'

She looked. So, beside her, did Saul.

Directly ahead, on a long island that seemed to rise like a great ship out of the watery marshland around it, was a building. Tall, imposing, its symmetry was only marred by the wooden scaffolding poles around one end.

Despite the many people scurrying round it — from this distance they were tiny and featureless — there was a sense of peace about the place. As if, up there on its low rise, it looked down on the world and gave its blessing.

And, into their awed silence, Augustine said quietly, 'That's Ely Cathedral.'

9

Having seen Brother Saul, Brother Augustine and the horses on their way to the guest lodgings of the monastery, Helewise asked one of the monks to direct her to the superior.

As she followed the black-robed figure along a maze of narrow corridors, she was cross with herself for her nervousness. This abbey might be very grand and have its own vast cathedral all but completed, she told herself, but Hawkenlye is equally important to God. Detecting a certain amount of worldly pride in the thought, she crushed it.

The monk tapped on a large oak door and, when a cool voice said 'Enter', opened it and stood aside to usher Helewise inside the room.

The monk who sat within, evidently busy with the sort of endless paperwork with which Helewise was all too familiar, looked up. His unsmiling face was thin to the point of boniness, and the light eyes under pale, almost invisible eyebrows and lashes had no discernible colour. Nor did they have any discernible warmth. He said curtly, 'Yes?'

She introduced herself. Trying to ignore the element of mockery in his incredulous 'All the way from Hawkenlye? In *Kent?*', she proceeded to state her business in Ely. Watching a hard, cutting smile spread across the thin face, she realised, too late, her mistake. 'Naturally,' she hastened to say, 'I did not expect to find that Sister Alba had actually been here in Ely, but I did wonder if — '

But he was not listening. Too busy enjoying her discomfiture, he interrupted her: 'We have no nuns here, Abbess. This is a *monastery.*' The slow delivery of the word 'monastery' — as if she were a halfwit and incapable of understanding — was insulting.

Anger gave her dignity, and told her what to say. 'I am aware of that,' she said calmly. 'I have come here merely to ask you to inform me of those foundations in the vicinity that are for women.' He opened his mouth — no doubt to say something else cutting — but she did not let him speak. 'Sister Alba was very sparing in giving details,' she went on, 'and so I must ask you, *if* it is not too much trouble, to give me a comprehensive list of all the convents you know of. Only when I am able to speak in private with her former superior is there any chance of my resolving this vexing situation, and so permitting my

133

community to return to our duty of serving God as He has ordained for us.'

Her determination seemed to have some effect; the abbot's supercilious expression relaxed slightly as he said, 'I understand your position, Abbess.' Then, after a pause as if to gather his thoughts, he said, 'You should, I advise, visit the nuns of Chatteris, and those in the priory at Cambridge, those being the two houses closest to us at Ely.' He frowned. 'Although why anybody would say Ely when their foundation was in Cambridge, I cannot say.' He was silent for some moments, apparently thinking. Then he said, 'Perhaps you might do better to go first to the small Benedictine house near to the Templar preceptory at Denney. Denney is between Ely and Cambridge; I therefore opine that it is more likely that somebody might possibly have described that location as being at Ely.' He gave a brief shake of the head, as if in incredulity at how anybody could be so ill-advised. 'Yes, Denney,' he repeated. Then, fixing hard and amused eyes on Helewise, added, 'The nuns there run a madhouse.'

His faint sneer said all too plainly that he thought Helewise might well be admitted to it.

'Is there no other convent nearer?' she asked, ignoring the sneer.

The disdainful look intensified. 'Nothing worth the name,' he said coldly. 'However, there is Sedgebeck.'

'Sedgebeck?'

He did not answer. Instead, he said, 'Your nun — this troublesome Sister Anne — '

'Alba.'

' — does not appear, you judge, to have absorbed the essence of the cloistered life?'

Untangling his pedantry, she said, 'No. I do not believe she has.'

Now he was actually smiling, probably, Helewise thought, at the pleasant prospect of imminently seeing the back of her. 'Then I would venture to suggest that, before Denney, to Sedgebeck you should go.'

She wasn't going to risk allowing him to snub her by asking why; in all probability, he would say something annoying such as 'That you must judge for yourself, Abbess, I could not possibly say'. Instead, she merely said, 'I thank you for your time,' and turned to leave the room.

He called out: 'Do you not need me to give directions?'

Feeling a small and totally unworthy sense of triumph, she said sweetly, 'Indeed no, Abbot, I shall ask someone who, unlike yourself, is not engaged in such all-absorbing work.'

* * *

She found her way back to the courtyard, where Saul and Augustine were waiting for her.

She said, 'We have to find somewhere called Sedgebeck, then a place called Denney, where Benedictine nuns run a madhouse. Do you know of either, Augustine?' The young brother shook his head. 'Then we need to ask for directions,' she continued. 'Have you met any friendly, Christian soul who might provide them?'

Augustine raised an eyebrow, and exchanged a swift glance with Saul. Both, Helewise noted, were too well disciplined to enquire why the Abbot hadn't told her which way to go.

'I shall ask the stabler,' Saul said. 'He says he is a local man.'

Soon he was back. 'For Sedgebeck, we have to go back the way we came, re-cross Wicken Lode, and go south towards a low isle that we'll see directly in front of us. That's Sedgebeck. Denney lies south-west of here, and it is a good road.'

Saul, Helewise noticed, looked pale. 'Thank you, Saul,' she said. 'Are you all right?'

'Yes, Abbess.'

'I suggest, then, that we leave straight

away,' she announced. 'We have several hours of daylight left, and if neither Sedgebeck nor Denney is the right place, then the sooner we establish that, the sooner we can get on with finding the one that is.'

Brother Saul's mouth had dropped open. 'Abbess, if we're heading for Sedgebeck, I really think we would be better to set out in the morning,' he said. Beads of sweat were standing out on his forehead.

'Why, Saul?' she asked gently, greatly surprised that her stalwart Brother Saul seemed to be showing all the signs of extreme terror. 'What else did the stabler tell you about the place?'

'Abbess, if it truly *is* where Sister Alba was, then it's no wonder the poor lass is losing her wits!' His voice dropped to a whisper, and he edged closer. Augustine, Helewise noticed, did as well. They must look, she reflected wryly, like a trio of witches.

'Sedgebeck has an evil reputation,' Saul murmured. 'People have got lost there in the marshes, and gone clean out of their wits! And there's shifting sands, too, in the waterways, that suck an unwary traveller in and don't give up the body till he's long dead and drowned! There's things that live in the water thereabouts that no man wants to encounter, unholy things, things that creep up out of the ooze and steal livestock. Steal babies, too, so the stabler says.'

Helewise straightened up and said firmly, 'Saul, you have been listening to superstitious gossip. Do you really think that Our Blessed Lord would allow such things on His earth, especially so near to the sanctified ground of one of His holy communities?'

'But that's just it, it seems they do say that Sedgebeck is not — ' Saul began.

'And that,' Helewise interrupted, 'sounds very like gossip of another kind, but just as reprehensible! Please, brothers, fetch the horses, see if you can beg some provisions from the good monks, and let's be on our way.'

With one last miserable look in her direction, Saul did as she commanded. Augustine went to follow him, but stopped. 'Abbess?' he said softly.

'Yes, Augustine?'

'It may not necessarily be just gossip, you know. We should take heed — these rumours don't grow up for nothing, not in my experience.'

She should have listened. Augustine's experience, having been brought up a child of the travelling people, was worth heeding.

But she was still suffering from the after-effects of her interview with the Abbot, and reasoning with two lay brothers, wide eyed with peasant dread, did not appeal just then. She said curtly, 'Please go and help Brother Saul. We leave as soon as we can be ready.'

* * *

The sun was low in the sky as they set out. A splendid sunset was painting the sky flaming orange, and small, brilliant pink clouds were puffing up from the cooling land. There were rustling sounds coming from the reed beds which, Helewise told herself, were doubtless waterfowl settling into their roosts.

They rode for some time. Then the weather changed.

A bank of cloud low on the horizon suddenly began to grow, blooming quickly like some weird, black fungus, spreading rapidly up the sky. There was a distant, ominous growl of thunder.

Saul, edging the cob up close beside Helewise, said urgently, 'Abbess, there's a storm coming!'

'Indeed there is, Brother Saul. What do you — ?'

But Augustine, in the lead, interrupted. Turning round, he called out, 'If we proceed to Sedgebeck, we're going to be drenched. It will take time — we have to find the way, and it's likely some of the dykes and ditches may flood if there's heavy rain. But it's a straight road to Denney, and only another four or five miles — should we not head there, Abbess?'

She thought quickly. Keep to the plan and seek out the convent hidden away in the fens? Or divert and go to Denney?

Another clap of thunder rolled towards them across the flat land. Swiftly making up her mind, she called out to Augustine, 'Lead us to Denney!'

★ ★ ★

They arrived as the first raindrops started to fall; big, round and hard as stones, they pounded agonisingly on to the three riders. Helewise tried to cover her head with one hand as she watched Augustine shouting at the porter above the sounds of the storm; he must have known exactly what to say for, after a moment, the big gate was thrown open and they all rode inside.

A couple of sacking-covered figures ran out to help, taking the horses and hurrying them under cover as another figure, also sheltering under a sack, peered out from a partly-opened door and beckoned the Abbess and the two lay brothers inside.

140

It was only as this figure was removing its sack and speaking words of welcome that Helewise realised it was a man. Hurriedly responding to the greeting, she asked, 'Is this not the Benedictine house at Denney?'

And the man, who, with the sack fully removed, was revealed as young, fresh-faced and dressed in a black habit, said, 'No. This is indeed Denney, but you are come to the Templar preceptory. Was it the Benedictines whom you sought, Sister?'

'It was,' she replied.

The man cocked an ear to another great rumble of thunder. 'Then I suggest you delay your mission until morning, and stay with us for this wild night.'

She could almost feel the relief coming off her two companions. With a bow to the black-robed monk, she said, 'Thank you. We gratefully accept your hospitality.'

★　★　★

The guesthouse of the Templars was luxurious.

Helewise, who was, she reckoned, probably the only woman under the preceptory's roof, had a room to herself. She was provided with hot water, a delicious meal and a jug of wine, and a fire was lit for her to dry her clothing.

She slept soundly, in a very comfortable bed with linen sheets and soft, woollen blankets.

Reunited with Saul and Augustine in the morning, the same monk who had received them the night before led them to a small room, where they were served breakfast. Helewise was just wondering why they were kept apart from the community when the monk said, 'Forgive us if we appear preoccupied. We are in the midst of grave afflictions that demand our Master's full attention, and that of our senior brothers.'

'I am sorry that we add to your burdens,' Helewise replied.

'Please, no need for apologies.' The monk smiled at her. 'I have been detailed to give you what help I can; may I take you to the Benedictine house, for example? Perhaps if you could reveal your business with the sisters there . . . '

Helewise saw no reason to ignore his invitation. She explained her mission but, before she had finished, the monk had begun to shake his head. 'Abbess — forgive me for having addressed you as Sister last night — Abbess, I can save you a wasted journey, for the nuns at Denney are most unlikely to have accepted your Sister Alba into their community. The nuns are all — er, *mature* in years, and without exception have been in the convent many years. Newcomers do not present themselves there seeking to join the community, for the work is arduous, and the Lord calls few to serve Him there.'

Helewise suppressed a sigh. Oh, dear, it looked as though she and the lay brothers were going to have to brave Sedgebeck. She met the young monk's anxious eyes. 'I see,' she said. 'In that case, we must go on to the convent at Sedgebeck, and enquire whether the nuns there know of our Sister Alba.'

'Sedgebeck,' the young monk repeated, frowning. 'I seem to recall the name . . . now where did I hear tell of the place?' His face cleared and he had just begun on a cheerful 'Yes, I recall now!' when the door opened and another, older monk entered.

Without preamble, the newcomer said curtly, 'Brother Timothy? Your presence is required in the dormitory, where Brother Adam needs you to help him repair the roof.'

The younger man had leapt to his feet. 'But I was just . . . '

'Now, please, Brother Timothy,' the older monk said, in a voice which allowed for no argument.

With a bow to Helewise, and a deeper bow to his fellow monk, Brother Timothy left the room.

The older monk said, 'You are bound for Sedgebeck, Abbess?' Helewise nodded. 'Then I recommend that you leave as soon as the rain stops.'

With no further speech — and no explanation of his remark — he, too, left the room.

Helewise and the two lay brothers saw no other monks before they left. Soon after midday, at last the rain eased up and allowed them to get on their way, and Helewise reflected that, whatever was preoccupying the brethren at Denney, it must be quite serious. Grateful for their hospitality, even if they had been somewhat aloof, she prayed that their troubles would soon be resolved.

★　★　★

They made reasonable progress along tracks made muddy and sodden with rain. Refreshed from a good night's sleep and a generous breakfast, they did not stop for more than a brief halt and, by late afternoon, Augustine reckoned they could not have many more miles to go.

In the lead as before, he drew rein and, shading his eyes against the sunset, stared out over the wetlands to the south. 'I can see a rise, there, straight ahead,' he commented.

144

Helewise looked where he was pointing. 'Yes, I see it. Do you think it is Sedgebeck?'

'Hope so,' Saul muttered.

'Come along, then,' she said decisively. 'It cannot be far. If we press on, we should surely be there before long.'

They pressed on. But, no matter how hard they tried to steer a straight line towards the rise, obstacles seemed to keep throwing themselves in their path. They would come to a lode just too wide for the horses to jump safely, or just too deep to ford. And, every time they had to divert to the east or the west, the growing darkness made it that much more difficult to discern the faint hump that was Sedgebeck.

After a long, anxious wait while Augustine stood up in the stirrups, peering into the gloom, Helewise said, 'Can you still see the place, Augustine?'

'I *think* so,' he replied, his voice sounding blessedly normal. Then: 'Aye. We must head along this bank,' — he indicated to the left — 'quickly find a place to cross, then go straight ahead. That should do us.'

Saul was muttering under his breath. It sounded as if he were praying.

They found a piece of reasonably firm ground and put the horses at the ditch crossing their path. All landed safely; perhaps,

Helewise thought, we should *all* join in with Saul's prayers, since the dear Lord seems to be listening.

They set out towards the island. The ghostly shape of a large, home-going bird flew across in front of them, a dark silhouette against the last of the light; Augustus said calmly, 'Heron.' And, as the warm, damp darkness seemed to settle around them, they heard the high-pitched, unmistakable whine of mosquitoes.

Slapping at her cheek, Helewise said urgently, '*Hurry*, Augustine!'

But, still calm, his voice floated back to her, 'No need for alarm, Abbess. It's best to make our way carefully, let the horses pick out their own path. Don't worry, they know where it's safe to tread.'

Fighting down her panic, Helewise took a couple of deep, steadying breaths, and began to pray.

★   ★   ★

It was fully dark when at last they climbed the slope up on to the island. The wet, heavy clay soil stuck to the horses' feet, and their hooves made a different sound in the still night.

From the low, reed-thatched buildings ahead that seemed to be the convent came

146

neither sound nor light. Oh, dear God, there's nobody here! Helewise thought. They've fled, or all died of the ague, or run from the demons and devils . . .

She heard a low moan from Saul. In front of her, Augustine sat on Horace's back as if turned to stone. They are my responsibility, these good, loyal men, she told herself. I must not sit here in dread — it is I who brought them here, and it is I who must try to rescue this awful situation . . .

Leaping into action before her fear could overcome her totally, she slid off Honey's back — the horses were not afraid, she noted almost subconsciously, so it couldn't be that bad — and, handing the reins to Saul, strode up to what looked like an opening in the low wooden stockade surrounding the buildings. There was a hurdle drawn across the gap, which she pushed aside. Immediately some animal that had been penned inside rushed past her and disappeared, with a splash of running feet, into the fen.

Oh, dear, she thought, hoping that the creature, whatever it was, wouldn't go far. She slid the hurdle back in place again, and went on towards the nearest of the buildings, which was the only one of any size.

Feeling foolish, she called out softly,

'Hello? Is anybody within? I seek the Abbess of Sedgebeck.'

From inside there was a rustling sound, as if someone were stirring in a bed of straw. 'Who's there?' a loud voice cried. 'Who comes to disturb our sleep? Be warned, we have dogs we shall set on you!'

'No!' Helewise exclaimed. She heard Saul crashing through the gap in the fence, and an instant later he was at her side. He had a cudgel in his hand which, she was sure, he hadn't been carrying when they left Hawkenlye.

'This is the Abbess of Hawkenlye!' he shouted. 'She comes on an important mission! Open up, in charity, and let us in!'

There was more rustling, and a pad of footsteps. Then a small wooden shutter in the door was slid back, revealing the sudden blinding light of a lantern. A pair of eyes peered out, narrowed in suspicion. 'Hawkenlye?' the voice said. 'Hawkenlye, where the Holy Waters are?'

'Yes,' Helewise said, trying to sound calm and reassuring. 'We mean you no harm, in God's name. We need shelter.'

'Hawkenlye,' the voice repeated. Its gruff tone made it difficult to tell whether it belonged to a man or a woman. 'Aye, that's a fair step away, I'll warrant.'

'We have been on the road a week,' Helewise began, 'and — '

Abruptly there came the sound of a heavy bar being drawn back, and the door swung open. 'Then you'd better come in, you and your manservant,' said their host.

Who, in the lantern light from within the building, was revealed to be a very tall, strongly-built woman, wearing the sleeping cap of a nun on her head and, covering her from chin to ankle, a voluminous, cream linen chemise, much darned and none too clean.

'I am accompanied by two lay brothers,' Helewise said, hesitating on the doorstep, 'and we each have a horse . . .'

The huge nun glanced outside, taking in at a glance the figure of Saul, just behind the Abbess, and, beyond him, Augustine holding the horses. 'The men and the horses can go in there.' She held the lantern aloft, pointing with the other hand towards one of the other two buildings, smaller and less well maintained than the main one. 'Hardly a stable, since we have no horse, but there's straw in there for our pig, and it'll keep out the mist and the fumes of the night air.'

'Will you be all right, Abbess?' Saul muttered in her ear.

'Yes, Saul. You and Augustine get some sleep. I'll see you in the morning.'

She watched them head off for the outhouse. Then she followed the nun inside and closed the door. The nun edged her out of the way and barred it.

Then she turned and stared at Helewise. Indicating a curtained-off area at the far end of the room, she said, 'The others are in there. I'll tell them who you are and why you've come, then I'll heat some water and make you a hot drink.'

'Thank you,' Helewise replied vaguely.

Tell them why you've come. But how could the big nun possibly know, since Helewise hadn't told her? She felt a shiver of fear run through her. This place, this desolate place, she thought, trying to be rational, must be affecting her. She must have misheard . . .

The nun was back within moments. Talking as she moved about, poking up the fire in the central hearth and suspending a pot over it from a tripod, she said, 'I've some chamomile, it will help you sleep. And perhaps a pinch of valerian. There, it'll soon be ready.' She fetched an earthenware mug, dusted it on the skirt of her gown, and placed it on the floor beside the hearth. 'Really,' she went on in the same conversational tone, 'we were quite sure we'd seen the last of Alba.'

10

The nun poured hot water on to the herbs she had put into the cup, stirred the mixture with her finger and, after a few moments, handed it to Helewise.

'Hmm,' she mused. 'Think I'll have one myself.'

Deliberately closing her mind to the filthy skirt and the finger that the nun had used to stir, Helewise sipped her drink. It tasted surprisingly good; there was the distinct sweetness of honey.

'Now,' the nun said, settling beside Helewise, 'you're here about Alba.'

'How did you know?'

The woman smiled faintly. 'We have our share of troubles here at Sedgebeck. Most of them — loneliness, not enough to eat, mist, damp, ague — we can cope with. Alba, however, was beyond our skills.' She sighed.

Desperately curious to hear more, nevertheless Helewise remembered her manners. 'Are you — forgive my asking, but are you the superior here? Only . . .'

'Only you should not speak of such private matters other than to another superior. Quite right, Abbess . . . ?'

'Helewise.'

'Abbess Helewise. Yes, I am the superior. I am Abbess Madelina.'

'And you are sure that our talking will not disturb your sleeping sisters?'

Abbess Madelina gave a quiet laugh. 'One is elderly and almost totally deaf, one is sick and has taken a sleeping draught, one is so deep in her communion with Our Lord that she will be hard put to hear the Last Trump when it summons her.'

'And the others?'

The Abbess gave her a strange look. 'There are no others.'

Four women alone in this wilderness! Helewise thought, aghast. Dear Lord, what a place! What did they do here?'

Abbess Madelina said, 'We work our small patch of land, we tend our animals, we pray.'

Stunned, Helewise said, 'How did you know what I was thinking?'

'We receive few visitors, as you will readily understand. Those who do persevere through the marsh, the mists and the biting flies all say the same thing. How do we cope with living out here?'

'I am sorry,'

'No need to be. In answer to the question, we always say the same words. That God has called us to this lonely, desolate place in order that His precious light shall illuminate the darkness, and that when He calls, we obey.' Abbess Madelina stood up. 'Now, will you have more to drink?'

No longer the least disturbed at thoughts of grubby skirts and dirty fingernails, Helewise held up her cup. 'Yes, please.'

'A bite to eat? There's a heel of bread and some salt pork.'

It would have been rude to reject the kind offer. Besides, Helewise was hungry, and her own provisions were out in the outhouse with the brothers and the horses. 'Thank you.'

'And now,' Abbess Madelina said presently, sitting down again, 'Alba. She is, I would guess, in some sort of trouble that affects you, or else you would not be here.'

'She is.' Quietly, Helewise told the Abbess of the struggle that the Hawkenlye nuns were having in trying to welcome Alba into their fold. She kept her account brief; there was a temptation to open her heart to this friendly stranger, but Helewise resisted it. She made no mention of Alba's attack on her youngest sister, and alluded only briefly to the blow that Alba had tried to land on her Abbess. 'So you see,' she concluded, 'I am in the difficult position of having been forced into doubting the vocation of a professed nun.'

'Hmm.' Abbess Madelina gave Helewise a look from clear blue eyes. Then: 'I am sorry for your troubles, Abbess Helewise. Our experience of Alba, distressing though it was, did not in general disrupt our little community quite as badly as recent events appear to have disrupted yours.'

And I have not told you the half of it, Helewise thought.

The bright blue eyes were studying her with compassion. Helewise found herself warming to this forthright Abbess, who appeared to accept her dismal lot with such fortitude and serenity. On an impulse, she said, 'How did *you* cope with Sister Alba?'

Abbess Madelina said, 'Not *Sister* Alba.'

'Not — but she told me she took the last of her final vows! Five years ago, she said!'

'She lied to you, Abbess. She was with us for under a year and, although I permitted her to take her first vows and embark on her novitiate, it was an error of judgement. After only four months, I suggested to her that she should not proceed with us. I requested the archbishop to release her from her vows, and she left the convent.'

'And made her way to us,' Helewise breathed.

'Not immediately.' Abbess Madelina's face was grim. 'First she tried to destroy our

154

chapel. With some determination, I might add.' She held out her right arm, in which the inner bone of the forearm was strangely crooked. 'I fear that is as good as it is going to get, she said, looking at the bent arm. 'She — Alba — broke a candlestick over it, and the bones did not knit together quite right.'

Helewise put out a tentative hand, touching her fingertips against the distorted arm. 'She must have hurt you.'

'I mended. What about you?'

'As I said, I managed to step out of the way.'

A silence fell between them. Helewise felt scant satisfaction in having been proved right about Alba; right or wrong, it didn't remove the terrible dilemma of what to *do* about her.

Again following the train of her thoughts, Abbess Madelina said, 'There is much I can tell you about Alba, Abbess, if you will hear me.'

'Gladly,' Helewise said. 'I need your advice, Abbess Madelina.'

'And you shall have it.' The big nun got to her feet and, towering over Helewise, said, 'But it is too long a tale for now. I will tell you in the morning.'

Within a short space of time Helewise — no longer hungry nor thirsty, and exhausted from the physical and mental

155

efforts of the long day — was settling down on a hard-packed straw mattress, drifting off to sleep.

★ ★ ★

She was awakened by the sound of a nun's voice, calling out with clearly audible joy, 'Praise be to God, who in His goodness has awarded us the gift of this new day!'

From close beside her, Helewise heard the crackle of straw mattresses as the other nuns flumped out of bed and on to their knees on the cold, beaten-earth floor, raising their voices in the morning prayers. After a few moments, she joined in with the familiar words.

Then, still in almost total darkness, she did as she presumed the others were doing and put on wimple, coif and veil, draping her robe over her undergown and fastening her belt. Stepping out from behind the curtained-off section of the room, she found that the main living area was lit by a pearly, early morning glow.

One of the nuns was laying out chunks of bread on five wooden trenchers, placing them equidistant apart along a rickety-looking table. Five earthenware mugs stood ready beside a pot of water that was simmering over the hearth. The nun looked up and, noticing Helewise watching, gave her a very sweet smile and beckoned her to be seated.

The sparse breakfast was taken in silence. Then Abbess Madelina stood up, led Helewise and the sisters in a brief prayer and, with a nod, dismissed her nuns.

Helewise looked out through the door as they left. It appeared to be a lovely day.

'They all have their allotted tasks,' Abbess Madelina said. 'And, Abbess, you will be pleased to hear that your two lay brothers are making themselves useful. One has already rounded up the pig — sensible fellow, he knew the animal would return as soon as she heard the rattle of the stick on the feed bucket — and the other is making good a damaged section of our enclosing fence.'

'They are reliable men, both of them,' Helewise replied.

'And the elder quite devoted to you.' Abbess Madelina gave her a smile. 'He asked how you fared, and was clearly anxious lest you had taken chill.'

Oh, dear, Helewise thought, I do hope Saul was diplomatic.

'Don't concern yourself,' Abbess Madelina added, 'he was perfectly courteous. Now' — she pressed on while Helewise was still reeling from yet again having had her

157

thoughts read so accurately — 'to poor Alba. I said I would tell you what I know, and indeed I shall. Although, in the light of experience of the woman, I do wonder how much will prove to be the truth . . . However, that remains to be seen.'

She paused, gazing into the corner of the room as she seemed to decide how best to begin. The action gave Helewise a strong sense of affinity with her; she, too, had been trained during her novitiate to assemble her thoughts before she spoke, so as to ensure both clarity and economy of speech.

'Alba came here early last summer — in May, I believe it was,' Abbess Madelina began. 'My first impression was that she sought admission with us because of some intolerable situation in the world, which is not, of course, the same thing as a vocation. However, I tried to maintain an open mind and, indeed, to begin with she did seem to adapt quite well to community life. One might almost say *too* well, for she was rigid in her self-discipline and also in her assessment of the discipline of others. For example, Sister Mary is elderly and deaf, and in addition suffers grievously from pains in her joints, and I turn a blind eye when she fails to hear a summons to prayer, or when she slips a piece of cloth between her aching knees and the cold, hard, damp floor of the chapel when she kneels to pray. Alba, in her single-mindedness, *always* brought these things publicly to my notice. And she would take our dear Sister Celestine to task over her absent-mindedness; she kept coming to me to report that Celestine was standing staring up into the sky when she should be working, or humming gently to herself when she should be engaged in silent prayer. Now, Abbess, I know Sister Celestine, and I understand that she is blessed with a rare and precious gift, that of communion with the Lord, whose voice she hears in the wind, in the beating of the rain, in birdsong, and in any number of other natural sounds. Who are we, her sisters, to interrupt when Our Blessed Lord chooses to speak? And, as I repeatedly told Alba — who just would not listen — Sister Celestine always makes up her share of the duties.'

'But over-eagerness is quite common among postulants,' Helewise remarked.

Abbess Madelina nodded. 'Yes, indeed it is. That was what I kept telling myself. And, as the weeks passed and Alba began pressing to take her first vows as a novice, I decided to ask her about her background. It can be of help, I find, to know what it is in a person's personal history that has given rise to certain

159

habitual behaviour.'

'What did she say?'

'She said she was from a wealthy family — which was in fact supported by the fact that she had arrived with a generous endowment including both money and goods — and that the richness of her home life had become a great burden to her. The lavishness of her father's hall sickened her very soul, she declared, when, within so short a distance of that warm, glowing place of abundance, the poor were dying of hunger and disease. She was called to a humble life of prayer, she told me, and fervently hoped that her own renunciation of wealth and comfort would mitigate against her family's state of self-indulgent comfort.'

'She must have been quite a trial to her family,' Helewise commented.

'Exactly what I thought, Abbess. I did wonder, although I am ashamed to confess it, whether the generous dowry was her father's way of saying that he would pay *any* price to be rid of her.'

'Quite.' Helewise was thinking, trying to remember exactly what Alba had told her on arriving at Hawkenlye.

As she had half expected before Abbess Madelina had even begun, it was totally different from what the woman had told the

Abbess of Sedgebeck. Alba had said that her family had farmed a smallholding — which they had not owned — and, when the parents died, the girls had been left homeless. And, presumably, penniless.

Where had the Sedgebeck dowry originated, then? And why had Alba made up the story about coming from a wealthy home?

Unless perhaps *that* story were the true one, and the tale of poor homeless orphans was the lie?

A thought occurred to Helewise.

'Abbess, what did Alba look like?'

The blue eyes held hers, a shrewd expression in them. 'Is the story she told us so very different that you question whether your Alba and ours are one and the same?'

Helewise smiled. 'Yes.'

'Alba is of medium height, but with a wiriness that gives the illusion that she is tall. Her face is habitually pale, save when she flies into a rage, when she takes on a violent flush. Her mouth is small, with thin lips that fold in on themselves when she disapproves of something. Her eyes — ' The Abbess broke off. 'Do you know, I cannot recall what colour Alba's eyes are.' She sounded as if it were cause to reprove herself.

'Neither can I,' Helewise agreed. 'They are rather small eyes, deeply-set.'

'Yes, that's right.' Abbess Madelina sighed. 'I do think, Abbess, that we refer to the same woman.'

'Yes, I am sure of it. And, as you rightly guessed, the story she told to me of her background was entirely different.' Briefly she related it. 'One similarity, however, does occur to me.'

'Yes?' Abbess Madelina said eagerly.

'Oh, it's only a small point! I was just thinking that, in both cases, Alba made herself out to be heroic.' No — that sounded far too accusatory. 'I should say, the circumstances that she related suggested, in each case, that she had acted with courage and a nobility of soul. When she came here, she said she had given up a life of luxury because she could not equate it with the sufferings of the poor. When she came to Hawkenlye, she said she had been forced to leave a community where she was very happy out of duty to her family. Her younger sisters were heartbroken over the death of their parents, and Alba took upon herself the responsibility for their happiness, removing them from the place where they had suffered their loss and taking them on to a new life elsewhere. And — Abbess, whatever is the matter?'

For Abbess Madelina, surprise quite

evident in her face, was slowly shaking her head. 'Abbess Helewise, we *must* be speaking of two different women after all. *Our* Alba had no sisters; she was an only child.'

11

It took a moment for the two Abbesses to reach the clear conclusion that Alba had lied to Abbess Madelina about being an only child, as well as about so much else.

But *why*?

'If the parents were living when Alba came here to Sedgebeck,' Helewise ventured, 'then, in truth, the little sisters were not her responsibility. But, once the parents were dead — and I should say, Abbess Madelina, that there are doubts about whether they died together, as Alba says, or whether in fact the mother died some time ago and the father but recently — then she could no longer ignore the girls.'

'Hmmm. I think,' Abbess Madelina said, 'that your next step must be to seek out the former family home. Assuming that you have been told where it was. I am afraid we were not.'

'I have been informed,' Helewise reassured her. 'Berthe told me.'

'Good. Much as I should like you to stay here with us and rest for a few days after your long journey, I do feel that we have told you

164

all that we are able to. And every day you remain here is another day for the trail, if indeed there is one, to go cold.'

'Indeed,' Helewise agreed. 'And another day that Meriel is missing and possibly in danger.'

'Missing?'

Helewise realised that she had not yet told Abbess Madelina about that. Nor, indeed, about the slain pilgrim found on the path in the Vale. Trying to minimise her distress — and with the distinct feeling that she was not succeeding very well — she explained.

Shaking her head in dismay, Abbess Madelina said as Helewise finished speaking, 'I shall pray for you, Abbess. I shall keep you with me in my thoughts, and, if you will permit, I shall ask Sister Celestine to ask the Lord to aid you.'

★ ★ ★

Helewise and the two lay brothers set out from Sedgebeck after joining the sisters for their noon meal. Helewise was quite sure that the kindly nuns had shared more of their precious stores with their guests than was prudent, for the meal was very good, and the portions were generous.

She had told the brothers where they were

165

bound for next. 'We only have the single name, Medely, to guide us,' she had said as they set out, 'and, for all I know, it may be but a tiny hamlet. None of the Sedgebeck sisters knew of it when we asked them over dinner.'

Brother Saul suggested enquiring at Ely. But Augustine said, 'I once went to a place called Medely Birdbeck. There was a fair there, and we put on a show for them.'

Wondering whether Abbess Madelina's prayers were already having an effect, Helewise said, 'Let's begin there, then.'

It was not a long ride to Medely Birdbeck. But, far from being the substantial and thriving place that Helewise had been expecting — fairs, after all, were not held in the middle of nowhere — it proved to be all but deserted.

There were more than twenty dwellings, set around a pond fringed with willows, and a crossroads met in the middle of the village. But most of the dwellings were quite obviously uninhabited. Smoke was coming out of only two or three chimneys.

'What has happened here?' Helewise whispered. The sense of dread before the unknown — never far away, all the time that she had been in the Fens — came rushing back.

'They suffer greatly from the ague here-abouts,' Augustine said, his face falling into lines of sorrow as he stared out towards the empty stretch of ground leading down to the pond. 'They do say it's spread by the biting flies, which bring the sweating, feverish sickness. It's accompanied by a trembling so violent that it fair shakes a man to pieces. The strong can survive, but the young and the elderly . . . ' He did not finish his sentence.

'And they have all died here?' Helewise said.

Augustine shrugged. 'I cannot say for sure, Abbess, but it seems likely. I've seen places like this before. We never used to stay around to ask, though. Better not to linger, where the sickness has already claimed so many.'

Helewise had a sudden sharp awareness of what she was asking of these two loyal men. 'You are quite right, Augustine,' she said. 'You and Brother Saul must retreat to — well, to whatever you feel is a safe distance while I go on and — '

Both the brothers spoke together. Brother Saul said, 'You must not go on alone, Abbess, there may be desperate ruffians lurking,' and Brother Augustine said, 'The biting flies are worst in the warm dampness of summer, there is nothing to fear from them now.'

Despite herself, Helewise laughed. 'How

convincing you both are,' she murmured. 'Very well. Let's see if one of those smoking chimneys belongs to the house of somebody who can help us.'

The first occupied house was temporarily empty, although there was a pot of something simmering over the fire, and a small child lay asleep under a patched blanket.

The door of the next house opened a crack as they approached, and an old man stuck his head out. 'What do you want?' he asked.

'We seek news of a family that once lived hereabouts,' Helewise said.

'Eh?' He stuck his head out further. 'A nun! You're a nun!' The sight of her seemed to reassure him, and he opened the door a little wider. 'What family? You'll be lucky if they're still alive, we had the sickness bad, lost many of our number. Some that didn't fall ill have fled. Couldn't say where.'

'I believe that the husband and possibly the wife of this family have died of the sickness,' Helewise replied. 'They were smallholders who rented their farm, and they had three daughters, one of whom became a nun, and — '

But the old man was already nodding enthusiastically. 'That'll be Alba,' he said. 'Aye, we all gave a cheer when *that* one ceased her meddling and took herself off to

168

take the veil, even though most folks reckoned it were no more than fear of the ague as drove her to it.'

'We know about Alba,' Helewise said. 'But can you help us over the rest of the family?' She was aware that she was holding her breath; the prospect of possibly getting some answers at last was making her tremble with anticipation.

'Well,' the old man said, drawing out the word and eyeing his eager audience, 'you've got it right about the lassies' father dying. Wilfrid took sick and, for once, his enemy wasn't someone he could bully into submission or cheat out of what was rightly his.'

'I see,' Helewise muttered.

'Do you?' The old man looked at her, a twinkle in his eye. 'Yes, Sister, I see that you do. Anyway, like I says, Wilfrid got the ague, and shook himself apart within the sen'night. Not that many mourned him.'

'What of the girls' mother?' Helewise prompted. 'We heard she died then, too, but — '

'No, no, no, *no*,' the old man interrupted. 'Whoever told you that got it quite wrong. Adela — now, *she* was a saint and no mistake, loving, gentle woman she was, God rest her. But the Almighty took her to her rest many a year ago. Ten years, was it?' He frowned at them in perplexity, as if they could answer his question.

'What happened to the younger sisters when their father died?' Helewise asked.

The old man put a gnarled finger alongside his nose. 'That'd be telling,' he said. 'We knows what we knows, but as to if we ought to *tell* . . . '

Brother Saul spoke. 'This lady is the Abbess of Hawkenlye,' he said stiffly. 'She has come all the way from Kent for the sake of Alba and her sisters, who have sought shelter there in the Abbey. If you have any information that can help her, then, in God's holy name, I ask you to give it!'

The old man shrank before him. 'All right, all right!' he cried. 'No need to take on! Meriel, she was planning to leave even before Alba came hurrying back from her convent all in a pother. Planning to take her little sister, too, I shouldn't wonder, they were always close, them young 'uns. But, like I says, up pops Alba, upsets whatever plans Meriel had made' — a distinctly shifty expression crossed his face just then, Helewise noticed, so that she wondered what it was he wasn't telling them — 'and whisks both the girls up and away, without so much as a farewell or a backward glance.'

'And you don't know where they went?' Helewise said.

'I do now!' He gave a catarrhal laugh. 'They went to *Hawkenlye!*' Convulsed with laughter at his own wit, he wiped tears from his eyes.

'You have been most helpful,' Helewise said when he had stopped laughing. Best to flatter him, she thought, it might predispose him in our favour. 'I wonder, though, if you could further aid us by indicating where the family used to live?'

'That I could.' He stepped outside and, raising his arm, waved it towards one of the ways leading out of the village. 'Follow the road for a while, then it'll become a track. It's muddy normally, but it's been dry recently — well, that's to say, up till the night afore last — so you'll probably do all right. Go on down the track, across the stream, up the bank the other side, and the farm's at the top.'

Helewise thanked him, and she and the brothers set off in the direction he had indicated. He called out after them, 'You won't find anybody there, you know!'

Brother Saul waved a hand in acknowledgement. Whatever else the old man said — they could still hear him shouting — was obscured by distance.

* ★ ★

The track was winding, and led through woodland. The trees were rapidly coming into leaf, and there were bluebells on the drier parts of the wood's floor. Birdsong filled the air.

It should have been a pleasant ride, but Helewise could not rid herself of her apprehension. It was gloomy under the trees, for one thing.

And for another, no matter how hard she tried, she could not rid herself of the irrational, unlikely and fear-induced suspicion that they were being followed. Trying not to let the others see, once or twice she spun round quickly, in a vain attempt to spot whoever — or whatever — it might be before it, or they, could slip into the shadows. But she didn't see anything.

Which, she told herself with rigid firmness, was because there was *nothing whatsoever to see.*

They found the farm — the old man's directions had been very accurate — and, just as he had said, it was deserted. Saul dismounted and went to peer inside one of the two tiny windows set either side of the door of the main building, returning to report that what he could see of the interior had been stripped bare.

'A dead place,' Helewise murmured.

Augustine looked at her enquiringly. 'Do you feel it, too, Abbess?'

'Feel what?' she asked anxiously.

'Death,' he replied simply. 'Wasn't that what you said? A *dead* place?'

'Yes, but I — ' How could she explain it? 'Never mind.'

They rode back in silence, in single file along the track through the woods.

Then, suddenly, Augustine pulled Horace to a sharp stop, jerking the horse's head. Dread overwhelming her, Helewise edged the mare close to him, glad to have Saul's guardian presence behind her. 'What is it?' she asked, battling to keep her dread out of her voice. 'Augustine, what have you seen?'

He pointed.

And, deep in the woods, down in a dell surrounded by trees and thick underbrush, was a burnt-out cottage.

'I'm going to look,' Augustine announced, sliding off Horace's back and looping the reins round a branch.

'No, Augustine, it might be dangerous!' The protest was out before she could stop it.

But Augustine took no notice. Neither did Saul, who, even as she spoke, was jumping off the cob and following Augustine into the woods.

It was surely better to be with them than left by herself on the track, so Helewise dismounted too and, making her way more carefully because of her long skirts, went into the still, dim interior of the woodland.

The dwelling could only have been very small, hardly worthy of the name cottage. The remains of four smoke-blackened walls stood up from a tangle of brush, and the new growth of rose-bay willow-herb — the country folk's 'fireweed' — was busy trying to cover the great black scar in the land. Anything that might once have been within the little house had been crushed to the ground by the beams from the roof, which had obliterated all beneath them as they fell.

Helewise shuddered. 'Come away,' she said, wishing her voice sounded more authoritative. 'This is an awful place, we — '

But, with an exclamation, Saul hurried forward into the dwelling. Her cry of 'Be careful!' was arrested in her throat as Saul bent down and, swinging up his arm, held aloft a human skull.

Augustine put his hand on her arm, and she was vastly comforted to feel his warm, firm touch. 'Abbess, stay here,' he said gently. 'I will help Saul.'

174

She should have gone with him. She was both men's superior, after all. But her legs had started to shake; she was afraid that, if she moved, she would fall.

Saul had carefully replaced the skull on the ash-soft floor of the dwelling. Now he and Augustine were crouching down, rummaging among the charred remains of beams and wooden wall supports. Saul murmured something — his tone sounded questioning — and Augustine replied. They were both picking up pieces of what looked like wood, holding them up to each other and then putting them back.

Suddenly Augustine let out a sharp breath, nudged Saul and pointed to what looked like a spike, sticking up out of the ground. His fingers were busy trying to pull something off it . . .

Then Saul stood up, ashen-faced, and swiftly crossed himself. Helewise heard him say, 'Dear God above, the poor wretch!' Then, bowing his head, he came out of the dwelling and returned to her side. Augustine stood quite still in the centre of the cottage, gazing down at whatever it was he held between his fingers as if he could hardly believe his eyes.

Helewise said, 'It *was* a human skull, wasn't it, Saul?'

He sighed. 'Aye, Abbess. I'm afraid it was.'

'And the rest of the body . . . ?'

'Aye, he's there, what's left of him. Only his bones, mind, and some charred remnants of his clothing and that. Leg bones, ribs, arms.' An expression of deep disgust crossed his face.

'It is a terrible thing to have seen, Saul,' she said gently.

He glanced at her. 'Oh, it's not that, Abbess, bless you. I've seen my share of dead bodies; they don't normally disturb me, beyond feelings of sorrow for the death. No, it's — he was — ' But, shaking his head, he did not seem to be able to go on.

Augustine had joined them; silent and soft-footed, he had made no sound. He stared at Helewise, and his face, too, was pale.

'That was no accidental death,' he said. 'Not a case of a man falling asleep while his supper cooks and, in his slumber, not noticing the fire spreading from the hearth and setting the house on fire. No. That's not what it was.'

'What, then?' She could hardly speak.

Augustine held up what he had been holding so carefully in his hand. It looked like . . . it looked like the frayed remains of a piece of rope.

'He was tied to a stake in the ground,'

Augustine said quietly and, instantly, the sense of dread that Helewise had been feeling grew till it all but floored her. Evil was there, right there, in that place where a poor man had been tied up inside a cottage and left to burn to death.

'Could — could it not have been somehow accidental?' she whispered. 'Might it not have been an animal that was tethered to the spike, not the dead man?'

Augustine shook his head. Then he held up his other hand, and the object that had been concealed behind his back came into Helewise's view.

It was a skeletal human hand, the fingers pulled up into a claw. Around the wrist was tied another length of rope.

12

They would have left the wood sooner, had Brother Saul not insisted that they bury the remains.

Helewise had resisted the temptation to suggest it; the expedition was under her command, and she was responsible for the brothers who were with her. She could sense peril all around them — and the sense that they were being followed, their every movement being observed, grew stronger by the minute — and, despite the clear Christian duty to inter what was left of the dead body, she felt it was an occasion when the living must take precedence over the dead.

But Saul insisted.

Augustine went to help him. They found lengths of wood to use as makeshift spades and, working hard, managed to dig a shallow pit within quite a short space of time; the recent heavy rain now worked in their favour, having softened the ground. Then Helewise helped them to pick up all the pieces of bone they could find and place them in the grave.

Augustine held up the pelvis. 'This was a man and no mistake,' he said quietly.

'How can you tell?' Helewise asked.

The boy gave a faint grin. 'My family have been gravediggers, in their time. I was taught about bodies when I was quite young, and told how the wider opening's for a woman's skeleton, the narrower, more pointed arch for a man's.'

Helewise felt quite faint. 'Thank you, Augustine. Shall we put those bones in with the rest?'

When they were as satisfied as they could be that nothing of the man had been left within the ruined cottage for animals to destroy, the two lay brothers filled in the grave. Helewise recited the prayers for the dead, and they all stood in silence for some time with bowed heads. Saul found two pieces of roughly straight wood, and he fashioned them into a cross, tying them together with a piece of twine taken from the cord around his waist. He stuck it into the ground above the dead man's head.

Then they returned to the horses.

It could reasonably be expected to be dark, in there under the trees. But, when they emerged into open countryside, to Helewise's dismay she noticed that the sun had almost set.

Dear God, where were they to sleep that night?

Saul kicked the old cob into a canter and overtook both Helewise and Augustine, disappearing up the track into the gloom. They caught sight of him again as they entered Medely; he had dismounted and, leading his horse, was tapping at the doors of each of the inhabited dwellings.

Nobody was answering his knock.

Even the house from which the old man had peered out was shut up and dark. If he were within, he was lying low.

Saul turned to her, a look of desperation in his face. 'I am sorry, Abbess, but I can't make anybody hear.'

'Never mind, Saul.' She was, she realised, feeling better now that they were out of the wood. 'We shall go into one of the empty houses. Should anyone come to ask what we're doing, we shall say, with total honesty, that we tried to ask for accommodation but were ignored. We shall not do any harm, and we shall be gone tomorrow.'

Then, kicking the mare into a trot, she led her party up the track to the furthest of the deserted dwellings. And there, out of the wind and the night time mist if nothing else, they spent the night.

★　★　★

Helewise was awake very early the next morning. She lay listening, but could hear no sounds of human beings other than faint snores from one or both of the brothers, over in the far corner of the room.

She huddled deeper under the warm, wool cover. She was thankful to have it; she had only packed it because Josse had said you never knew when you might have to spend a night in the open, and it was better to go prepared.

Josse. How was he? I wish he were here right now, she thought, I could do with his good sense and his insight. Not that I am criticising dear Saul and Augustine, she added to herself, they have been exemplary companions. But Josse and I have puzzled over many a problem together . . .

She dozed for a while, then had a half-sleeping, half-waking dream in which she sat before Josse and told him that she had brought him a hand and a pelvis, and that he must put the dead man together again. But Josse held up his wounded arm and said he couldn't manage such a task just then, and instead snapped off two of the skeletal fingers and made them into a cross.

It was quite a relief to wake up.

* ★ ★

When all three of them were awake and had eaten a sparse breakfast, she asked Brother Augustine to prepare the horses. When he had done so, she said, 'I think, my brothers, that it is time we went home.'

'Is there nothing more that we can find out here, Abbess?' Saul asked.

She smiled at him. 'Many things that I should *like* to find out, Saul. But who is there to ask?'

Slowly he nodded, gazing out at the empty track outside. 'Aye. And the three people who we know to be most closely involved are back at Hawkenlye.'

'Do you think that Alba and her sisters knew of that place in the woods?' she mused. 'It is so close to their father's farm that it is hard to believe they did not. They will be distressed to know of the fire, and even more so if we tell them that we found a body inside. The poor man might even have been somebody they knew.' She thought for a while. 'In fact I think, brothers, that we should not tell them.'

Both the brothers nodded.

Then, leaving Medely as silent as it had been when they arrived, they mounted the horses and turned their heads for the long road home.

★ ★ ★

Josse's days of convalescence seemed interminable. He was bored, sick of the sight of the four walls of the infirmary, and longed to be up and out in the fresh air. He was quite sure he was ready for such an excursion, but had not yet managed to persuade Sister Euphemia. At least he was now visiting the latrine, though, and spared the ignominy of using a bottle to pee in.

As his spirits and his health recovered, Sister Euphemia allowed him more visitors. He was relieved to discover that talking no longer exhausted him. He enjoyed long conversations with many of the nuns and quite a few of the monks; Brother Firmin brought him a daily phial of holy water, praying solemnly with him while he drank it. Whether it was the water, or whether he was catching Brother Firmin's sincere and fervent belief in it, the daily drink always left Josse feeling full of vitality.

His most frequent — and, he had to admit, most beloved — visitor was Berthe. She came to see him at least once every day, and often managed to slip back in the evening when the infirmary was meant to be closed to visitors. He began to think that she might treasure their time together as much as he did for, although she never said as much, he guessed that she was

183

lonely, worried and very unhappy.

Their conversation had steadily become more wide-ranging as they relaxed in one another's company. Berthe never mentioned the sister penned up beneath the infirmary, and she seldom speculated about where Meriel was. That in itself was a little suspicious, Josse thought; while she easily might not be too disturbed to have the bullying Alba unable to get at her, surely she must be desperately anxious about Meriel? The two younger sisters had appeared to be so close.

Puzzling over the problem one morning, a thought occurred to him. Perhaps Berthe wasn't worrying about her sister because she knew quite well that Meriel was safe . . .

Feeling only a little ashamed of himself, Josse resolved to do some gentle probing the next time Berthe came to see him.

★   ★   ★

He did not have long to wait. Towards the end of the morning, he heard her light step coming down the long ward of the infirmary and, leaning forward, he saw her approaching his bed.

'I've brought you some bluebells,' she said, proffering a small bunch. 'Alba used to forbid

184

us to pick them, because they would always droop so quickly and then she had to throw them away and wash out the jar. But Meriel says — Meriel used to say the smell was so perfect.'

A pink blush was creeping up the girl's face. Dear child, Josse thought, lying doesn't really suit you. 'Thank you,' he said, pretending he hadn't noticed either the slip or the blush. 'Have you been into the forest?'

'Yes! But only a little way, the nuns told me it's easy to become lost.'

'The nuns were quite right.' He pretended to be preoccupied with the bluebells while he thought how to proceed. Berthe was on her guard, he realised, so questions pertaining directly to Meriel were probably not the best way. After a moment, he said, 'There were woods near where I grew up. One of my earliest memories is of picking flowers with my mother.'

'We used to do that, too, Mother and Meriel and me!' Berthe responded, with such innocent pleasure that Josse cringed at his own duplicity. 'Sometimes when Father wasn't there, Mother used to pack up food, and we'd be out all day. Once we made a pretend house out of dead branches and stuff, and Mother even let us have a fire. We had to make a proper hearth — she showed us how, using stones from the stream as a surround so that the fire didn't burn out of control. After Mother died, sometimes Meriel and I — '

Too late, she heard her own words.

Josse began to say, 'It's all right, Berthe, we'd already — ' But, observing with alarm the girl's face, he stopped.

Berthe had gone deadly white, and had thrust her knuckle so hard into her mouth that she had drawn blood. She was rocking to and fro in a compulsive, persistent rhythm that was dreadful to watch, emitting all the time a soft, high-pitched keening.

Josse opened his arms to her. After an instant's indecision, she threw herself against him and began to sob.

She even sobs quietly, he thought, compassion for her drenching his heart. As if crying out loud were likely to earn her a punishment. Poor lass, what can her life have been like?

When the crying subsided, he said very softly, 'Berthe my love, we had guessed that some of what you have told us wasn't quite true. We also understand that sometimes people have to tell a lie. It may be to protect somebody else, or it may be because someone is threatening to hurt them if they tell the truth. Which means, sweeting, that a lie isn't

186

always a bad thing.'

She said, her voice muffled, 'Father beat us if we lied. He beat us with a belt, and the buckle used to cut our shoulders.'

He stroked the thin back with his left hand. 'Your father can no longer hurt you, Berthe. You don't have to tell lies for him any more.'

'Alba can hurt me,' Berthe whispered.

'Not all the time she's imprisoned.'

Berthe raised her face and stared at him. 'How long will that be?'

'I don't know,' he replied. 'She certainly won't be released until Abbess Helewise comes back.'

'I like Abbess Helewise,' Berthe remarked.

'She likes you, too.'

'Does she? How do you know?'

'She told me.'

'You're friends, aren't you? You and the Abbess?'

'We are.'

She frowned. 'I didn't like it when she asked me about Alba. Before she went away, I mean. She asked if I knew the name of the place where Alba went to be a nun, and I couldn't tell her because I don't know.'

'If you didn't know, then you couldn't possibly tell her,' Josse said reasonably.

'Yes, but you see, there were other things I *could* have told her but I didn't,' Berthe persisted. 'And it's not fair, when she's been so kind to me.' The girl was still half-lying on Josse's bed; now she drew up her legs and settled against him, like a puppy curling up to its dam. 'I wish she were here.'

Josse sensed the thought forming in her. He held his peace; if he were to suggest it, she might clam up . . .

She said presently, 'I suppose I could tell *you*. You're her friend, you just said so, and so telling you would be almost as good. Wouldn't it?'

This child is suffering from a heavy conscience, Josse thought. The urge to unburden herself is strong.

Hoping he was doing the right thing, he said, 'Yes, Berthe. And whatever you tell me, I promise to pass on to Abbess Helewise, as soon as she gets back.'

Berthe gave a soft little sigh. Then: 'My mother died a long time ago. I don't know why Alba said we had to say she died when Father did, and I didn't like saying it. Mother was loving and kind. Father wasn't kind at all, and it didn't seem right to pretend that they'd died together, because if Mother *had* died just recently, when Father did, then we'd really be grieving for her. I didn't like people seeing I wasn't sad, and thinking it meant I hadn't loved my mother. Do you see what I mean?'

'Very clearly.' Josse gave her a hug. Then he asked, 'Berthe, you just said you didn't know *why* you had to pretend your mother had only just died. But, if you're really clever, and puzzle at it terribly hard, do you think you could have a guess?'

Berthe though for a while. Then she said tentatively, 'Perhaps it was because Alba knew we weren't really unhappy over Father dying. So if people knew the truth — that it was really only Father who'd just died — they'd think there wasn't any real excuse for her taking us away from our old home.'

Josse thought he understood. 'She needed a convincing story to cover her action in getting you all away from the area,' he said slowly. 'And so she said it was the shock and the grief of losing both your father and your greatly-beloved mother.'

'Mm,' Berthe said. She was humming gently to herself, and he sensed that the confession had done her good. With a gentle push, he said, 'Berthe, will you go and find a jar? The bluebells need to be put in water.'

'All right,' she said.

He watched idly as she went off towards the bench where jugs of water were kept. She approached Sister Beata, who bent down to listen, then pointed towards a shelf under the bench.

He was thinking hard. Yes. It was beginning to make sense. The father's death would have made the girls homeless, but, without the false grief, there was no reason for the sisters to go so far away. The logical thing would surely have been for Alba to find some place locally for her sisters, then return to her Ely convent.

Josse was coming to the conclusion that arranging a new home for Meriel and Berthe had not been the reason behind Alba's actions at all. What she had been desperate to do was to get herself or her sisters, or possibly all three of them, away from their old home.

A very long way away.

And *why*?

Suddenly he understood why Alba had been so agitated when Berthe was sent down to work with the pilgrims visiting the Holy Shrine in the Vale. She was terrified that somebody from their old home would arrive and recognise the girl.

Something else was tapping at the edge of his mind . . . something that had worried him before, the day Helewise had told him about the murdered pilgrim . . .

It would not come into focus. Deliberately he thought about something else. Look at

Berthe down there, stopping to let that old woman with the crippled foot smell the bluebells — enchanting, sweet-natured child she is . . .

And into his mind flashed the word *Walsingham*.

Yes! Of course! The dead man had worn a badge from the Shrine of Our Lady at Walsingham.

And Walsingham was only fifty miles north of Ely.

Was it relevant? Had he stumbled on something really useful? He concentrated, trying to see a way through the strands of the mystery. The murdered man could surely be nothing more than he seemed, an honest pilgrim who had travelled to several holy places and, with the visit to Hawkenlye, was adding another to the list.

But they had said he spoke with a strange accent! Could that have been the accent of eastern England?

Oh, Josse thought in frustration, this is useless! Every time I think I have found an answer, two more questions arise from it to vex me!

Berthe had returned, and was placing the jar of bluebells carefully beside his bed. 'There! I've put them close, so you'll be able to smell the lovely scent.'

'Thank you, Berthe.'

She answered his smile. 'I have to go now, Sir Josse. But I'll come back soon.'

'Please do.' He leaned forward as she bent to give the now-customary kiss on his cheek. 'Goodbye.'

★ ★ ★

When she had gone, he made himself summarise what he had discovered.

Although Berthe's mother had died some time before the death of the father, Alba had pretended that grief for *both recent deaths* had been her motive in taking the girls so far from what was known and familiar.

For some strongly compelling reason, Alba had needed to remove herself and her sisters far from their home.

Alba was so terrified that someone from that home would come to Hawkenlye and recognise Berthe, working in the Vale, that she had been driven to that outrageous, violent reaction when thwarted.

A man who was known to have been to Walsingham had been murdered in the Vale.

And, although Berthe's much-loved sister Meriel had gone missing, Berthe just didn't seem too dreadfully anxious about it . . .

Sister Euphemia appeared, carrying Josse's

midday meal. 'She hasn't tired you out, has she? Lovely lass she is, to be sure, but she *is* a bit of a talker.' She put the trencher down on Josse's lap.

'She hasn't tired me,' Josse said. 'I enjoy her chatter.'

'Aye, she's a breath of spring all right,' the infirmarer agreed. 'She has a gentle hand, too — she's been helping me change the dressing on some of my less badly-afflicted patients, and they've all told me they prefer her touch to mine.'

'I find that hard to believe, Sister,' Josse said loyally.

'Ah, it's not the touch, Sir Josse, so much as the lively, pretty little face and the winning smile,' Sister Euphemia said shrewdly. 'Now, eat your meal while it's hot!'

Josse went on thinking while he ate. But, try as he might, he could not tease out anything more from the assembled facts than what he had just concluded.

I have only half of the puzzle, he thought, reaching down to set the empty trencher on the floor and settling for the prescribed post-prandial nap. There will only be a chance of solving it when the other half is added.

And for that, he would have to wait until the Abbess returned.

13

Helewise returned to Hawkenlye in the evening of the first full day that Josse had spent out of bed.

He had awoken that morning with a strange certainty that today would be the day that the Abbess and her party came home, and he had been unshakeable in his determination to be sitting outside waiting when they rode through the gates. Not that the infirmarer had tried very hard to dissuade him; she could see for herself that lying fretting in bed would probably do him more harm than sitting outside in the sunshine.

After breakfast, he went — carefully — out through the infirmary door.

He was dismayed at how very slowly his strength was coming back. That alone made him face up to how ill he had been. Now that mental clarity was starting to return, he had been spending much time wondering how they were faring at New Winnowlands without him. Sister Euphemia had told him how Will and Sir Brice had brought him to Hawkenlye, and how they had stayed until reassured that he was out of danger; her words had moved him at the time to the ready tears of the invalid. Even now, when he was so much better, the thought of his manservant and his friend keeping vigil for him still had the power to touch him deeply.

Should he, he wondered as he walked slowly across to the cloister, send for Will? Have a talk with him, make sure all went well at home?

No, he decided finally. Will was quite used to managing without his master. In fact, Josse accepted ruefully, Will probably only ever made a show of consulting him out of kindness.

Ah, but it was good to be out in the fresh air again! He stood still for a moment, flinging out his arms in a wide stretch, but the sudden movement caught him unawares; as the dizziness swept through him, hastily he moved to the stone bench that ran along inside the cloister and sat down.

I am, he concluded, far from fully fit yet.

He tried not to dwell on it. Instead, settling himself comfortably so that he could keep an eye on the main gate, he ran through the additional small facts which he had managed to pick up from his conversations with Berthe.

They were mainly to do with her family. Alba, she said, was a *lot* older than her two younger sisters — which, Josse imagined, those at Hawkenlye who had seen all three would already have known — and the girls' mother had been afraid of her.

'She's very like Father,' Berthe had told him. 'Like him to look at, and like him in her hot temper and her tendency to fly into rages and go bright red in the face.'

No wonder, Josse had thought, the poor, gentle mother had been afraid.

And, on another occasion: 'Alba's terribly proud, Sir Josse. She's always on at me and Meriel about the good name of the family, which she drags into the argument whenever she wants to give us orders. Like not to laugh and shout in public, not to go out in less than perfectly clean and mended clothes, not to associate with this person because they're beneath us, whatever *that* means.'

To that, Josse had been prompted to ask why the father and the mother hadn't been the ones to discipline the younger girls. Berthe had replied, a remembered anger and hurt making her pretty face flush, 'Father said we were like an army. He gave orders to Alba; she gave them to us. As for Mother' — the girl's expression softened — 'she never interfered. It sometimes seemed as if she were another sister, kinder, more loving, who left the bossing about and the issuing of punishments to Alba. Who was, after all, far better suited to it.'

Once, Josse asked her whether Alba had left home to enter the convent before or after the mother had died.

'Oh, after,' Berthe replied.

'I wonder whether your mother's death prompted her to take the veil?' Josse mused aloud.

'Oh, no, I shouldn't think so, she . . . ' But, with a perplexed frown, Berthe trailed off. Josse waited, and after a moment she said, 'You know, it's strange, but, now I come to think of it, I think you might be right.' She was staring at him, her face intent as she tried to put a vague idea into words. 'She was — Mother and Alba were — well, it was Alba, really. It always felt as if she was sort of *vying* with Mother for control. For who was head of the household after Father. But, of course, when Mother died, that left Alba with nobody to vie with.'

'Didn't that make her happy? After all, the way was then clear for her and your father to rule between them, which you imply was what they wanted?'

'It *ought* to have made her happy.' Berthe sounded puzzled. 'But having nobody to fight with didn't seem to suit her at all. I remember that, when she made up her mind to enter the cloister, she said something about having won her battle, so there was no need for her to stay at home.' She shrugged. 'I really have no idea what she meant.'

* * *

Berthe had sought him out in the cloister this morning. She came bearing a cushion and a warm woollen blanket; when he protested that he had no need of either, she ignored him as completely as Sister Euphemia would have done, and made him stand up while she placed the folded blanket beneath him and put the cushion between him and the rough stone wall. He had to admit he was far more comfortable like that.

He glanced at her face, trying to judge if she was up to a little gentle teasing. Her serene expression suggested that she was, so he said, 'You know, Berthe, you really are picking up infirmary ways. If I hadn't known it was you, I could have sworn that commanding voice and that refusal to listen to my protests was pure Sister Euphemia.'

To his delight, Berthe burst out laughing. 'I'm delighted, Sir Josse!' she said. He watched the dimples appearing and disappearing in her cheeks. 'I have been modelling myself on her, but I had no idea I was doing so well!'

She had brought some needlework with her. Settling herself beside him, she took some garment in soft white cloth from an embroidered workbag and, threading her needle, began to repair a seam.

They made the occasional comment to one another but, in the main, sat in a happy, companionable silence.

She sat with him for much of the day. She was quite radiant, Josse noticed; he was now as sure as he could be that she knew perfectly well that Meriel was safe. And, probably, that the two were in contact. Berthe, he observed, never spoke to him of Meriel's disappearance. He liked to think it was because she was now too fond of him to tell him lies.

For the fifth time, he made her put aside her sewing and hurry across to the gates, to look out along the road and see if there were any sign of three weary riders approaching the Abbey. The first four times, she had come hurrying back shaking her head.

This time was different.

He could tell by the way she stiffened as she looked down the road that she had spotted something. Watching, he saw her put up a hand to shade her eyes. Then, when she was certain, she started jumping up and down, waving her arms and shouting, 'It's her! It's Abbess Helewise! She's *back*!'

⋆ ⋆ ⋆

He did not push forward to greet the Abbess straight away. Others had precedence. From his seat in the cloister, he watched her go through what appeared to be a routine, as if, in this regimented life of devotion, there was even a prescribed way for an Abbess to return to her community.

He saw the senior nuns go in turn to see the Abbess in her room, and he assumed that they were reporting to her all that had happened in their particular departments during her absence. Some, it appeared, were more succinct than others; or perhaps less had happened in their areas of convent life.

Then there were the Offices; she would naturally be eager to attend those with her sisters.

All in all, it was dusk before she put her head out of her doorway and said, 'Sir Josse? Will you come and speak with me?'

When the door was closed behind him, she came towards him with her arms open and said, 'I am so happy to see you looking well! You have been in my heart all the time I have been away, and I have prayed for your recovery.' She gave him a wide, beaming smile. 'Sister Euphemia tells me you have been a model patient, listening to her advice, working with her, and with God, to bring about your healing. And now we see the result! Up and about all the long day, so I hear, and you look *fine*!'

He was responding to her delight, a smile spreading over his face. 'I thank you for your concern, Abbess. Aye, I am well on the way to recovery.' He studied her; she looked tired. 'But what of you? Did you find Sister Alba's convent? Were they able to answer your questions?'

She went to sit down in her chair, motioning him to be seated on the wooden stool that she kept for visitors. 'We found the place, yes. And, although the good nuns did indeed provide some answers, those in turn posed more questions. Such as, why did Alba describe a totally different background to the Abbess of Sedgebeck from the one she revealed to me? According to *that* Alba, she was a spoiled, only child of an indulgent father.' She sighed. 'A *very* different woman from the one who tore herself from the place where she was so happy, in order to take her grieving, poverty-stricken, homeless younger sisters away to a new life.'

'Which tale is the true one?' he asked.

'Have you any idea?'

She stared at him. 'Yes. We managed to find the former family home. We spoke to a villager who confirmed that the girls' mother died long since, and — ' Something in his expression must have alerted her. 'But I think that you already know that, Sir Josse.'

He didn't want to interrupt her story, so he just said, 'Aye. Berthe told me. But I'll explain when you've finished.'

She nodded. 'Very well. The village has suffered recently from the sickness and many died, including the girls' father. That part of Alba's account is true. The farm was abandoned, the house empty. But, Sir Josse, our informant said that Meriel was already planning to take Berthe with her and leave the village, before Alba returned from Sedgebeck and brought them all here!'

'Was she, now?' Josse said slowly. That would fit, he thought, wouldn't it? He wished his brain were not so sluggish; it seemed to work far less swiftly than before his illness. If Meriel's plans had been torn apart by the bossy Alba, throwing her weight around and dragging her sisters far away into the depths of south-east England, would that not be grounds for Meriel's subsequent misery?

A misery that, perhaps, was even now being relieved . . .

He felt that he was on the very edge of understanding the mystery. If only, *if only*, he could *think*!

He gave the Abbess a rueful grin. 'I wish I were more use to you than simply sitting here saying is that so? and was she really?' he said. 'I do believe that we have sufficient information between us to solve this puzzle. Indeed, I feel that I already have the answer, but my mind is so foggy that I can't reach it.'

She gave him a sympathetic look. 'Don't distress yourself, Sir Josse. It is the way with fevers, to leave the brain like a tangle of sheep's wool. Do not push yourself so hard.'

'I must!' he exclaimed. 'There are matters that cannot be resolved until we *know*.'

'Yes, of course.' A worried frown creased her brow. 'Meriel is still missing, I am told.'

'She is safe, Abbess,' he said softly. 'I cannot say where, or with whom, but I would stake my life on her being both safe and well.'

And he explained about Berthe.

She nodded slowly. 'You make good sense, as always, Sir Josse. The child does not appear to be a habitual liar, I agree. And, now that your friendship had progressed so well, I am sure you are right when you say that she does not speak of Meriel because, in the face of your kind-hearted concern, she could not bear to uphold the fiction that she doesn't know where her sister is.' She paused. Then: 'But there is still Alba.'

He had noticed that she no longer referred to *Sister* Alba; fearing that he might have guessed why, he asked her why not.

When she had told him, he let out a long breath. 'What do you do with her now, Abbess? If she is no longer a nun, then surely you can't go on imprisoning her here in the Abbey?'

'Indeed not,' she agreed. 'And while on the one hand I should be relieved to be rid of her, can I, in Christian charity, turn her out into the world when she has nowhere to go?'

'I don't know,' he said gently.

Turning her mind with an obvious effort from the problem of Alba, the Abbess straightened up and said, 'Has Sheriff Pelham made any progress with the murder in the Vale?'

'None,' Josse said in disgust. 'He asked some of the pilgrims a few fairly pointless questions, and he now seems to have settled on the man having been attacked by a traveller on the road who is now miles away.'

'A typical Sheriff Pelham solution,' the Abbess murmured.

'Aye.' He remembered what it was about the dead man that had struck him as significant. 'But there *is* one thing, Abbess.'

Instantly she looked alert. 'Yes?'

'He wore a pilgrim badge from Walsingham. Which is only about fifty miles north of Ely.'

'And so you conclude that he was connected with the girls? With Alba and her sisters?'

'Ah, not necessarily!' he protested. 'I dare say many of our visitors wear such badges. Walsingham is a popular place.'

'But to have someone from the same area of the land killed, here, where the sisters fled to, must be more than coincidence,' she insisted. 'Mustn't it?'

'My reason tells me no,' he said bluntly. 'But yet it keeps coming back to me, as if some part of me doesn't want me to forget about it.'

'That is God's voice speaking directly to you,' she said. 'We must *always* listen when God speaks, Sir Josse.'

'Aye, Abbess.' He felt duly chastened. 'I'll keep that in mind.' She opened her mouth to say something more, but before she could speak, he hurried on. 'Now, if I may, Abbess, I'll summarise the picture that emerges when we add your findings to what I have concluded from talking to my ingenuous little friend, Berthe.'

He thought briefly, then began.

'A bullying man and his gentle, timid wife had three daughters, one much older than the other two. The mother and the two younger ones form an alliance, but they are under the domination of the father and the oldest girl. She, among her other bullying ways, is insistent on the family keeping up high standards in the way they appear to the outside world. Then the mother dies and the oldest girl, no longer having anybody to compete with for the role of her father's second-in-command, takes herself off and joins a convent. But she is not suited to convent life, and she is asked to leave. In the meantime, the tyrannical father succumbs to illness and dies, leaving the middle sister free to make her own plans for her and her little sister's future. But, before those plans can be implemented, the big sister comes back from her convent, decides that her sisters' grief for their father is too strong to be assuaged there, in their former home with all its memories, so she drags them away and brings them all the way south to Hawkenlye.' He paused for breath. 'Have I left anything out?'

'Only that Alba lied to us to make her story more convincing,' the Abbess said.

'Aye, she did. She told us both parents had recently died.'

'And that — Oh! You've also omitted

something I have thought of; that something had happened in their former home which Alba was desperate to run away from,' she said. Her voice had dropped to a whisper, and her face, he noticed with a stab of anxiety, had paled. 'Oh, dear God, Sir Josse, I — ' She put a hand to her mouth, as if physically holding back her words.

'I had concluded the same thing,' he said. 'That the reason Alba showed such an extreme and uncontrolled reaction to Berthe working down in the Vale was because she feared somebody might have followed them from East Anglia and would recognise the girl.'

The Abbess was nodding. 'Yes, that is true, of course.' She hesitated. Her hands, he noticed, were trembling. 'But I'm afraid I was thinking of something far more terrible than that.'

He waited while she got herself under control. She lifted her chin, closed her eyes as if in a brief prayer, then said, 'Josse, I haven't yet told you everything. I hope and pray that this last discovery was pure chance, and has nothing to do with the girls. However, I am very afraid that . . . ' She broke off. 'But I must tell you, then you can judge for yourself.' She paused. 'We found the farm where the family used to live, as I have said,

207

and it was not at all a cheerful or welcoming place; indeed, we sensed the presence of death quite strongly. We were riding through the woodland which surrounds it, on our way back to the village, when we spotted a cottage deep in amongst the trees. It had suffered a devastating fire.' She paused again, folded her hands tightly together, then said, 'The roof had collapsed, and there was little left that was recognisable. Except that we found a human skeleton.'

'A — *what?*' Great heavens, no wonder she was agitated! 'You're sure it was human? Not some animal caught inside when the place went up in flames?'

She was shaking her head. 'No, no, that's what I hoped. But Brother Augustine knows about bones. He insisted the skeleton was human. A man, he said.'

Again, Josse wished with all his soul for his usual speed of thought. A dead body, in an out-of-the-way location so close to the girls' former home? What did this *mean?* 'Perhaps the fire and the death happened years and years ago,' he suggested.

'No,' she said again. 'We discussed that on the long road home, and Brother Saul remarked that the small degree of regrowth of vegetation bore witness to the fact that the fire can have been but recent.'

'I was afraid you'd say something like that,' Josse muttered.

He met her eyes. She was looking at him with an almost compassionate expression, as if about to give him very bad news.

As, it proved, she was. 'Sir Josse,' she said very quietly, 'we cannot even console ourselves with thinking that it was a dreadful accident. This was murder.'

'How can you be so sure?'

'The dead man had been tied to an iron stake set into the floor of the dwelling,' she said dully. 'Brother Augustine found what was left of the rope, knotted very securely around the bones of the wrist.'

And Josse, momentarily overwhelmed, dropped his head in his hands.

She let him be for a while, for which he was profoundly grateful. So much to assimilate! There *was* a pattern behind it all, there had to be, and he kept having the frustrating, nagging feeling that it was there for the seeing, if he could only *think*!

Presently he heard her get up and move round her table to stand beside him. 'Sir Josse?' she said gently.

He raised his head. 'Abbess?'

'Sir Josse, there is a further matter I should tell you about,' she said, face creased in anxiety. 'I hesitate to do so, since it is but a

suspicion, without any real substance. But . . . '
She did not continue; she seemed to be
waiting for him to invite her to.

'You had better tell me anyway,' he said
dully.

A fleeting smile lit her face, there and gone
in an instant. 'Try not to sound so eager,' she
murmured.

He managed a grin. 'Sorry. Go on. What
was this suspicion of yours?'

She straightened, took a breath and said, 'I
am almost certain that we were being
followed.'

'Followed? Where? When?'

'I first sensed it when we were going to
Medely — the girls' old home. I was
convinced somebody was watching us in the
woods, where we found the body, although
that was such a creepy, eerie place that it
would have been surprising *not* to have
thought someone was there, hidden away.
Then there were times on the road home
when I . . . Oh, this is silly! I shouldn't have
mentioned it! When I stop to think, of course
there were people following us! It's a warm,
sunny April, and the whole of England is
probably on the move!'

He understood her sudden emotion. But
knowing her as he did, he did not dismiss
what she had just revealed. Weighing his

words, eventually he said, 'I'm glad you told me. Perhaps it was nothing, perhaps there really was someone following you. If the former is true, then there's no harm done. If the latter, then sharing your suspicions with me means that now we shall both be on our guard.'

Her face fell. 'Against what?'

He gave a helpless shrug. 'Abbess dear, I have no idea.'

14

Staring at her old friend's hopeless expression, Helewise had a moment's urge to wave her arms and shout, We have to get to the bottom of this, right now! Two men are dead, a young girl is missing, and we two must go on thinking until we know *why*!

But he's still convalescing, she told herself severely. I have no right to push him so hard when he has been so ill. And I, too, am exhausted. Neither of us is at our best at the moment.

She stepped away from him and, making herself move slowly and calmly, walked round her table until she was once more in front of her wooden chair. Raising her head so that her eyes met his, she said, 'Sir Josse, I am sorry that I have kept you here for so long, tiring you out by talking. Please, go back now to Sister Euphemia, and surrender yourself into her care once more. We will speak again tomorrow.'

He raised an anguished face to hers. 'There have been two deaths, Abbess! *Two!* We must — we ought to be ... ' But his resolve seemed to have run out.

'To bed, Sir Josse,' she insisted. Still he did not move; she realised that she was going to have to help him. 'Come,' she said, returning to his side, 'I will walk with you to the infirmary. I shall confess to Sister Euphemia that it was I who exhausted her poor patient, and that you are not to blame.'

He stood up, managing a weak grin. 'Oh, I shouldn't go doing that, Abbess; Sister Euphemia's like a mother hen with her patients, she'll have you scouring out slop bowls for the next week as a punishment.'

'One that I richly deserve,' Helewise murmured.

She noticed, as they went across to the infirmary, that he was leaning on her. Deeply touched at this evidence of his physical weakness, she could not bear to linger; almost pushing him towards a surprised Sister Beata, she said somewhat gruffly, 'I've tired your patient, I'm afraid. Please look after him.'

Then she turned abruptly on her heel and strode back to her room.

Soon afterwards, it was time for the evening devotions. Joining her voice with those of her sisters in the beautiful words and sounds of Compline, eventually she began to feel a little better.

★   ★   ★

The next day saw an end to the spell of warm, sunny weather. The sky was overcast, and a light drizzle was falling. The weight of clouds massing over the forest suggested that heavier rain was not far away.

Helewise's mind was racing and, eager to implement the plan she had worked out while lying sleepless in the early hours, she had little appetite for breakfast. But she made herself eat; she knew that she would be less well equipped to face the challenge of the day on an empty stomach.

As soon as she could get away, she set off for the Vale to find Berthe.

The monks and the pilgrims were all in the little shrine that had been built over the holy water spring. They were in the middle of a service.

Helewise stood at the back of the shrine, at the top of the short flight of rough-hewn steps that led down to the pool. Even above the soft murmur of praying voices she could hear the gentle, steady sound of the water, falling from where it seeped out of the rocks into the pool below.

On a plinth, set into the rocky walls over the spring, stood a wooden statue of the Virgin. She was raised above the floor, so that her small, bare feet were at eye level. Her arms were outstretched and her hands were spread out with the palms uppermost; she seemed to be giving a constant gesture of invitation, and this benevolence was echoed in the gentle smile on the softly curving mouth.

Helewise, who was always moved by this beautiful image of the Holy Mother, breathed a sigh of pure happiness.

It was such a wonderful place, this shrine, she thought. For a few precious moments, she put her pressing preoccupations aside and opened her heart and her soul to the kind blessing that seemed to be present in the very air of the shrine.

The service ended, and Helewise stood back as the monks escorted the pilgrims out of the shrine and into the lean-to shelter adjoining it. The able-bodied visitors stood at the back; the infirm were helped to sit down on roughly made wooden benches that the lay brothers had placed ready in a semicircle. Then Brother Firmin gave out small, earthenware cups of the precious healing water.

Helewise studied Brother Firmin's lined old face. As he raised each cup to a pilgrim's lips, it seemed that a light shone from him. The strength of his faith, she thought, is an example to us all.

She had been so entranced by the simple

service and the giving of the waters that she had all but forgotten why she had gone to the shrine. Forcing her mind back to her anxieties, she looked around for Berthe.

And, after a while, saw her. She was crouched on the beaten earth floor of the pilgrims' rest house, whose wide doors had been thrown back to air it after the night. She was playing with two small children, whose laughter was bringing a smile to the faces of quite a few of those who heard it. Beside her, the crossed legs and sandalled feet of another figure could just be seen.

Helewise went over to the rest house. The other person was Brother Augustine; as Helewise went inside, both he and Berthe got to their feet and bowed to her.

She returned their greetings. Then she said, 'How lovely to hear the children laughing! It must have been a good game.'

Brother Augustine grinned. 'It was, Abbess.' He glanced at Berthe, who was blushing furiously. 'But — er . . . '

Helewise guessed at the cause of the confusion. 'But a little vulgar, dare I suggest?'

Both young people nodded. The children, overawed at having the Abbess of Hawkenlye herself visit them, sat on the ground with their mouths open, staring up at her.

'Please do not let me interrupt,' Helewise

went on. 'Augustine, may I borrow Berthe for a few moments?'

'Of course, Abbess.'

She beckoned to Berthe to follow her, and led her a little way along the path leading on down the Vale. When she was sure they were far enough away not to be overheard, she stopped. It was still raining, although not very hard, so she indicated to Berthe that they should stand beneath the shelter of a chestnut tree.

She studied the girl. There was, she decided, a definite look of apprehension in the young face.

'Berthe, I have come to tell you what I have discovered during my travels,' Helewise began. 'I found the convent where Alba was; it is called Sedgebeck. But I am afraid I must tell you that Alba was excused from her vows and she left the community. Her behaviour was — ' Oh, dear, was there a diplomatic way of telling the poor girl? 'She was not suited to convent life,' she said. Then, before Berthe could press her for more, she hurried on, 'Then I went to Medely, and I was given directions to your farm. It is, as presumably you are well aware, now quite deserted.'

Berthe was watching her closely. 'Yes, Abbess. We understood that there was not to be a new tenant. The land, you see, is not very good.'

'No, indeed.' Helewise paused, thinking hard. Berthe had, she realised, just given her an opening . . . 'No, we noticed that yours was the only farm in the immediate vicinity. The only dwelling, in fact, for some miles around. My, but you were isolated out there, weren't you, you and your family?'

Berthe's eyes were fixed on hers. Was there a hint of fear? Did the girl know why Helewise was saying all this about being so alone?

Slowly Berthe nodded. 'Yes, Abbess. It *was* isolated. The village, as you saw for yourself, was some distance away. And there were no other inhabited dwellings nearby.'

Very neat, Helewise thought. No other inhabited dwellings. Which tells me nothing for sure, but which *suggests* that Berthe knew there was a cottage in the woods, but also knew it to be empty.

Should I press her further? Helewise wondered. Why not? At the least, Berthe's reaction might reveal whether or not she was aware that her empty dwelling had become a dead man's pyre.

'You were aware, of course,' she said, trying to keep her tone casual, 'of the old cottage deep in the woods? I dare say that it was uninhabited when you lived at the farm.'

Berthe was nodding. 'Yes, I know it. A very old couple used to live there — I can just remember them from when I was small. Sometimes Mother and I used to call on them. Mother would take them something — some eggs, or something from the vegetable plot — and once the old man made a garland of wild flowers and crowned me with it.' A soft smile of reminiscence briefly lit her face. 'But they died,' she finished. 'A long time ago.'

'And nobody took over the cottage?'

'No. It was tumbling down around them even when the old folks were there. When they died, it was too far gone for anyone to bother. We used to use it as a camp, when we could escape from Alba's vigilance, and, later on, Meriel — '

But she must have realised that she was about to say something she shouldn't. She shut her mouth abruptly, turning away from Helewise and staring out towards the lake that filled the bottom of the Vale.

'Meriel?' Helewise prompted. 'What about her?'

Berthe spun round to face her. 'Abbess Helewise, I *can't*!' she cried. 'You mustn't ask me, because if you really press me for an answer, I'll have to lie to you, and I don't want to do that. But I can't break my promise!'

She was sobbing now, violent, convulsive sobs that made her whole body shake. Helewise put her arms round the thin shoulders, and for a few moments Berthe leant against her. 'I know, Berthe, I know,' she murmured soothingly. 'You must understand that I do not pry from mere curiosity — I am trying to help you.'

'I *know* you are!' Berthe cried. 'But I — '

'Yes, yes, I understand,' Helewise interrupted. 'You can't break a promise, even though you may well feel it would be better if you did. Yes? Am I right?'

Berthe broke away from her and looked up into her eyes. She did not speak, but slowly she nodded.

'Poor child,' Helewise said gently. And, although she did not further dismay Berthe by saying so aloud, she feared that things would have to get quite a lot worse before they got better.

Especially if she could convince herself that she would be justified in implementing a certain course of action she had just thought of . . .

'Come along, let's get you back to work,' she said bracingly, giving Berthe a little shake and brushing the tears from her cheeks.

'There, that's better. You hardly look as if you've been crying — I don't expect anyone will notice. Not those happy little children, anyway!'

Berthe managed a watery smile. 'No, *they* won't,' she agreed. 'But Gussie will.'

Gussie? Ah, yes, Brother Augustine's nickname was Gus, Helewise recalled. And that had been softened by this sweetnatured girl to Gussie. 'Will he?' She was hardly surprised; Augustine, she had perceived, missed very little. 'Well, I'm sure he won't tease you about it.'

'No, he won't. He's very considerate, actually.' Berthe was looking a lot more cheerful, probably, Helewise thought, at the prospect of imminently being with 'Gussie' again. 'He doesn't tease me at all. He's very kind to me.'

Was that, Helewise wondered, because the lad had seen what was in that cottage in the woods? And, having seen, was concerned and sorry for this young girl, who must surely be somehow caught up in the wretched business?

Good for Augustine, if so, she thought. To have realised Berthe's need, and to turn himself into a kind and supportive friend, was Christian indeed.

Was it likely Augustine had spoken to

Berthe about the journey to East Anglia? More particularly, about the visit to her old home? Instinct told Helewise that it wasn't; the boy was responsible and obedient, and surely would have held his peace unless specifically told that he might break it. Nevertheless . . .

'Berthe, has Augustine told you anything of our trip?' she asked casually.

Immediately Berthe gave a brief *tsk!* of irritation. 'No, Abbess Helewise, not a word! I've pressed him and pressed him, tried to wheedle out a few remarks, but he just shuts his mouth up tight and says it was Abbey business and he's not allowed to gossip. *Gossip!* Really! And it was my own village he went to! Well, amongst other places.'

'Now, now, don't be cross with Augustine,' Helewise soothed. 'He is right to be cautious. And anyway, Berthe,' — she crossed her fingers and hoped God would understand the lie — 'there wasn't much to see.'

Only slightly mollified, Berthe said, 'Huh!'

Helewise took the girl's hand as they went back to the shrine, hurrying now for the rain was coming down harder.

She watched her go back inside the rest house — and the laughter from within suggested that the same game was still in progress — then, accepting Brother Saul's offer of a piece of sacking to cover her head and shoulders, she walked quickly through the rain back to the Abbey.

As she ran in through the rear gate, a clap of thunder detonated right overhead. Hoping that it was not an omen of dire happenings ahead, she headed for the shelter of the cloister and made her way to her room.

15

Josse had expected to feel very tired after his first whole day spent outside. But, when he woke the next morning, he was delighted to find that he was full of energy.

Sister Euphemia was sceptical when he told her. 'Are you sure you're not just telling yourself that because you want to go racing off to help the Abbess sort out these wretched sisters?' she asked. 'Mind, I'm not suggesting she couldn't do with a bit of help; they do say trouble comes in threes, and it certainly has done with Alba, Meriel and poor little Berthe.'

'Aye, that it has,' he agreed. 'But I promise you, I really do feel well, Sister Euphemia. After all,' he added craftily, 'I would be of little help to the Abbess if I were to collapse at her feet from exhaustion, now, would I?'

Sister Euphemia gave a snort of laughter and dug him in the ribs. 'Go on with you!' she chuckled. 'You've always got a plausible answer, haven't you?'

Agreeing that he had, he shooed her away while he put on his tunic and his boots.

★　★　★

He was sitting on a bench outside the infirmary when, some time later, Helewise came to look for him. The side of the long building which faced into the courtyard was lined with a deep cloister and, tucked in against the infirmary wall, he was sheltered from the rain. Sister Beata had thoughtfully brought out a sheepskin fleece, which she had draped over his legs, and he was adequately warm.

He knew from the Abbess's face that she was troubled. He shifted along to make room for her to sit down beside him, then said, 'What is it?'

Without preamble she said, 'I have thought of a plan. I intend to tell Berthe that I must release Alba — indeed, that Alba will have to leave the Abbey — and then I shall have Berthe followed. She will, I am quite sure, go straight to find Meriel, to tell her that Alba is once more to be on the loose.' Before he had time for even the briefest comment, she rushed on. 'Oh, there's no need to tell me I'm being cruelly devious, and taking advantage of a suffering girl's confusion and concern! I *know* I am, and I just hope it will prove worth it. But I must speak to Meriel, and I cannot think of another way.'

She finished, turning an angry, defensive

face to Josse. He said mildly, 'I think it's a splendid plan.'

'Oh! Do you?'

'Aye, Abbess. I understand how you feel. I wouldn't like to think I was making use of Berthe, either. But look at it this way: she must be suffering agonies, trying to keep Meriel's secret and worrying about how she's managing, wherever she is. And your scheme, although possibly hurtful to her in the short term, will ultimately help both Berthe *and* Meriel. Won't it?'

The Abbess's face was clearing. 'I hadn't thought of that,' she said. No, he thought, you wouldn't. You were too busy accusing yourself. She gave him a brief bow. 'Thank you, Sir Josse.'

'Think nothing of it,' he murmured. Then: 'Who have you in mind to act as hound to Berthe's hare?'

She gave a short laugh. 'I should like to go myself, but a nun's habit is hardly the garb in which to go creeping through the under-growth trying to be quiet and inconspicuous. I thought I might ask Brother Augustine. He is young and lithe and, because he accompan-ied me on my travels, he is already aware of many of the finer points of the situation.' She hesitated, then went on, 'In addition, he is, I believe, fond of little Berthe, and thus may be

226

eager to help her.'

'A good choice,' Josse agreed. He wished yet again that he were fully fit. He would have argued her out of appointing any other man but himself, had he been able to go. But, even assuming he were able to walk into the forest, he certainly wasn't up to doing so stealthily. Trying to be sensible and ignore the childish protest clamouring, send me!, he said, 'When do you propose to put your scheme into action?'

'I was only waiting to discuss it with you,' she said.

Moved, he muttered, 'You do me too much honour, Abbess. You do not need my advice, when your own decisions are so sound.'

'Oh yes, I do,' she countered.

There was a moment's rather weighty silence between them. Then, deliberately lightening his tone, he said, 'You'll have to brace yourself if you're really proposing to go and see Alba. Or will you just tell Berthe you've done so, and not actually inform Alba that she's to be released?'

'Oh, I intend to visit Alba first,' the Abbess said. 'And I know what you mean about bracing myself; the nuns who have had the care of her report that she is increasingly restless, and that they have had to resort to the threat of depriving her of her daily excursions.'

'Humph.' Josse privately thought that it had been overcharitable to allow a violent and possibly unbalanced woman out twice a day to take the air. But, knowing the Abbess would not agree, he merely said, 'I hope you're not planning to go in to see her alone. Take Saul, and maybe one of the more robust nuns with you.' Then, realising what he had just said; 'I apologise, Abbess. I did not mean to give you orders.'

But she was smiling. 'Apology accepted. And thank you for the advice.' She got up.

On an impulse, he said, 'May I come with you to Alba's cell?'

She studied him for a moment. 'Yes. Provided you do not attempt to form part of my bodyguard.'

He grinned back. 'I promise.'

★ ★ ★

They sent for Brother Saul, and Sister Martha came over from the stables; the Abbess made her leave her pitchfork behind. Then the four of them went down the steps into the undercroft beneath the infirmary, and the Abbess unlocked the stout door of Alba's prison.

Josse, keeping his word and remaining

228

behind the Abbess and her two guardians, peered round Brother Saul and caught his first glimpse of Alba.

He was shocked.

He had been prepared for her to be considerably older than her two sisters; he'd already been told that. But he had not expected the pale face, thin to the point of emaciation, nor the bleak look in the deep-set, dark eyes. Sister Martha must have heard his intake of breath; turning, she whispered, 'They do say she has not been eating, poor wretch.'

And, to prove her point, Josse saw that on the floor was an untouched tray of food.

The Abbess stepped forward. At Sister Martha's gesture, Alba got reluctantly to her feet and faced her.

'Alba, I must tell you that I have visited your convent at Sedgebeck, and I have been informed that you have been released from your vows as a nun,' she said, her voice level and unemotional. 'Since I now know that you are not in holy orders, I have no authority to keep you imprisoned here. You are not under my jurisdiction and, as soon as we can find a place for you, you will be free to go.'

A range of emotions ran across Alba's gaunt face. Shock, shame, a brief flaring anger and, finally and most enduringly, horror.

'You *can't* make me go, Abbess!' she said in a whisper. 'I am a nun! That is my vocation, and I shall be the best nun ever! I shall rise, just like you, to be Abbess — just wait and see!'

'You are no longer a nun, Alba,' the Abbess insisted firmly. 'You knew that when you presented yourself to me, and yet you told me you had been fully professed for years.'

'Yes, yes, I'm sorry,' Alba said impatiently, as if brushing a minor matter out of the way. 'But I'll just have to begin again. Here.'

'You cannot, Alba!' The Abbess sounded aghast.

'Ah, but I must!' Alba countered. 'You see, it's my sisters. They are to take the veil, I've told them so, and I must be here, senior to them, to tell them what they may and may not do.'

'But they — you wouldn't — ' the Abbess began. Then, as if, like Josse, she realised she was addressing an irrationality that verged on mania, she stopped. 'You have heard my decision, Alba,' she said with dignity. 'We shall do what we can to find you somewhere to go, then you will be released and you will leave Hawkenlye. That is final.'

The Abbess turned and left the cell, and

Brother Saul swung the door shut and bolted it.

But, as the four of them walked away, they heard the dreadful sound of Alba hurling herself against it.

★ ⋆ ★

Josse could see that the Abbess was shaken. As Sister Martha and Brother Saul returned to their duties, he said to her, 'Why not leave it for a while, Abbess? Sit and compose yourself, rest, go and pray, and — '

She turned to him, and the expression in her clear grey eyes silenced him. 'I cannot stop until I see this through,' she said coldly. Then, her face softening: 'Oh Josse, forgive me! You meant only to help me, I know. But would you advise a general to have a little rest just when the battle is at its height?'

'No.'

'Well, then. All the time this awful, disturbing mystery remains with us, there can be no rest, for me or for any of my nuns. No. I shall speak to Brother Augustine and entrust to him his vital mission, then I shall find Berthe, and tell her what I have just told Alba.'

He nodded. 'Aye. That's for the best.' He put out his hand and touched her wrist.

'Good luck, Abbess. God be with you.'

Her muttered 'Amen' floated back to him as she hurried away.

⋆　⋆　⋆

The early afternoon was a quiet time down in the Vale. As Helewise approached the little clutch of simple buildings, she noticed that several of the pilgrims were resting under the overhanging roof outside the shelter; it was all part of the cure, she reflected, for them to be encouraged to take naps. As Sister Euphemia often said, going to sleep allowed the body to get on with the work of healing itself without any distractions.

She could see Berthe in the distance, sitting at the waterside further along the Vale. She had a clutch of children with her, and, from their rapt faces, it looked as if she were telling them a story.

Some of the monks and lay brothers were about, engaged in various tasks. Nobody seemed to be in a hurry. It was all most peaceful . . .

Helewise told herself to stop daydreaming and remember why she had come. She wondered where Brother Augustine was. She was just about to send a monk to go and find him for her when one of the pilgrims got up from where he had been sitting, leaning against the front wall of the shelter, and came over to her.

She stared at him as he approached. She didn't think she had seen him before, although it was hard to tell with so many people passing through all the time. And there *was* actually something vaguely familiar about him.

She said pleasantly, 'Good day to you, pilgrim.'

He stopped a few paces from her and made her a deep reverence. She noted fleetingly that it was exactly the way that the professed greeted one another; the man must have a good eye for detail. Then, straightening, he met her eyes. His, she noticed, were dark, as was his short-cropped hair. And, unlike most men, he wore a beard.

He said in a low-pitched voice, 'I believe I have the honour of addressing the Abbess of Hawkenlye.'

Helewise bowed her head briefly in acknowledgement, and his serious expression lightened momentarily into a smile.

'You have arrived just today?' she asked.

He nodded, but then said, 'Er — yesterday.'

'Have you yet taken of the precious, holy water?'

'No.'

She was about to ask whether he was there for healing — not that he looked anything but the picture of health, but you could not always tell — or to offer prayers at Our Lady's shrine. But she stopped herself. It was not usually her way to question visitors; why should she do so now?

The stranger was still staring at her. Beginning to feel a little uncomfortable, she said, 'Excuse me, please. I must — '

But again she stopped herself. She was not in the habit of explaining her movements to the pilgrims, either. Giving him the smallest of nods, she turned away.

As she hurried off to find someone to locate Augustine for her, she was surprised to find that her heartbeat had quickened.

Why? she wondered. She tried to analyse the emotion coursing through her. It was not exactly fear, but it was quite close. Apprehension?

Yes.

Then suddenly she thought, it's as if I've just had to go before a superior with an inadequate excuse for some fault!

Amazed at herself — it was a long time since she had been in *that* position — she put the image of a pair of disturbingly penetrating dark eyes to the back of her mind and beckoned to Brother Saul.

Brother Augustine, who had been helping one of the pilgrims treat his old mule's cut foot, came hurrying to find her as soon as he was told of her summons. She explained what she wanted him to do and, putting her trust in his shining honesty, told him why.

He frowned as he absorbed her words. 'You're really going to use Berthe to lead you to her sister,' he said slowly.

'I am, Augustine,' she replied. She kept her eyes on his. 'I do not like myself for doing so, but I feel that a greater evil is perpetuated by allowing Berthe to continue living this life of pretence.'

He nodded. 'Aye. She's not happy, poor lass.'

'I don't suppose that she has confided in you?' Helewise asked.

'No.' He grinned briefly. 'And that's the truth, Abbess.'

She laughed softly. 'Oh, Augustine, I believe you. Really, I never knew a pair so transparently honest as you and Berthe!'

'Thank you,' he said gravely. Then, after quite a long silence: 'I will gladly go for you, Abbess. And, when this is all over, I will explain to Berthe why I did so. Is that all right?'

Thankfully she said, 'Yes, Augustine. Indeed it is.'

* * *

She gave him a little while to find himself a hiding place from which he could observe Berthe. Then, trying to control her excitement, she walked along the path to where the girl was still sitting with the group of children.

Catching sight of Helewise, Berthe leapt up to greet her.

'Abbess, how nice to see you!' she said ingenuously.

'Good day, Berthe. Will you walk with me? I have something that I wish to tell you.'

'Of course!'

She led the girl further along the path, away from the shrine. Then she said, 'Berthe, I told you yesterday that Alba is no longer a nun. This means that I have no authority over her, and therefore I cannot keep her imprisoned. I have informed her that, as soon as we can find her somewhere to go, she will have to leave Hawkenlye.'

Berthe's rosy face had gone dead white. 'You — ' she began. Then, trying again, 'But surely she wants to stay?'

'What she wants is not relevant,' Helewise

said gently. 'Berthe, she is not at all suited to life as a nun, nor indeed to living in a convent as a lay sister. She is too disruptive an influence. I have the well-being of all my community to consider and, although it is hard on Alba, I have no alternative but to send her away.'

'I understand, Abbess.' Berthe's face had set into a strangely adult, resigned expression, which looked incongruous on one so young.

Helewise's heart turned over with pity. 'But *you* may stay here, Berthe,' she said. 'Without becoming a postulant, I mean. Sister Euphemia is always on the look-out for suitable young girls to train as lay nurses, and you are certainly suitable, she tells me.'

For a moment, Berthe's face lit up. But then the depression fell again. 'It is a lovely idea, Abbess,' she said politely. 'But not possible.'

'Because of Alba?' Helewise asked. The girl nodded. 'But you can be free of her, if she is sent away!'

Berthe turned sad eyes to her. She said dully, 'We can *never* be free of Alba.'

Hating herself, wanting above all to talk to the child, give her what consolation she could, instead Helewise gave her a short adieu and, turning away, set out back to the Abbey.

She could not bear to sit in her room while she endured the prolonged wait. There was work she could have been getting on with — there was always that — but she could not concentrate. Her mind kept filling with images of Berthe slipping away, running to find Meriel, and breaking her heart as she sobbed out her story. Of Augustine, following her, watching from behind some great tree and recording everything with his observant eyes to report back to his Abbess.

In the end, she went over to the Abbey church, slid into her accustomed place in the stalls and opened her burdened heart to God.

★ ★ ★

While the Abbess prayed, Berthe and Augustine were engaged in almost exactly the actions she had imagined.

But somebody else was following behind Augustine. Someone whose involvement, had she been aware of it, would have surprised the Abbess greatly . . .

★ ★ ★

Augustine came to find her sooner than she had expected. She was back in her room, calmer now, about to go through the cellaress's latest report when there was a soft tap on the door.

In answer to her response, Augustine came in. Trying to read his face as he greeted her, she thought perhaps he looked relieved.

'Did the plan work?' she asked.

'Aye, Abbess. First, let me tell you that Meriel is safe and, as far as I could tell from a brief glance, seems to be none the worse for a spell of living in the open.'

'Thank God,' Helewise whispered.

'Amen. You were right, Abbess,' Augustine hurried on, the story seeming to burst out of him, 'soon as you'd left the Vale, Berthe slipped away. I only managed to trail her because I was expecting her to go off somewhere — she was very clever, she went *inside* the lean-to and got out through a loose panel at the back. Anyway, like I said, I managed not to lose her.'

'Where did she go?'

'I thought at first she was heading up to the Abbey but, before she got to the rear gate, she turned off to her left, circled round the side of the Abbey, then crossed over the track that leads off to Tonbridge and went into the forest.'

'The forest!' Dear Lord, Helewise thought. She knew only too well what dangers lurked in the great Wealden Forest.

'Aye.' He seemed hardly to have registered the brief interruption. 'She headed off down a deer path, and it led right into the trees, through thick undergrowth. Then it met a wider track, which led into a clearing. Really, Abbess, you'd never have found it if you didn't know where to look, or unless, like me, you were following somebody. It was so well hidden.'

'And what was in the clearing?'

'There were some shelters. Rough sort of shelters, made of a few poles covered with branches and turfs. Charcoal burners' camp, I reckon it was, although there hadn't been fires there in a long while. Well, no more than a little cooking fire, which was burning away nicely. Cooking somebody's dinner, I'd say, from the appetising smell.'

'Meriel's dinner?' Helewise hardly dared breathe.

With a wide smile, Augustine nodded. 'Aye. Meriel's dinner. She came out of one of the huts as Berthe ran into the clearing.'

'And she looked well, you said?'

'She did that. Much better, I'd say, than when she was here in the Abbey. She looked radiant. She raced over to Berthe, hugged

240

her, and she was starting to say something, laughing all the while, when Berthe stopped her. Must have told her about Alba, I reckon. Because, whatever it was, it stopped the laughter on an instant.'

Helewise's mind was racing. The great flood of relief at hearing that Meriel was alive and well was receding a little, and now other anxieties had shot up. I know of folk who dwell in the forest, she thought. I have encountered them, and lived to tell the tale. But that does not mean that I have forgotten how perilous they can be . . .

'She was happy?' she asked Augustine. 'Radiant, didn't you say?'

'Aye, both of those.'

If she has already encountered the forest folk, Helewise thought, and still appears so cheerful, then perhaps I am worrying needlessly, and they are no threat to her. But, oh, I am afraid for her!

One thing she could and must do, she decided, was to prevent any more harm. 'Augustine, thank you,' she said, smiling at him. 'You have done very well. You have, in fact, achieved all that I asked of you. But now I have to give you an order which you may not like.'

'Anything, Abbess,' he said stoutly, bracing

himself as if preparing for some risky, exacting task.

She hated to disappoint him.

'You must return to the Vale, and you must stay there,' she said firmly. 'You must not reveal to Berthe that you followed her, and you must not follow her again. *Whatever* happens.'

His face had crumpled into a ferocious scowl. 'But, Abbess — '

'There *are* no buts here,' she said with quiet finality. 'You may go, Augustine.'

Obedience made him bow to her before he left. Observing the resigned set of his shoulders, she was quite sure he would do exactly as she had commanded.

Now, she thought, I must visit Sir Josse. I hope and pray that I shall find him rested and willing to accompany me on an excursion.

She crossed the courtyard and approached the infirmary. As she went inside, it occurred to her also to hope that Josse's fever hadn't affected his memory, and that he still remembered the way to the charcoal burners' camp.

16

Having the Abbess visit him was, Josse thought, no rare occurrence. But to have her propose that they set out together into the forest, right this minute before it became too dark, and could he lead them to the charcoal burners' camp, now that *was* unexpected.

'Will you go with me?' she repeated, face taut with anxiety.

'Of course, Abbess.'

'You are strong enough? It won't be too much for you?'

He wasn't entirely sure about that, but he was prepared to take the risk. 'Aye, I'll manage,' he assured her. 'Only — '

'Only what?'

He had been about to say, only we'd better be sure Sister Euphemia doesn't spot us, but he decided against it. Whatever had prompted Helewise to make this urgent request was obviously of great importance to her, or she would not have asked him. Best not to distress her by suggesting that the infirmarer might not consider him up to it.

'Nothing. I've been up and about today, and I'm feeling stronger every minute! A walk in the woods in the evening air will do me good. Er — is it still raining?'

Assuring him it wasn't, she hurried off towards the door, pausing only to beckon to him to follow her out of the building.

★ ★ ★

It became easier, he discovered, once he got into his stride. To begin with, even the gentle slope out of the Abbey and into the forest had him panting, and it was difficult to conceal from the Abbess that he couldn't catch his breath.

But then, as they followed the deer track in under the trees, he began to feel better. The air in the forest smelt wonderful after the day's rain: he could almost taste it, and he was quite sure it was putting new heart in him.

And, after so long in the infirmary or, at best, penned within the walls of the Abbey, it felt marvellous to be out in the great, wide world again.

He realised presently that he had been so preoccupied with testing his legs and his endurance that he had hardly spared a thought for where they were going. Not that it was difficult to work it out. Stopping — he was in the lead — he turned to the Abbess and said softly, 'Your plan worked, I take it? We're on our way to wherever it is that Meriel has been hiding out?'

'Yes,' she whispered back. 'Augustine says she's quite all right. Looking very well, in fact.'

'And camping in one of the old charcoal burners' huts?'

'Yes.'

He remembered somebody else doing that. He sent up a brief prayer that, this time, it wouldn't end as it had done then.

He was about to move on when she stopped him by catching hold of his sleeve. 'Sir Josse, we need to — That is, I fear for Meriel's safety, as for that of any young girl in the forest alone. I'm sure I do not need to say any more.'

He knew exactly what she meant. He, too, remembered. He said, 'No, Abbess. You don't.'

Moving on, in his mind he saw again — although he tried not to — what he and the Abbess had once witnessed, not many miles from the place to which they were now heading. And, remembering, he understood her urgency. She was quite right; an isolated hut deep in the Wealden Forest was no place for a young girl all on her own.

★ ★ ★

He slowed down as they approached the clearing. For one thing, it wouldn't be kind to surprise Meriel by crashing unexpectedly into the silent grove. For another — well, the forest somehow seemed to *command* a reverent pace; you never quite knew what you might surprise out of its hiding place . . .

He stopped on the edge of the clearing. The Abbess was at his shoulder, and he thought she seemed to be holding her breath. Together they peered through the undergrowth into the open space beyond.

The least dilapidated of the ancient dwellings was clearly occupied. There was a small fire burning outside it, within a neatly built hearth of stones. Garments of some sort had been hung on some bushes; had Meriel been doing the washing? Surely not!

Adopting the Abbess's tactic of holding her breath, the better to listen, he cocked an ear in the direction of the clearing.

Carrying quite clearly on the still evening air came the sound of voices.

A girl's voice — Meriel's? — speaking softly, a question in her tone.

And, answering, a different voice. Warm with love, it seemed to give reassurance in response to Meriel's anxiety.

It was, quite unmistakably, a man's voice.

Beside him, Josse felt the Abbess stiffen in

outrage. 'She's got a *man* in there!' she hissed. And, before Josse could stop her, she pushed her way through the last belt of undergrowth, strode across the glade to the hut and cried, 'Meriel! Meriel, answer me, it's the Abbess. What on *earth* do you think you're doing?'

Trying to hurry after her, Josse tripped and almost fell. Recovering, his eyes ever on the tall, erect figure of the Abbess standing there alone, he stumbled on. But before he could reach her, do whatever he could to defend her, a figure shot out of the hut.

A figure as tall as the Abbess, much broader in the shoulder, and holding a sword.

With a last huge effort, Josse hurled himself forward. The man saw him coming, turning towards him and swiftly raising his sword to defend himself all in one easy, practised movement. But it was that trained eye and obedient body that saved Josse; the young man observed instantly that Josse was unarmed, and dropped his weapon. Instead of running into the sword, Josse found himself falling into the man's outstretched arms.

The young stranger said, 'Sir Josse d'Acquin, I greet you.' And he dropped on one knee, bowing his head as if he were swearing fealty.

Panting, the stitch in his side feeling as if it were cutting him in two, Josse slumped to the ground. His eyes almost on a level with the young man's, he said, 'Forgive me for not standing to receive your greetings as I should. But I don't think I can.'

With enormous relief, he lay back on the welcoming forest floor and closed his eyes.

★ ★ ★

But not for long.

He heard the Abbess call again, 'Meriel! Are you all right, child? *Meriel!*' And then, as he opened his eyes, he saw the girl emerge from the hut.

It was only then he noticed that both of them, Meriel and the young man, were not dressed. They had both wrapped themselves in covers of some sort, and they both looked as if they had just got out of bed.

Josse sat up. After a moment, his head stopped spinning and he said, 'I believe, Abbess, that we intrude. Let us move away some distance, and perhaps Meriel and — ?'

'Jerome,' said the young man, raising his head with dignity. 'Jerome de Waelsham.' Some achievement, Josse thought wryly, to maintain such presence when clad in nothing but a blanket.

'Perhaps Meriel and Jerome will come to speak with us when they are ready?' Josse went on.

Jerome glanced at Meriel, who nodded. She was wide-eyed with fear, and Josse noticed that the young man swiftly went to her side, putting a protective arm around her bare shoulders.

The Abbess, still fuming, began to say something. 'Don't you try to — '

Josse interrupted. 'Come away, Abbess,' he said quietly. 'We are embarrassing them. They will talk to us when they are ready, I am sure of that.'

The young man shot him a grateful look, collected the garments from the bush and followed Meriel inside the hut. Josse took the Abbess's arm — she was rigid with tension — and led her over to the far side of the clearing. They sat down on the trunk of a fallen tree.

'They were lying together!' she said with furious indignation.

'Aye,' he agreed. 'That they were.'

She turned on him. 'How can you be so calm?' she demanded. 'Two young people — she's scarcely sixteen! — out here in the wilds, all self-control thrown to the winds, and she's only just left the Abbey!'

'Where she was not a nun,' he reminded

her, 'so she has broken no vow of chastity.'

'But — but — ' Helewise spluttered. Then, with an indignant, 'Humph!' she folded her arms and lapsed into wounded silence.

I have let her down, he thought ruefully. She expected my support in her condemnation, and I am unable to give it.

He saw them again in his mind's eye, that handsome, loving pair. Saw how she looked to him for comfort, saw how he hastened to show her how much he cared. There was love, right enough, he thought. And, for the life of me, I can't condemn it as a sin.

After a while, the young couple came out of the hut. They were fully dressed, Meriel in a simple golden-yellow gown and Jerome in hose and tunic. His hair, Josse noted absently, looked as if it had been cropped very short not long ago.

The pair stopped in front of the Abbess and Josse, who both rose to their feet. The Abbess — sounding once more in control of herself — said, 'Meriel, will you please tell me — us — what is going on?'

Meriel took an audible breath, then said, 'I had to run away, Abbess Helewise. I know how much trouble I must have caused, and please believe that I deeply regret it. You took us in, you didn't let Alba turn you against us with her rantings and ravings, and I believe you intended to side with Berthe and me over whether or not we had to become nuns.'

'Indeed I did!' the Abbess exclaimed. 'No girl or woman is *ever* put into the community against her will, Meriel.'

'Yes. That's what I thought.'

'You should have come to me,' the Abbess said kindly. 'I was only waiting for you to ask for my help. I would have given it wholeheartedly.'

There were tears in Meriel's eyes. 'I'm sorry, Abbess. It's just that — just that Berthe and I aren't used to trusting people.' Her voice broke. Instantly, Jerome hugged her to him, stroking her hair and speaking soft, soothing words into her ear.

'But you trust Jerome, here,' Josse put in. Meriel nodded, disentangling herself. 'So, when you knew he had come to find you, it was best, you thought, to run away from the Abbey and put your faith in him.'

'Please, she's been through enough!' the young man protested. 'You don't know — '

But Meriel said, 'It's all right, Jerome.' Then, turning back to Helewise and Josse, she said simply, 'I thought he was dead. When I found that I had been wrong, how could I not come here to be with him?'

'You thought he was *dead?*' the Abbess repeated. 'But why — ' Then, light dawning in her face, she breathed, 'That was why you were so grief-stricken! Nothing to do with your father's death, or having to leave your home, or Alba threatening to make you be a nun.' She looked from Meriel to Jerome, and back again. 'You believed your lover was dead.'

'Yes. And I wanted to die, too.'

She spoke with such honesty that Josse, for one, entirely believed her.

'I know something of your story,' the Abbess was saying. 'I have been to Sedgebeck, where Alba was briefly in the convent. I know, too, that she is no longer a nun. As I believe Berthe has reported to you, I shall have to ask Alba to leave Hawkenlye. As soon as arrangements can be made to find her a home, she will go.'

Meriel was shaking her head. 'Abbess, you don't know what you're doing,' she said. 'Forgive me for being so blunt, but I must. Alba has — I fear that Alba may do untold harm, if she is free to pursue — if she is not controlled. She takes things upon herself that are not her responsibility, and she does not give up. Believe me!'

'I am aware that she has assumed far too much control over you and Berthe,' the Abbess said, 'and, indeed, over your late mother. Berthe has revealed something of her background to Sir Josse and to me, and we sympathise deeply with what must have been a most difficult childhood.'

'*Difficult!*' Jerome said incredulously. 'Clearly, Abbess Helewise, you have not heard everything. She used to — '

'Jerome,' Meriel said gently. Looking at her with impatience that was quickly replaced by a smile, he stopped. 'Abbess, Alba is not sane,' Meriel continued. 'Her unreasoning insistence on maintaining the good name of our family led to the death of my mother. Having seen off the person she saw as her rival in my father's affections, Alba decided it was safe to leave us all alone, and she went away to become a nun, by which she meant she was going to be an Abbess. Great Lord, she'd have aimed for Pope, if they allowed women to hold the post! Then, when word reached her of Father's death and — and of what Berthe and I were planning to do, she came rushing back to Medely purely to stop us! She even — '

'No, Meriel,' Jerome said warningly. 'Not that. Not until we *know.*'

She nodded. 'Very well. But, Abbess' — she turned back to face Helewise and Josse — 'she was *ruthless*. Berthe and I were about to leave when she arrived at the farm, and she locked us both in the cellar overnight to prevent us going! We were there for the rest of that day and all of the night, and Berthe is afraid of the dark.' She shuddered. 'Then, the next morning, she let us out and told us Jerome was dead. She even showed me — ' Another, more violent shudder shook her, and she left the sentence unfinished. 'As she had no doubt predicted, I went to pieces. Then it was quite easy for her to bundle us both up — Berthe and me — and take us away. I don't think there was as much as a squeak out of either of us, the entire way from Medely to Hawkenlye.'

'And you managed to pick up their trail?' Josse asked Jerome.

'Yes. It was not difficult. And I had — ' He broke off. 'People seemed readily to remember a wild-looking nun and two girls with tears in their eyes,' he said instead. There was a great deal of bitterness in his tone.

Josse felt a stab of sympathy. 'So, once you realised they were here at Hawkenlye to stay, you set about making a camp, then you sought out Meriel?'

'Yes.' He glanced at Meriel, his face full of joy. 'Our reunion was — well, it was a relief to find her.'

'I imagine it was.' Josse swallowed the lump in his throat. 'And you, Meriel, informed Berthe of Jerome's miraculous reappearance, swore her to secrecy, then slipped away to join him?'

'Yes,' she agreed. 'I know it wasn't very fair on Berthe, making her live a lie and pretend she didn't know where I was. If I was safe, even. But, honestly, I don't think she really minded. I wouldn't have done it if I'd thought it would make her suffer.'

'No,' Josse agreed. 'I don't imagine you would. And we can assure you, the Abbess and I, that Berthe has not been suffering. On the contrary.'

'I agree,' the Abbess said.

Josse was just thinking thankfully that her attitude to the young couple seemed to be softening, when suddenly she stood up. Folding her hands away in the opposite sleeves, she had, he observed, adopted her disciplinarian stance.

'Abbess, don't — ' he began.

But she took absolutely no notice.

'I understand, Jerome,' she said severely, 'that there are particular circumstances governing your actions, and I also understand that, probably, you felt you had no choice. But, nevertheless, it remains the case that, for *whatever* reason, you have taken a young girl away from her family and her home, brought her out into the wildwood to make camp with you where, as Sir Josse and I could not help but witness, you have — you are — '

'I have been making love to her,' Jerome supplied. 'Abbess, I cannot deny it.' He glanced at Meriel, who appeared to be suppressing laughter. 'We *have* been making love, as often as we have been able.'

'Jerome,' Josse said warningly. 'Please remember to whom you speak. She is Abbess of Hawkenlye, and you must show her respect.'

'I am sorry, Abbess.' He bowed to her. Josse thought he saw a swift look of surprise cross her face as he did so but before she could speak, he went on, 'I meant no disrespect. You are, of course, quite right. It would be most immoral — and it would in all likelihood also indicate a taking of advantage — for a man to spirit a girl away into the wild-wood, as you so poetically call it, and seduce her.'

The Abbess was looking increasingly disapproving. 'But that is what you have just done!' she said, exasperation sharpening her tone. 'Can you not perceive the sin in your actions?'

Jerome smiled at her. Then he took hold of Meriel's hand, raising it for the Abbess and Josse to see. 'No sin has taken place, Abbess.' His face was ecstatic. Pointing to the brand-new, shiny gold band on her finger, he looked at the tousled young woman beside him and said, 'Meriel is my wife.'

17

Helewise and Josse had stayed longer than they had planned out in the forest; Jerome's revelation had been so startling — and, Helewise reflected, so moving — that it had given rise to a great deal of talk.

By the time she and Josse were back at the Abbey, dusk was well advanced. She was worried about Josse; he had been walking more and more slowly for the past half mile, and she was very afraid that the excursion had exhausted him. Not that he complained. She was very relieved when, back inside the calm, restful atmosphere of the infirmary, she was able to thank him, wish him good night, and hand him over to Sister Euphemia's care.

Even had she been ready to discuss with him the implications of what they had just discovered, she reflected as she crossed over to the Abbey church, he was far too weary.

And I, she thought as she knelt to pray in the empty church, need first to talk to God.

Which, for the spell of peaceful silence that endured until the nuns entered the church for Compline, was exactly what she did.

★　★　★

In the morning, Helewise rose with her day's tasks clearly outlined in her mind. There was much for her to do and, she had always found, setting about a busy day with a welldefined plan of campaign was of great benefit in terms of efficiency.

Between Prime and breakfast she remained in the Abbey church, in private prayer. There were many matters over which she needed God's help, but uppermost of her concerns was what to do about Alba.

What should I do, dear Lord? she asked, eyes fixed on the simple wooden cross on the altar. She begs to stay here, in this community, but for the sake of everyone else here, how can I let her?

But if I send her away, where is she to go? I cannot simply turn her loose, for, if Meriel and that passionate young husband of hers are to be believed, she will seek them out. Even if I cannot make myself accept what Meriel said about Alba doing them actual harm, I do see that her interference could be very unwelcome. New marriages need privacy, while the couple become accustomed to one another. To the state of wedlock itself. It would not aid the progress of either adaptation to have a bossy and quick-tempered elder sister hanging around.

Helewise closed her eyes, trying to empty her mind, trying to listen to whatever guidance might be sent to her.

Trying, if she were honest with herself, to face up to the insistent little voice in her head that said, you *should* believe Meriel.

She pictured Meriel's face, transformed by her happiness from the haggard pallor of misery into radiant loveliness. And Jerome's words, as he interrupted something Meriel was about to say, kept echoing in her ears: *No, Meriel. Not until we know.*

What had the girl been about to say? Whatever it had been, it was to do with Alba, clearly; for just afterwards Meriel had said of her, *she was ruthless.*

Oh, dear Lord, did it mean what Helewise was so dreadfully afraid it meant?

I must not start suspecting that, she told herself firmly. I have no proof and, in Christian charity, I must prevent myself believing the worst purely for the excitement of the sensation, like some superstitious peasant listening to an ancient legend of ghouls and monsters for love of the fear-induced thrill down the spine.

She prayed aloud for some moments, repeating the familiar words until she felt calmer.

By the time she rose from her knees to leave the church and go over to the refectory, she had convinced herself that she was right to ignore Meriel's warning, and that the best thing she could do for Alba was to send out word that the Abbess of Hawkenlye needed a place in some good household — the further away, the better — for a young woman who had lately been living in the Abbey. It was something she had done many times before, usually with success; Hawkenlye had an excellent reputation, and when its Abbess asked for a situation for somebody, her request rarely went unanswered.

Next on Helewise's list of tasks was to visit Josse. To her relief, she found him quite well; he was up and about, helping a man recovering from a fever to take his first steps outside. Having settled his patient on a bench, Josse came over to the Abbess, and they moved out of earshot.

She told him what she had decided to do about Alba.

Frowning, he said, 'Are you quite sure, Abbess?'

'Sure of what?' She felt herself stiffen; her tone, she realised, had not been exactly friendly.

Josse's frown had deepened. 'Sure that you will not be sending something into this distant household you envisage that they will wish you had kept well away,' he said bluntly.

Some*thing*, she noted. Not even some*one*. 'You have decided to judge and condemn Alba all by yourself, have you?' she demanded, anger rising. 'When you do not know her? When, but for one brief visit, you have not even *met* her?'

'I am going by what you have told me!' he cried, angry in his turn. 'And, indeed, by what Meriel said.'

The little flame of doubt flared again in Helewise's mind. Meriel . . . *she was ruthless* . . . Swiftly she doused it. 'Meriel was distraught,' she said firmly. 'And also in a highly charged emotional state. I do not feel we should place too much credence on what she said.'

Josse was nodding knowingly, fuelling Helewise's anger. 'I see,' he said. 'Aye, I see.'

'What?' She had an uncomfortable feeling she knew what was coming.

'Abbess, you still can't get over those two in the woods, can you?'

'I — ' she began.

But he did not let her interrupt. 'They really discomforted you, didn't they, when they emerged from their lovers' bed and stood before you? And even though you know they are man and wife and perfectly entitled, even in the Church's eyes, to share a bed, you haven't forgiven them. Have you?'

His face wore an expression she had never seen before. Confused, she said, 'Of course I have!'

But even to herself she did not sound convincing.

And Josse, with a muttered, 'Abbess Helewise, I never took you for a *prude*,' turned his back and walked away.

⋆ ⋆ ⋆

Shaken, she went through the office of Tierce struggling to keep her mind on her prayers.

Then, with difficulty dragging together the ragged remnants of her fine plan for the day, she announced to her senior nuns that she wished to work alone and was only to be disturbed in dire need. Then she went to her room and firmly closed the door.

Having solved the problem of Alba — I *have*, she insisted to herself — she pushed her recent preoccupations to the back of her mind and surveyed everything else awaiting her attention. Oh, but it was depressing! The new system of delegating tasks to her deputies was working, after a fashion, but both the senior nuns and Helewise herself were finding it difficult to adapt to new ways after so long in the old ones.

But Helewise, she reminded herself, had promised Queen Eleanor that she would do her best to employ the system that Eleanor had outlined. It was early days yet. And the Abbess had been away from Hawkenlye, throwing everything out of kilter . . .

Resignedly she reached for the heavy accounts ledger, now kept by Sister Emanuel, and began going through the neat entries. When she had worked her way through three weeks of Hawkenlye's material comings and goings, there would be the reports of her deputies to consider. Then it would probably be time for Sext, and then the midday meal.

All in all, Helewise reflected, the day was going to be well advanced before she got round to the next item on her list, which was telling Berthe that she knew about Meriel and Jerome.

She had a vague sense that she ought to do that sooner rather than later, but dismissed it as a temptation she should ignore — she would far rather have sought out Berthe than ploughed her way on through the ledger. With a sigh, she bent her head and got on with her work.

★   ★   ★

In the end, it was late afternoon before Helewise finally went to look for Berthe.

She went first down into the Vale but, as it turned out, she could have saved herself the trouble. Berthe, Brother Firmin informed her, had gone to see Sir Josse up in the infirmary.

Oh, Helewise thought. Walking slowly back up to the Abbey, she felt a rush of shame. I shouted at Josse this morning, she reminded herself. For saying something that I didn't like. But which, I have to admit, was perfectly true.

I must apologise. Tell him he was right.

As she approached the infirmary, she caught sight of Josse and Berthe sitting outside. They were laughing.

Wondering if Josse had already told Berthe of the visit to Meriel, Helewise quickened her steps. He should not have done that, she thought crossly, it was up to me to tell her . . .

Josse looked up and greeted her with his usual smile. 'Good afternoon, Abbess,' he said. 'Berthe and I were playing at riddles.'

Sorry! she said silently to him. What was it about her today, she wondered, that she insisted on misjudging her old friend?

'Sir Josse, I have come to steal your young companion away, I am afraid,' she said. She met his eyes. Would he guess what she was going to do? 'I have a fancy for a stroll in the forest,' she went on, keeping her gaze on his as she improvised, 'and I wondered if Berthe would like to come with me?'

He gave a faint nod of understanding. 'A good idea, Abbess. Berthe?' He turned to the girl.

'I would love to walk with you, Abbess Helewise.' Berthe had shot to her feet. 'Now?'

'Now,' said Helewise.

They fell into step, walking out through the Abbey's main gates and off towards the fringes of the forest.

'If we go *that* way,' Berthe said after a moment, pointing along a path that circled the trees and that led in a completely different direction from the charcoal burners' camp, 'we shall stay in the sunshine.'

'Indeed.' Helewise was thinking. Taking Berthe's arm and turning her firmly in the opposite direction, she said, 'But that is not the way I wish to go.'

Holding the girl as she was, she felt the sudden tension. They walked in silence for a while, then Helewise said gently, 'Berthe, as you have doubtless guessed, we are not merely going for a pleasant stroll.'

'Aren't we?' Berthe sounded desolate.

'Child, do not despair!' Helewise gave her hand a squeeze. 'You have borne a heavy burden these many days, and you have borne it long enough.'

'But I can't tell you! I can't!' Berthe was sobbing.

'Berthe, there is no need for you to break a confidence, since I already know what you are trying so hard to keep from me.' Helewise gave the girl a little shake. 'Sir Josse and I came out here to find Meriel yesterday.'

'You can't have done! You didn't know where they — where she was! Nobody did but me!'

Feeling distinctly sheepish, Helewise said, 'I must confess that I asked Augustine to follow you. He told me where you had gone, and whom you met there.'

Berthe's face had darkened. 'Augustine?'

'Yes.'

The girl said, with a catch in her voice, 'I thought he was my friend.'

'He *is*!' Helewise insisted urgently. 'Berthe, he realised that matters could not go on as they stood, purely *because* he is your friend! You are not a natural liar, child, and it was not right for you to be forced to go on bearing another's secret.'

'I didn't mind! Meriel's my sister, I'd do *anything* for her!'

'Even lie to Sir Josse?' Helewise asked shrewdly. 'How did that feel, Berthe, to pretend to someone as fond of you as he is that you had no idea where Meriel was, pretend that you were worried sick about her?'

Berthe's resistance collapsed. 'I couldn't lie to him,' she said softly.

Helewise threw her arms round the slumped shoulders. 'I'm very sorry, Berthe. This — setting Augustine to follow you and reveal your secret to me — was entirely my plan.'

Berthe disengaged herself and stared up into Helewise's face. 'But then you're tougher than him,' she said quietly.

'I — ' Helewise found she couldn't go on. What, indeed, was there to say?

'Come on, then,' Berthe said, leading the way off along the track. Stopping again and turning round, she added, 'That is, if you really want to pay them a visit, and this wasn't just a way of getting me on my own for a private talk?'

Such cynicism! Helewise thought. And the child still so young. 'Indeed I do wish to visit Meriel and Jerome,' she assured Berthe. 'And in your company, too. Much has been going on that has been damaging to you both, and I wish to set matters right.'

Berthe did not reply. But the look she gave Helewise over her shoulder rather suggested she doubted whether setting these particular matters right was within any one person's power.

Even if that person was the Abbess of Hawkenlye.

*　*　*

Berthe was still in the lead when they came to the clearing.

'Meriel!' she called out. 'Jerome! It's me, Berthe, and I've got the Abbess with me!'

There was no answer.

Berthe turned round to Helewise. 'They're probably off checking the snares,' she said confidently. 'Jerome's getting very good at snaring; he got a hare the other day and Meriel cooked it beautifully! Meriel!' she called again, more loudly. 'Where are you?'

But Helewise had walked over to the little hearth. No fire burned; none was laid ready. She put her hand to one of the pieces of turf that had been neatly cut and placed where the fire had been, gently moving it aside to feel beneath.

Cold.

Hearing Berthe's calls echo from the edge of the trees, she straightened up and went across to the shelter which Meriel and Jerome had been using.

It was empty.

Other than the edges of the scar left by the recent fire, the glade and the charcoal burners' camp looked deserted. Looked, moreover, as if nobody had been there for weeks. Months.

Helewise called softly, 'Berthe, come here.'

After some time, Berthe obeyed.

Helewise stared at her. 'Child, they've gone. Meriel and Jerome have gone.'

Berthe was shaking her head, her eyes filling with tears. She said, '*No!*'

'Now, Berthe, don't cry!' Helewise tried to hug her but she would not suffer herself to be hugged. 'We'll find them, I promise, and then you'll — '

'We *won't* find them!' Berthe shouted. 'Don't you understand? I only found them here because they told me where they were, and *you* only found them because you followed me! If they don't want to be found, then nobody will find them.'

'They don't know the forest,' Helewise said, trying to sound calm and in control, 'whereas I — ' No. She could not say, whereas I do, even to reassure this poor child. It was a lie. And for some reason Helewise didn't like to fathom, it felt as if it would be a dangerous lie . . .

Berthe was looking at her. 'The forest is

vast,' she said. 'I know it is, Jerome said. Big enough for two people to disappear and *never* be found.' Two fat tears rolled down her cheeks.

Helewise's heart broke for her. 'They won't leave you behind, Berthe.' She wished the girl would relent and let her approach. 'Your sister won't abandon you.'

'She will if she has to,' Berthe said. 'And anyway I told her about the infirmary, how I really like working there and how Sister Euphemia says maybe one day I can be one of her proper nurses.'

'So?' Helewise didn't immediately see the connection.

Berthe gave a faint sigh. 'So she knows I'll be happy. Even if she has to go.' But the tears, momentarily halted, were flowing again. 'Even if I never see her again as long as I live.'

Helewise could no longer resist the urge to comfort. Stepping forward, putting her hands on Berthe's shoulders, she said, 'Berthe, it will not come to that! I am quite sure it won't!'

Berthe shook her off. 'Abbess Helewise, I know you mean well, but you don't understand!' Her voice rising to near hysteria, she cried, 'That's been the trouble, all along! You've tried to help, but you can't. You just don't know what's at stake!'

'Then tell me!' Helewise implored. 'Let me help you, all of you!'

For a moment of stillness, she thought Berthe was going to relent. Waiting, she found she was holding her breath.

But then Berthe said, 'No.' With a resigned look, she straightened her shoulders, and the gesture almost undermined the Abbess. Managing a weak smile, Berthe went on, 'Please don't think I don't long to tell you. But the secret isn't mine to reveal.'

Turning away from the camp, she headed out of the deserted glade and back along the track.

And Helewise found she was left with no option but to follow.

18

By the time Helewise and Berthe were safely back inside the Abbey's gates, the nuns were already making their way to the church for Compline. As Sister Ursel carefully barred the gate behind her, engaging the Abbess in a few brief words of conversation as she did so, Helewise wondered if there was anything she could say which would have the effect of sending Berthe more happily to her bed.

She couldn't think of anything.

And when she turned from Sister Ursel and walked on towards the church, she saw that Berthe had already hurried away. The child was not even going to have the solace of prayer before she went to bed.

Helewise, while not entirely sure what she could have done differently — done better — was nonetheless filled with the feeling that she had failed Berthe. Failed her badly.

Since Meriel and Jerome undoubtedly would not have fled had the Abbess not announced that she was about to set Alba free, she probably had.

★   ★   ★

The nuns dispersed after the Office, most heading for the dormitory and a well-earned night's sleep, but some going off to various parts of the community for night duty. Helewise knew she should go to bed — she was worn out — but her mind was still racing.

It is no use my going to bed, she realised, for I shall not sleep.

She slipped away from the rest of the sisters and, walking in the shadows of the great church, made for the rear gate. Perhaps some time spent looking out over the Vale, absorbing its serenity and its peaceful, natural beauty, would calm her.

She unbolted the gate and went outside. It was almost fully dark now, but there was a half moon in the clear sky, and she could make out the details of the familiar landscape. Strange, she thought, I hardly ever come out here unless some matter has called me to visit the shrine. I wonder why I should have felt drawn to come and stand here this evening?

Perhaps it was because there had been a death down there on the path that led off along the Vale. A death that seemed to have gone out of most people's heads, driven away by other, more pressing problems.

Why do I think of that poor soul *now*?

Helewise wondered.

But there was no answer.

After a while, she went back inside the Abbey walls and fastened the gate.

★   ★   ★

She was back in her room, tidying away her earlier attempts to complete her tasks and leave a perfectly clear table to greet her the next day, when there came a knock on the door.

It was so soft that at first she doubted whether she had really heard anything. Stopping what she was doing, standing perfectly still and holding her breath, she waited.

The tapping came again.

Clearing her throat, which seemed to have gone quite dry and closed up, she said in a low voice, 'Come in.'

The door opened slowly. Against the dark backdrop of the deserted cloister, she could not see who stood there. But it was a tall figure, broad-set . . .

Alarm making her sound shrill, she said, 'Step forward into the candlelight and show yourself!'

Instantly the figure obeyed.

And, once again, the bearded stranger from

the Vale made her that deep, graceful reverence.

'I regret having alarmed you,' he said as he straightened up again. 'I did not mean to. I thought about approaching you just now, when you were outside the gate, but I feared that would scare you even more.'

'I am not scared!' she said crossly, swiftly removing her hand from where she had pressed it against her wildly thumping heart. Then, as a worrying thought occurred to her: 'How did you get in? I barred the gate when I came back inside!'

He gave her a quick grin, momentarily making him look like a boy caught out in a misdemeanour. 'I know. I heard you do it. But there is a place just along from the gate where a convenient tree branch allows a determined person to climb over the wall.'

'Is there, indeed,' she said coolly, making a mental note to tell Brother Saul to make sure all such branches were ruthlessly lopped off. 'And why, may I ask, were you so determined to get in?'

'I had to speak to you,' he replied. There was no mistaking the earnestness that now filled his face. 'I have been watching out all afternoon and evening, waiting for my chance to catch you alone. But you kept disappearing, Abbess. You are, indeed, a hard woman to follow.' He smiled briefly. 'When I saw you step outside the rear gate, I believed that my prayers had been answered, and that *you* had come to find *me*.'

'It's strange,' she said musingly, 'but I *did* sense a weird and quite unprecedented urge to go and look out over the Vale . . . ' Then, hearing what she had just said, mentally she pulled herself together and demanded, 'Who are you? And what do you want with me?'

'My name is Bastian.' There was the briefest hesitation, as though he were usually more forthcoming but, in this instance, had chosen not to be. 'I have heard tell that you propose to release the former nun known as Alba, and I have come to beg you to reconsider.'

How did he know about Alba? Helewise wondered. Had he overheard Berthe and Augustine discussing her? But that was not the most important thing; waiting for a moment until she was sure she could speak calmly, she said, 'I have no choice but to let her go. She is not a nun, as you appear to know already, and I cannot contemplate her joining the Hawkenlye community. As either a nun or a lay worker.' He started to speak, but she did not let him. 'Rest assured, however, that it is not our way to turn people away without first ascertaining that they have somewhere to go. A place will be found for Alba.' Whatever business it may be of yours, she wanted to add.

He closed his eyes briefly, and his lips moved silently. It looked as if he were praying. Then he said, 'Abbess Helewise, I appreciate that this is not how I should be doing this. You do not know who I am, and anything I tell you of my background could, as far as you are concerned, be a pack of lies. All I can do is beg you to put your trust in me.'

His dark eyes seemed to connect with hers, and she found herself staring right *into* him. It was uncanny but, she discovered, not frightening. After a moment, deliberately breaking the contact, she said, 'About what do you ask me to trust you?'

A look of relief crossed his face, prompting her to add, 'Be aware that I have not yet decided if I *will* trust you,' eliciting another of his smiles. The contrast of his dark beard against his revealed teeth, she noticed, made the teeth look extremely white. They were very good teeth, evenly sized, with no gaps . . .

'It is to do with Alba.' His voice interrupted her musings. 'As no doubt you have guessed, I know her. Or rather, I should say, I know *of* her; she and I have never met. She is irrational to the point of mania; she was instrumental in the death of Adela, wife of Wilfrid of Medely; and I believe she was personally responsible for the murder of a young man who burned to death in an abandoned cottage.'

Oh, *no*! Oh, dear God, Helewise prayed, help me! Here is a stranger putting into words the things that I have been dreading might be true. Am I to believe him? Does he bring the proof that I have been so desperately searching for?

The stranger seemed to understand her inner conflict. He said no more, and gave her the courtesy of turning away, appearing to study the bare wall to his right, while her frantic thoughts chased each other round and round inside her head.

Deliberately, she stilled them.

And waited.

Then she looked at Bastian. Just at that moment, he turned to look at her. Their eyes met. I believe him, she realised. I do believe him! Is that God's answer, to make me confident that I can trust this man?

She said, 'We found the body in the cottage. We knew it to be that of a man. I had — without proof I could not be sure, but, ever since then, I have been haunted by the fear that Alba was involved.'

'More than merely involved,' Bastian said. 'She followed him there, to the empty cottage. She crept up behind him, hit him on the back of the head and knocked him unconscious, and tied his wrists to a stake in the floor.'

Helewise knew what was coming next. She did not want to hear. 'No,' she whispered.

But he was relentless. 'I must tell you, Abbess, in order that you recognise Alba for what she is. Having rendered the young man helpless, she fetched the dry fuel she had prepared and set light to it. Then, while the cottage and its human contents burned, she stood and watched.'

'How do you know this?'

'Because somebody saw her do it.'

'Why didn't they intervene?'

'The witness was a child. Who, God be thanked, thought that Alba had done nothing worse than set her supper on fire. The boy could not tell the smell of burning human flesh from roasting beef or lamb. But he did wonder why she had filled the cottage with bales of hay and put a flame to them.'

'A child,' Helewise whispered. Oh dear Lord, what might Alba have been driven to do if she had known a child had seen her perpetrate a murder?

'The child told his mother — who is known

to me — and she told me,' Bastian went on. 'But not until some time later. By then, Alba had disappeared, taking Meriel and Berthe with her. The mother refused to allow the child to lead us to the spot — reasonably enough, I suppose.' He glanced at Helewise, who nodded her understanding. 'Although we searched for the place, we were unsuccessful. The child's account was unclear; I did not realise that he spoke of a location which in fact I knew. We decided our prime concern should be to hunt for Alba and her sisters, and — ' He stopped himself, and a brief frown darkened his face, as if at some ill memory. 'Er — we sent people to track them. And when I discovered that — that is, as soon as I could get away, I followed.'

Only half hearing him, suddenly Helewise had remembered what Jerome had said, when Josse asked if he had managed to pick up the sisters' trail. *Yes. It was not difficult. And I had —*

What had he been going to say? 'And I had help'?

'Jerome followed them!' she exclaimed. 'Jerome and somebody else, somebody more experienced?'

Bastian's frown lifted; for an instant Helewise thought he appeared relieved. 'You are perceptive, Abbess,' he said smoothly. It

280

was only later that she realised he had not actually answered her question. 'And I see that you have met young Jerome. He is well, I hope?'

'He's married,' she said before she could stop herself. 'He and Meriel are man and wife.'

'I know.' Bastian gave her a calm smile. 'They were wed before they left Medely.'

'*What?*' But it was not the moment to ask that; recalling what they had been discussing, she said, 'Jerome must have found the burned body in the cottage, and realised that Alba had to get away from the farm before anyone else came across it, in case she was suspected of being involved.' She paused. 'I do not believe Jerome knows the truth,' she said slowly. 'He and Meriel may have their suspicions, but I believe they have no proof.'

'I believe you are right,' Bastian put in quietly.

But she barely heard. 'He — Jerome — would surely have hurried to the farm. But before he had time to prevent her, Alba had swept up her sisters and fled — Jerome would have found nothing but an empty house. Since Alba must have known that Meriel wouldn't go with her otherwise, she told her that Jerome had died in the cottage.' *She even showed me.* 'Oh, God,' she murmured. 'Alba made Meriel *look*. And how convincing she must have been in persuading the girl that the poor, dead youth was Jerome!'

Bastian was looking at her sorrowfully. 'Alba was convincing because she believed he *was* Jerome. It was her intention to murder Jerome, and she thought she had done so.'

'But *why?*'

Bastian gave a deep sigh. 'It is all to do with the person that Alba is,' he said, 'or, perhaps, the person that her life has made her.' His eyes on Helewise's, he asked, 'Will you hear the tale?'

And, late though it was, surreal though it seemed to be sitting here with a stranger in the silent, candlelit dimness of her room, she nodded.

★ ★ ★

'Alba,' he began, 'is considerably older than her sisters, as you will have observed. This meant that, when Meriel and Berthe were born, Alba developed a rivalry with their mother, Adela, over who had the greater responsibility for them and, indeed, for their father. Alba had been used to caring solely for Wilfrid, and he allowed a far greater intimacy to develop between the two of them than he ought to have done. But he was a weak man.

282

An autocrat within his own four walls, but without the moral strength to recognise a developing wrong and correct it.'

'You speak of the two of them, Alba and Wilfrid,' Helewise put in. 'What of Adela?'

'Adela was not Alba's mother. In his young manhood, Wilfrid took a village whore to his bed and impregnated her. She died giving birth to the child, and my predecessors — that is, those who had overseen events made sure that the baby was placed where she belonged, with her father. Wilfrid was faced with the baby, Alba, and he had no choice but to accept his responsibilities. Village gossip being what it is, Alba grew up in no doubt about the identity of her mother, who was, indeed, a loose-living, indolent soul with few, if any, saving graces.'

'Only God can know that,' Helewise put in gently. 'We receive many prostitutes here, Bastian, and their profession does not necessarily remove them from God's love and favour.'

'I know, Abbess. I accept your reprimand.' He bowed his head briefly. It was hardly a reprimand, she thought. He went on, 'And in any case, I am only repeating what others said, which I should not do.'

She had, she realised, interrupted the flow of his story. 'Please, continue,' she said.

'Thank you. Alba, the child of a whore, began early in her life her attempt not only to better herself, but also to raise up the family into which, on her father's side, she had been born. He was, as I have said, a weak man, and it was easier for him to go along with Alba's high-flying aspirations than to argue her out of them. Indeed, he probably enjoyed her flattery and her insistence that only the best would do for *them*. There was an adequate living on the farm and Alba, for all her faults, was a good manager. She was apparently horrified when Wilfrid announced he was going to marry Adela, who, decent and loving woman that she was, came from very humble stock.'

'Then, when Meriel and Berthe were born, Alba would have sensed that she was being thrust into the background, and doubled her efforts to make herself and her family shine,' Helewise said thoughtfully. 'Because she saw them as *hers*, any achievement of theirs reflected back on to her.'

'Precisely. With Wilfrid's support, Alba became bossy, then dogmatic, and finally domineering to the point of tyranny. She instigated a system of punishments, and even Adela sometimes suffered, although never as much as the girls. Wilfrid, one gathers, was vastly amused at the sight of his middle child being penned up outside with the hounds because she had forgotten to feed them, and by the howls of little Berthe shut in the cellar for answering Alba back.'

'Meriel said Berthe is afraid of the dark,' Helewise said pityingly.

'Is it any wonder, when Alba worked on that childish fear to increase Berthe's suffering? It was a dreadful life, Abbess, and, although Wilfrid was perhaps even more to blame, he is dead and gone. Alba, on the other hand, is very much alive.'

But Helewise was following another thought. 'Meriel, too, said that Alba was instrumental in Adela's death,' she said. 'Is that truly so?'

'It is.' Bastian's face was grave. 'The girls used to use the old tumbledown cottage as a sort of play house, and, I suspect, as a refuge. Alba rarely went there — whenever the girls and their mother were out of the farmhouse, she used to bask in being in sole charge. One day, Adela took the girls to the old cottage for the day, and they were having such fun that Adela forgot the time. She rushed home to start on Wilfrid's dinner — he used to be violent if his meals were late — and all would have been well except that Alba told him. She said something like, what a shame we have to have this stew again! Had Adela not been so late home, she would have had time to prepare something fresh! Wilfrid ordered his wife to cook something else, but she had nothing to cook. She was going to slip out, run all the way down to the village and try to beg something from kindly people there, but Alba said slyly that it surely wasn't fit for a wife of Wilfrid's to be seen *begging*. Wilfrid agreed and told Adela instead to go and dig up some vegetables from their own plot. He wouldn't let her back inside until he was satisfied she'd got enough to feed them all. It was raining, and dark, and cold, and Adela took a chill. Weakened by it, she succumbed to the ague.'

'They were *monstrous*, Alba and her father!' Helewise cried. 'Especially Alba!'

'Monstrous?' Bastian seemed to reflect. 'Yes, perhaps. But we have to look at it from Alba's viewpoint, Abbess. Unwanted at birth, thrust on to a father who didn't want her either, then, as soon as she began to make some progress in her life, the father ousts her by taking a wife and begetting two enchanting little girls. Whose mother, incidentally, adored them both and worshipped the very ground they walked on. Whereas Alba's mother was a reviled, hapless woman who had died at her birth.'

'I do see what you mean,' Helewise acknowledged. 'But her distressing background cannot be allowed to condone her behaviour.'

'I did not intend to suggest that it should,' he said. 'But what happened to her when she was young can perhaps explain why she grew up as she did.'

'She murdered a young man.' Helewise felt the horror begin again. 'Whom she believed to be Jerome. Did she know they were married, he and Meriel?'

'No. Nobody knew except Berthe. She knew about Jerome from the start, and was sworn to secrecy. But the poor child inadvertently let the secret out to Alba that Meriel and Jerome were in love. They all knew Alba would make a fuss, both because she couldn't bear to lose control over any of her family, and also because, although she had never met Jerome, she had heard that he was an orphan, brought up by distant kin and very much a poor relation.'

'What did they do?'

'Jerome had a constant companion; another orphan brought up in the same place. He was a splendid youth, by the name of Felix, and he suggested that, to put Alba off the scent, they pretend that *he* was Jerome and Jerome was Felix. The idea was that Felix would be pointed out to Alba as if he were Jerome, and he would lead her off on a wild goose chase and give Jerome and Meriel a chance to slip away and be married.'

'But didn't they realise the risk they were taking?'

Sadly Bastian shook his head. 'I do not think that anybody believed Alba capable of actual murder,' he said. 'She has deteriorated far further into her own private world than any of us suspected.'

'So, believing this poor Felix to be Jerome, she followed him to the cottage, and — '

'The cottage was Meriel and Jerome's trysting place,' Bastian said.

'Yes. I see. So she followed Felix there, and presumably believed he was waiting for Meriel. Then — '

'Alba knew Meriel wouldn't disturb them.' Once more, he interrupted. 'She'd seen Meriel and Berthe set out. Although Alba didn't know it, they were on their way to meet Jerome, for Meriel to marry him.'

Helewise was picturing the deserted cottage. In her mind's eye, a young man sat there, alone. Perhaps he was smiling, both at the sheer fun of fooling Alba and because, through his suggestion, he was giving his great friend this precious time to be united with his Meriel.

Then through the underbrush came Alba, some heavy weapon in her hands . . . she swung it up high, then brought it crashing down on Felix's unsuspecting head. And, while he was out cold, she manoeuvred the body until she could tether the hands to that hard, firm stake.

And then . . .

No. It was too dreadful to contemplate.

Pushing her fists against her eyes to blot out the images of flame and smoke, Helewise gave a low moan.

From across the room, Bastian spoke.

'I regret that I have had to burden you with this terrible tale.' There was deep compassion in his voice. 'But it was, as I am sure you appreciate, necessary.' He paused. 'Necessary,' he went on quietly, 'in order that you understand what a danger Alba is. To her sisters, and even more to those who threaten her by taking her sisters from her.'

She thought he had finished. She lifted up her head and looked at him. Meeting her eyes, he gave a brief, almost apologetic glance. 'Felix was very special to me,' he said quietly. 'As is Jerome. Felix was born to my late sister, and Jerome is the son of my younger brother, who died when Jerome was a child.' For a split second, she saw a flash of fury in his face, but he controlled it.

Then he said neutrally, 'Alba has murdered one of my nephews. I do not intend to let her have the other.'

Part Three

A Predestined Death

19

The Abbess arrived to see Josse very early the next morning. He was up and dressed, and perched on a bench pulled up at the foot of his bed. Moving along to make room, he beckoned for her to sit down beside him.

He could see immediately that she was deeply troubled; instinctively he put out his hand to her, and she grasped it, giving it a brief and intense squeeze before letting go.

She said, 'Josse, I don't know what to do. Meriel and Jerome have vanished — they have abandoned their camp and disappeared without trace. And there is a pilgrim in the Vale who says he has proof that Alba murdered the man we found in the burnt-out cottage. There was a witness. A child.'

Oh, Lord, he thought. Faced with the two calamities, his first thought was to attempt to quieten her very obvious anxiety over Meriel. 'Do not worry too much for the girl,' he said. 'For Meriel, I mean. Abbess, I was very impressed with young Jerome. Truly, I do not believe he would do anything to risk her safety. She is quite clearly far too precious to him for him to do that.'

'Do you think so?' Her face was a picture. She looked, Josse thought, as if the very thing she most wanted was to believe him, but she wasn't quite sure she could let herself.

'I do,' he said firmly. 'He had made a comfortable, well-concealed camp for her, hadn't he? And when you and I burst in on them, he was all set to defend her with his sword, mother-naked though he was.'

He was relieved to see a swift smile cross her face. 'Not *quite* naked,' she murmured.

'No,' he agreed.

'But by now they may be deep in the Great Forest!' she said with renewed alarm. 'And you and I, Sir Josse, know full well what they may find there! Or, rather, what may find *them*. Oh, and it's all my fault, because if I hadn't told them I was about to free Alba, they would still be safe and snug in the charcoal burners' camp!'

Worried at seeing her usual calm desert her, he said swiftly, 'Helewise, whatever happens is *not* your fault! We are all responsible for our own actions. You, as Abbess of Hawkenlye, have every right to decide to send Alba away, whatever the consequences!'

'But — '

He overrode her. 'And as to the perils of the forest, I cannot say that I believe Jerome

294

and Meriel to be in danger.' He hesitated, aware that he was venturing on to delicate ground. 'Would you not say,' he went on softly, 'that such a pair would be more likely to meet with the Forest Folk's approval than their enmity, given what you and I know of them and their ways?'

'I — ' she began. And stopped. Slowly she nodded.

With relief, he hurried on to the second part of her news. 'Now, to your mysterious pilgrim and his accusations. Do you believe him?'

For a moment, she seemed still to be thinking of Meriel and Jerome. Then, bringing herself back with an obvious effort, her eyes met Josse's.

'I do believe him, yes,' she said. 'He says Alba murdered the young man because she had been duped into believing him to be Jerome.'

'And she could not bear to have one of her sisters seduced away from her,' he concluded. 'Presumably this pilgrim wishes to take Alba away to face the consequences of her action, back in East Anglia, where the crime happened?'

'I suppose he must do,' the Abbess whispered. 'All that he has said so far is that I must not on any account release Alba, since if

I do, she will find Meriel and Jerome and she will kill Jerome.'

'As she well might, in the light of her previous behaviour,' Josse said. A thought struck him. 'Did you tell him that Jerome and Meriel had been living in hiding nearby? That they have now fled?'

'For shame, Sir Josse!' She managed a weak smile. 'Mistrusting him as I did — as I still do — of course not!'

'I apologise, Abbess.'

'There is no need.'

'Is he a sheriff, this pilgrim of yours?' he asked.

'I don't think so.' She frowned. 'I was so taken up in his tale that I confess I didn't think to ask him.' She paused. 'He was — that is, he gave the air of being a man of quality. For all that he dresses as a pilgrim, he is not a poor man, nor an unimportant man. Of that I am quite certain.' She met Josse's eyes with a brief apologetic grimace. 'I regret that I cannot substantiate my remark, Sir Josse. It is purely an impression.'

'Your impressions, Abbess, are good enough for me,' he said gallantly.

She smiled faintly, but it was clear her thoughts were elsewhere than on his little compliment. 'He said something about his predecessors having made Alba's father take responsibility for her when her mother died,' she said. 'She — Alba — was the child of a village prostitute; the younger girls' mother was in fact her stepmother.'

'I see.' That explained quite a lot, Josse thought.

'And he also referred to both Jerome and the friend who died being orphans, looked after by distant kin. They were cousins, and they were both Bastian's nephews; one the son of his late sister, one of his dead brother.'

'Bastian is the name of your stranger?'

'Yes. Didn't I say?'

'No.' He was thinking hard. 'Abbess, what about this? Your Bastian, although he's dressed as a poor pilgrim, is in fact in disguise. He is really a knight, with his own household. If he's sufficiently rich and influential, he may well be responsible for law and order and the administration of justice in his area, as his forefathers were before him. That would explain why he said that it was his predecessors who arranged for the baby Alba's placement with her father. It would also suggest that both his nephews might well have lived with him. That this place where they went to be cared for by distant kin was actually their uncle Bastian's house. Does that tally with what he told you?'

She hesitated, clearly deep in thought.

Then she said slowly, 'I *think* it does. But . . . '

'What is it?'

'Oh, probably nothing. It's just that I can't see Bastian as a rich and influential knight. He's too . . . too . . . ' Giving a helpless shrug, she trailed off.

This, Josse thought, was getting them nowhere. 'Can you describe him?' he suggested. 'I think you're going to have to try to put these impressions of yours into words. It might help you isolate exactly what it is about him that says he is not a knight.'

She gave him a grateful smile. 'What a good idea.' She closed her eyes as if picturing the stranger. Opening them again, she said, 'Quite tall, slim, strong-looking. Dressed simply in a rough brown robe, worn over something quite bulky underneath. Bareheaded, with short cropped hair. Dark eyes, tanned face, bearded, and he has this way of bowing that reminds me of — '

But Josse had stopped listening. '*Bearded?*'

'Yes. Like the pilgrim who was murdered in the Vale.'

'*He* had a beard too? Why didn't you tell me?' Aye, he was thinking, aye! It all begins to fall into place!

' . . . cannot think why it was important,' the Abbess was saying.

'Eh? What did you say?'

'I *said* that I expect I didn't mention the dead man's beard because I can hardly think it was relevant,' she repeated rather frostily. 'Really, Sir Josse, I can't think why you're being so — '

'Abbess,' he interrupted her, 'in an age where the fashion for men is to wear their hair long and their faces clean-shaven, who, can you think, habitually go against the general tide? Who are well known for their cropped hair and their uncut beards?'

At first she shook her head in denial. 'I don't know who you mean!' But then, as realisation dawned, she whispered, 'The warrior monks!'

'Aye,' he agreed. 'The Knights Templar. Your Bastian, Abbess, is a Templar, I'd bet a tidy sum on it. As was the fellow who was killed.' Another thought struck him. If the dead pilgrim was indeed a Templar, then in all likelihood Bastian was not solely there to look after his nephew Jerome and make sure Alba did not attack him.

Bastian was also there because one of his brother monks was killed in the Vale.

'There are Templars at Denney!' the Abbess cried suddenly. 'The monk whom I saw at Ely told me about them and, when Saul and Augustine and I were threatened by an approaching storm, we took shelter with them! We thought they were the Benedictine nuns,' she said, with the air of one giving an explanation; her remark left Josse quite foxed. 'Oh, let me think! What can I recall of them?' She was wringing her hands together as she tried to remember.

She does not serve herself well by this near panic, Josse thought. Reaching out a steadying hand, he said, 'Abbess, take it slowly. Someone at Ely directed you to this house, did they? Denney, was it?'

She stared at him for a moment. Then, as if realising what he was doing, she smiled faintly, visibly relaxing. 'Yes, that's right. The monk at Ely said there was a home for the insane at Denney, run by Benedictine nuns, and also a Templar preceptory. Running from the coming storm, Saul, Augustine and I ended up at the wrong place. The Templars put us up for the night, in some comfort, I should say.' She was frowning, clearly thinking hard.

He waited.

After some time, she said, 'We only saw two of the brethren. The young monk who saw to our needs said something about the members of the community being preoccupied with some serious trouble, and that was why more of the monks did not socialise with us. Then when we were leaving — ' She broke off. The sudden light in her eyes made him suspect she had thought of something important.

'Abbess?' he prompted gently.

'I asked the young monk if he knew of Sedgebeck — that was Alba's convent, if you recall?' He nodded. 'We were headed there next. He — the young brother — said he thought he knew the name, and he'd just remembered *why* he knew it when another, older monk came into the room and shooed him away.' A wondering expression flooded her face. '*As if, whatever it was he knew about Sedgebeck, the older man didn't want him to reveal it!*'

Catching her excitement, Josse said, 'Can they have known about Alba?'

'If my young monk did, then he kept it from me,' she replied. 'I told him of our mission. I am almost sure that I even mentioned Alba by name.'

'Perhaps your monk didn't know the whole story,' Josse suggested. 'It's possible, surely, that he had overheard the name Sedgebeck mentioned, but had not been told the details.'

'Indeed it is,' she agreed. 'He was, as I have said, young. No doubt serious problems, such as the business of Alba and her family, are not made common knowledge in a Templar community.'

'If the Denney Templars *are* somehow involved,' Josse said slowly, thinking it out as he spoke, 'then it increases the likelihood of your Bastian being one of the brethren. Don't you think?'

'Indeed I do.' She raised troubled eyes to meet Josse's. 'Oh, it all seems to fit!' she exclaimed. 'Bastian must have meant that the two boys — his orphaned nephews — were at Denney, brought up and cared for by him and the other Templars.'

'I was not aware that the Templars took in orphans,' Josse remarked. Too domestic for them, he thought to himself; protecting the unarmed along the great pilgrim routes and weighing in against the infidel was one thing, acting as nursemaid to orphaned children quite another.

'But if they were his own kin, and they had nowhere else to go,' the Abbess said, 'in Christian charity, Bastian owed them his protection.'

'And I suppose they could have been looked upon as two new recruits for the brotherhood,' Josse added. 'So, Abbess, does that alter the picture? If we are right, how do you feel about releasing Alba into the care of a Knight Templar whose nephew she murdered?'

'I don't know.' She met his eyes. 'Yes, I do.

Although I should not speak ill of the fellow avowed, I must admit that I fear for Alba, if she is to be judged and sentenced by the Templars.'

'I, too,' he agreed. 'And, Abbess, consider this. If the man who was slain in the Vale was indeed of Bastian's community, then it is almost certain that he, too, was here because of Alba and her sisters. And I think we must not rule out the possibility that Alba recognised him — or he recognised her — and, knowing why he was here, she attacked him.'

'She was terrified when Berthe was sent to work down in the Vale,' the Abbess said.

'If she feared somebody would come looking for her because they knew she'd murdered the youth in the cottage, then her fear is understandable,' he replied. 'She'd know that everyone from her old home knew all three sisters. Someone searching for Alba would only have to spot Berthe or Meriel to know that Alba was nearby.'

Abruptly she stood up. 'Sir Josse, I have agreed to receive Bastian again after Sext. I should be most grateful if you would agree to be a party to our discussion.'

He gave her a smile. 'Gladly.'

★ ★ ★

303

He stood back against the wall of the Abbess's room, behind her as she sat at her table. Bastian, who had just arrived, was invited to sit on the visitors' stool.

It was a relief, Josse thought, to have this confrontation at last. Although it was not long past noon, the day had already seemed endless. Although Josse knew quite well that *he* was not guilty of spreading rumours, and he was equally certain that the Abbess would not have done, somehow word seemed to have leaked as to who Bastian was and what he was there for. An uneasy mood had permeated the Abbey; it was time to stop the speculation and take action.

Josse studied Bastian. He noted the formal bow which he gave to the Abbess — I'll wager that's what told her he was no knight, he thought — and he took in the strength in the slim, wiry frame. There was power in the man, he concluded. Both physical and spiritual power, and a great deal of it.

'I have considered your request that I do not release Alba from her imprisonment,' the Abbess said after having returned Bastian's greeting, 'and I would like to ask you a question.'

'Please,' Bastian said.

Without even glancing at Josse — to whom Bastian had been introduced, and whose presence he had acknowledged with a brief, wry smile — she said, 'You tell me that you have a witness who will presumably attest to the fact that Alba murdered your nephew, Felix.'

'As I told you, Abbess Helewise, the witness is but a child,' Bastian said gently. 'But yes, he will attest before us.'

Us, Josse thought.

The Abbess had picked that up too. 'Bastian, who exactly is *us*?' she asked.

'The people with whom I lodge,' he said smoothly. 'My — er, my household.'

'The Knights Templar of Denney,' she said, equally smoothly.

For a moment, Josse thought he would deny it. But, with a brief apologetic bow, he said, 'I see that my disguise of a simple pilgrim has been penetrated. Yes, Abbess. I am Bastian de Waelsham, Knight Templar, from the house of Denney.'

'And you know quite well, for all that you have not mentioned it to me,' the Abbess said, 'that one of your brethren, also in the guise of a pilgrim, died in our Vale recently.'

'I do,' he admitted. 'I regret, Abbess, that I made no mention of it last night. But, as I am sure you will appreciate, to reveal that I knew of the death would have made you suspicious, since I did not arrive at the shrine until well after the event, and your monks, you will be glad to hear, do not gossip with new arrivals about matters pertaining to those who preceded them.' He sighed. 'However, as it transpires, I might as well have told you, since you have discovered who I am without assistance.' He shot a glance at Josse. 'Without *my* assistance, anyway.'

The Abbess said coolly, 'Sir Josse and I are used to working together. He has often been my confidant, and his advice has been instrumental in the resolution of many grave problems.'

'I see,' Bastian said. 'Well, Abbess? Now that you know the whole story, what have you decided to do about Alba? Not that it is in truth your decision,' he added softly, 'since, as you said, she is no longer a member of your community. She is no longer even a nun.'

'I am aware of that, thank you, Brother Bastian,' the Abbess said. Josse noted how, once his identity had been confirmed, she addressed Bastian by his proper title. 'What concerns me is this, if I may speak plainly. Alba is guilty of the murder of your nephew, Felix, you tell us, and, although you have not said so, I guess that you believe she may also have attacked your brother monk in the Vale.' Bastian began to speak, but she held up her hand for silence. 'I fear that the emotions of you and your brethren will run high, and this is understandable since one of your own has died, but — '

'*Two* of our own,' Bastian put in. He gave her a sly look. 'Felix was about to enter the Order.'

'Very well, two of your own.' She was staring straight at Bastian, Josse noted. Brave woman, he thought; he had an idea of what she was about to say. 'And I very much fear, Brother Bastian, that, under the circumstances, Alba may not receive a fair trial. My inclination, therefore, is to keep her here until she may be tried in this area, where we may — '

Bastian's face was pale with anger. 'Not receive a fair trial?' he repeated. 'Abbess Helewise, remember to whom you speak! I am a Templar, and we do not pervert the course of justice!'

'Brother Bastian, I have learned much of Alba and her sisters over recent days and weeks,' the Abbess said. 'I accept that she may be responsible for these acts of extreme violence, but, in the name of God's holy mercy, should we not bear in mind that the woman has had a dreadful background, which may well have affected her adversely? You told me yourself that her mother died in giving birth to her, and you spoke of the character of Wilfrid, and — '

But Bastian could contain himself no longer. 'These matters *will* be addressed, Abbess!' he cried, 'and you insult both me and my Order by implying that they will not! And, besides, what choice do you really have? You cannot release Alba to freedom, now that you know what she has done, and it may be months before she can be tried here in Kent. Put her in my care, and I will take her straight back to Denney, where her fate will be decided immediately!'

'Brother Bastian, it serves no purpose merely to repeat your arguments,' the Abbess answered, with what Josse thought was admirable calm. 'I believe that the best thing — '

But neither Josse nor Bastian were to hear what she thought the best thing was. For at that moment there came the sound of running footsteps from the cloister outside. After a token thump on the door, it was flung open and Sister Martha stood there, red faced and panting.

'Abbess, oh, Abbess, I'm sorry to interrupt but you have to know, right away! I just went down to take Alba some fresh food and water, and the door was wide open — she's gone!'

20

Brother Bastian, his face working, demanded instantly, 'Who let her out? Do they not *know* the danger?'

'Danger?' Sister Martha echoed, staring blankly at Bastian and clearly wondering why a pilgrim visitor to Hawkenlye was being so pushy and rude. Why, indeed, he was standing in the Abbess's room.

The Abbess, already getting to her feet, said, 'Sister Martha? Have you any idea how this has happened?'

'No, Abbess, indeed I have not!' Sister Martha said hotly, as if she felt Bastian were accusing her of being personally responsible. 'Only the three of us have been taking turns seeing to poor Alba, and we're all very careful, I can assure you! Why, we usually make sure we've got — '

'That will do, Sister Martha,' the Abbess interrupted gently. 'You found the door open when you went down into the undercroft, you said?'

'Yes, wide open, and no sign of the woman!'

'Then somebody must have let Alba out

before you got there, and it can hardly be called your fault,' the Abbess concluded. With a swift glance at Brother Bastian, fuming beside her and giving the impression that he wanted to wrest authority from her hands and take over, she went on calmly, 'The important thing now is to find her. Sister Martha, summon three lay brothers and six nuns and divide them into three search parties. Sir Josse here, Brother Bastian and I will form a fourth. We shall meet in the courtyard as soon as we are all ready, and I will tell each party where to go. Hurry up!'

With a last glance at Bastian — *Brother Bastian?* she seemed to be wondering — Sister Martha sped away.

★ ★ ★

While the search parties were gathering, Brother Bastian excused himself and hurried off towards the Vale. When, a short while later, he returned, he had removed his coarse brown robe; now he wore openly the white surcoat of the warrior monks, emblazoned on the breast with a red cross. At his side hung a sword.

'Brother Bastian, for pity!' Helewise exclaimed as she saw the latter. 'We hunt for one miserable woman, not a band of murderous brigands!'

'I pray my sword will remain sheathed, Abbess,' he replied grimly. 'But I intend to take no foolish risks.'

Angrily she turned away from him, and her eyes met Josse's. Be calm, he seemed to say.

As always, his very presence was a comfort. We shall be with Bastian to watch what he does, she thought, cheered, and he will not make any over-reckless move against Alba before two witnesses.

Will he?

When the nuns and the lay brothers were ready in their groups, she issued her instructions, giving each group an area to cover and ordering them to locate and inform the other groups if they found Alba.

Then she led Josse and Brother Bastian out of the Abbey's main gates and off towards the forest. Josse, coming to walk closely beside her, said quietly, 'Do you think she has run this way?'

'I do,' she muttered back. 'If I am any judge of her state of mind, she is very nearly frantic.'

'Aye,' he agreed. 'I am still haunted by the sound of her flinging herself against the door of her prison.'

'As I am. Do you not think, then, Sir Josse, that the Great Forest would appeal to a fugitive? Plenty of concealment, and — '

'I believe, Abbess,' he interrupted, 'that it would all depend on why our particular fugitive has run away. If it is because she has heard whispers of Brother Bastian's intentions, then she has fled in order to hide from him. But we must not forget what has been, until now, her prime concern.'

'Her family!'

'Aye. It may be — indeed, I think it *must* be — that she has gone to search for Meriel and Jerome.'

Oh, dear God! Helewise felt a growing dread. Suppose the young couple have returned to the charcoal burners' camp?

'That area of the forest — where they made camp — must be searched,' she said, relieved to hear that her panicky fear was not evident in her voice. 'We shall go there straight away, Sir Josse. If, by a miracle, we find Jerome and Meriel, we can tell them what is happening.'

We can protect them, she added silently.

'But what about *him*?' Josse indicated Brother Bastian, striding along behind.

She hesitated. Was she doing the right thing? She still wasn't entirely sure. 'He will have to be told that they were here sooner or later,' she replied eventually. 'And what if Alba is heading straight for them? If, by some chance, they have come back, and she has discovered where they are, then — '

312

Brother Bastian had caught them up. 'I know where we are going,' he announced. 'You are heading for the camp where Jerome and Meriel are living.'

Helewise shot Josse a quick glance, and, almost imperceptibly, he nodded. No. It was not the moment to inform Bastian that Meriel and Jerome had gone.

She turned to Bastian, adopting her most formidable manner. 'You knew of their presence?' she demanded. 'Why did you not tell us?'

'Why should I?' He sounded as if he were suppressing rage. 'I followed along behind that young lay brother of yours, when you sent him to trail Berthe, but neither of them was aware of me. And, before you ask, I did not let Jerome or Meriel see me, either. But let us make haste! If Alba finds them, we do not know *what* will happen!'

Pushing past Josse and Helewise, he rushed on along the path, not waiting to see if they were keeping up. Not pausing, either, to look to his left or his right.

Which was why, when a small and dejected figure stepped out from behind a tangle of undergrowth, it was Helewise who saw her first, and to whom she rushed, weeping, for comfort.

'I meant no harm to Meriel, Abbess, nor to

Jerome!' Berthe sobbed. 'I *love* them, both of them, Meriel's my dearly beloved sister, and Jerome promised he'd be a real brother to me! And anyway they're not there any more — Alba won't find them now. They've gone, they've gone and left me all alone!' A loud wail ripped from her, its sudden shrill noise shattering the still silence of the forest.

Helewise hugged her. 'Hush, child! You're not alone, we will take care of you.'

Berthe did not seem to hear. 'But, oh, Abbess, Alba's my sister, too, and when I heard about that monk wanting to take her back for trial, well, I couldn't just let him have her, could I? I love her, too, really, and they'll hang her, those Templars in Denney, I just *know* they will!'

The sobbing rose towards hysteria, and Helewise held the girl tightly against her, muttering soothingly, 'Yes, Berthe, I understand.' She let her cry for a few moments, then, giving the girl a gentle shake, she said, 'Berthe, stop this now. Does Alba know that Meriel and Jerome were out here in the forest? Did you tell her where they had been living?'

'Of course I didn't!' Even in her pitiful state, Berthe managed to sound indignant. 'She doesn't even know Jerome's still alive — I didn't tell her, I know better than *that*.

But actually, she didn't even ask me if I knew where Meriel was. She just rushed off, in the other direction. Down there.' She pointed.

Helewise, following the direction of the waving hand, felt a wave of relief flood through her. Glancing at Josse, she saw that he was thinking the same. Unless Alba turned sharp right off the track Berthe was indicating, she would go straight past the charcoal burners' camp and not even suspect it was there.

Even if the young lovers had returned, Alba would not find them.

'Come on,' Helewise said firmly, taking hold of Berthe's hand. 'We'll follow her. You, me and Sir Josse. Don't worry, Berthe, I'm sure we'll find her.'

But before they could set off on Alba's trail, there was a rustling in the undergrowth and a figure appeared from the path behind them.

It was Bastian.

He ran towards them, shouting as he ran, 'They've gone!'

Waiting until he had slid to a halt, Helewise said calmly, 'Yes. We know.'

Bastian's mouth opened and shut. 'But you — why — ?'

Berthe, looking from Helewise to Bastian and back again, wailed suddenly, 'I don't

315

understand! Oh, why don't you stop arguing and *look* for them! Both my sisters are lost in the forest, and it's all my fault!'

Once again, she flung herself against Helewise.

Josse, stepping forward, put a gentle hand on the girl's shoulder. 'You must not take blame on yourself, Berthe,' he said. Helewise flashed him a look of gratitude. 'These are matters whose roots go a long way back, and — '

'It *is* my fault, whatever you say,' Berthe cried. 'If I hadn't let Alba out, Meriel wouldn't have had to run away!'

Oh, but the child's logic has deserted her! Helewise thought. 'Berthe, that is not right,' she said firmly. 'Meriel and Jerome ran away *before* you opened the door to Alba's cell.'

'But — ' Berthe began.

Bastian cleared his throat. Glancing at him, Helewise noticed on his face an expression she had not seen before. It was . . . it looked as if it were pity.

He, too, came to stand beside Helewise and Josse. In a rather clumsy gesture, briefly he put his hand on Berthe's head. It was almost as if he were bestowing a blessing.

'Berthe?' he said.

She raised her face and looked up at him. 'Yes?'

'The blame is mine. I thought I could return alone to the camp, and speak to Jerome. As God is my witness, I meant no harm — in fact, quite the opposite. But I am not as stealthy a tracker as you, or young Augustine — Jerome heard me coming. He and Meriel disappeared into the trees and, try as I might, I could not find them. I called out till I was hoarse, but they would not come out of their hiding place.'

Berthe was the only one to be comforted by Bastian's announcement; Helewise, totally perplexed, saw from Josse's face that he was equally puzzled.

'What business did *you* have with Jerome?' Josse asked.

'And,' Helewise added, 'what was so alarming about it that Jerome was driven to run away from you and hide?'

Bastian gave a sigh. 'Should we not put this aside for now and proceed with our search?' he asked hopefully.

Together Helewise and Josse said decisively, 'No.'

He sighed again. 'Very well. Abbess, when I said that my nephew Felix had been on the point of joining our Order, I was sparing with the truth; it was but a lie of omission, but a lie nevertheless. Jerome, too, was destined to join us.'

'*Jerome* was?' Berthe said incredulously. 'But he's in love with Meriel! He's *married* to her; I saw them wed, I was there!'

'Yes, I know.' Bastian smiled kindly at her. 'However, there was a time before he knew her when he believed he had a call from God. When he met and fell in love with Meriel — and I gather that the two events were very nearly simultaneous — he believed he was doing a great wrong, both to God and to our Order. He thought that he had no option but to run away, which is exactly what he did. He married Meriel, and the young couple were planning to leave, with Berthe, when Alba — that is, when Alba acted.'

'She told Meriel that Jerome was dead,' Berthe whispered. 'It broke Meriel's heart. And then — '

Very gently, Helewise put a hand to Berthe's face and pressed it to her chest. 'No, Berthe,' she said firmly. 'There is no need for any more. We all know.'

She met Bastian's eyes, trying to urge him to hurry on with his tale. Understanding, immediately he did so.

'Jerome set off to follow Alba and the girls, and I set someone to follow him,' he said. 'I was relieved, Abbess, when you jumped to the conclusion that Jerome had been *helped* by another, more experienced monk; in fact,

318

Jerome needed nobody's help. Indeed, he threw Brother Bartholomew off the trail quite early on. It was only an inspired guess that brought Bartholomew on to Hawkenlye.' His expression fell into sadness.

'Brother Bartholomew is the man who died in the Vale?' Josse said.

Bastian nodded. 'Yes, that was him. A fine man, loyal, willing. And a good monk.'

'We have prayed for him, Brother Bastian,' Helewise said.

Bastian nodded.

After a brief and rather awkward pause, Josse said, 'Brother Bastian, how did *you* find your way to Hawkenlye?'

Bastian gave a brief smile. 'I followed the Abbess.'

Before she could stop herself, Helewise burst out, 'I *knew* we were being followed! Did I not say so, Sir Josse?'

'Aye, Abbess.' He, too, seemed to be suppressing a smile.

'I knew, naturally, that you were going from Denney to Sedgebeck,' Bastian said. 'In fact, Brother Timothy told me a great deal about you and your mission. He also, incidentally, almost gave away to you why the name Sedgebeck was familiar to him; I managed to send Brother Matthew to distract him just in time. It would not have done for you to find out that the Templars at Denney knew all about Alba of Sedgebeck. Now where was I? Ah, yes. I was telling you how I managed to follow you. I merely had to ensure that I did not miss you when you left the Sedgebeck nuns and, after that, it was easy.'

'You were watching in the wood at Medely?' Helewise demanded. 'When — '

'I was. It was you, Abbess, who led me to that terrible discovery in the burned-out cottage. My heartfelt thanks are due to you and the brothers for undertaking a task there that should have been mine.'

She whispered, 'The burial?', and he nodded.

Stunned, she could not think what to say.

But Josse, she was relieved to find, was not so easily distracted. 'You still have not told us why you had to find Jerome,' he said. 'Nor explained why you blame yourself for making him flee.'

Bastian stared at Josse. 'Have you not guessed?' he asked gently.

'I imagine you intend to take him back to Denney by force,' Josse began, 'and make him honour whatever vow he has made to your Order.'

There was a small silence. Then Bastian said, 'Sir Josse, we do not force men to become Knights Templar.' A wry expression briefly crossed his face. 'Usually we have no need. And Jerome has no vows to honour; as yet he has taken none.'

'Then why — ?' Helewise began.

'Abbess,' Bastian said, 'I needed to seek Jerome out to tell him he had run away needlessly.' He put his face closer to hers, as if by so doing he might more readily convince her. 'I *had* to find him. Don't you see? Unless I did, he would always carry a needlessly guilty conscience, believing he had committed a grave sin where there had been, in fact, no sin at all.'

Swinging round, away from the little group, he said in exasperation, 'Abbess Helewise, Sir Josse, I did *not* want to haul Jerome back to Denney, fling him in a punishment cell and turn him into a Templar! I sought him so as to give him and Meriel my heartfelt blessings on their marriage!'

21

Helewise was finding Bastian's revelation quite hard to take in.

'You mean,' she said slowly, 'that all this — Brother Bartholomew's arrival, and his death, then your coming after him — has been purely to let Jerome know he is free to wed Meriel, and to give him the Templars' blessings for a long and happy life?'

'That was how it began, yes,' Bastian agreed. 'Although, of course, things took altogether a more desperate turn when we found out what Alba was capable of. When we guessed she had — ' He glanced at Berthe, then resumed. 'When Felix went missing and our terrible suspicions dawned about what that child might really have witnessed, then there was another, more pressing reason to find the runaways.'

Josse, Helewise noticed, was studying the monk. 'You really do care for Jerome, don't you?'

'I do,' Bastian said. 'He is, as I believe you know, my kinsman. But I should care for him anyway. He is a good lad. Headstrong and impetuous, perhaps, but still a good lad.'

Helewise pulled herself out of her reverie. 'Sir Josse, Brother Bastian,' she said, 'we have stood here talking for long enough. I intend to keep Berthe close to me' — she took firm hold of the girl's hand — 'but now, if you please, we must resume our search for Alba. Berthe, which path did you say she took?'

'That one.' Berthe pointed.

'Then that is where we, too, must go.'

And striding out with firm steps, Helewise led her little party away.

★　★　★

The great forest was uncannily silent.

Helewise, walking ahead of Josse and Bastian, with Berthe clutching tight to her hand, felt a growing sense of oppression. We have introduced a discordant element here, she thought, a shiver of dread going through her. And the forest doesn't like it. The birds have fallen quiet; the breeze no longer stirs the young leaves on the trees. It's as if — as if the whole place is holding its breath. There is no air.

Panic fluttered in her. Then, with her free hand, she grasped the plain wooden cross that hung over her heart. This is still Your place, dear Lord, whoever else may live and worship here, she thought, comforted. This new harm that has been brought in is not of our instigation. Please, of Thy mercy, protect us as we try to redress it.

Berthe gave her hand a squeeze. 'Are you praying, Abbess?' she whispered.

'I was, yes. I've finished now. I was just asking God for His help.'

'Did He hear you?'

'He always hears.'

'And will he help us?'

Helewise looked down into the earnest little face. It was not really the moment to explain how God's help sometimes takes an unexpected guise, and that we must have faith that what happens is always for our ultimate good. So she just said, 'I hope so, Berthe.'

Behind them, Josse gave a muted gasp. Instantly turning to him, Helewise said, 'What? What is it?'

Wordlessly, he pointed.

Ahead of them, the narrow track led into a small clearing. One or two ancient trees had died, and were lying at odd angles against their living neighbours. The space above, which had been opened up by their falling, had allowed new growth on the forest floor; a beam of sunshine lit up the glade, and the clearing was full of bluebells.

In one of the largest of the living oaks,

astride a sturdy branch leading out from the wide trunk, sat Alba.

Her habit, stained and torn from her scramble up through the lower branches, was crumpled up around her bare thighs, but her coif and veil were neatly in place. In her hands she held her rope belt.

Helewise turned to Bastian, who was right at her shoulder. 'Please, Brother Bastian,' she said, very quietly. 'I understand your urge to confront her, but please let me speak to her alone. At first, anyway.'

'She may be violent,' Bastian hissed back.

'I do not believe she will be violent towards me,' Helewise replied; she had no idea *why* she should believe that so strongly, but believe it she did. She stared into the Templar's passionate face. 'And if she threatens me,' she added with a small smile, 'then you have my full permission to come to my aid.'

For an instant he went on glaring at her. Then, grinning, he said, 'Very well.' He added something else, which she thought might have been, 'God go with you.'

Gently pushing Berthe towards Josse, Helewise walked on into the glade alone.

Alba was humming softly to herself. She did not notice Helewise until she was standing right beneath Alba's tree. Then, peering down, she said, 'Abbess Helewise. Greetings.'

'Greetings, Alba,' Helewise replied. 'We have been worried about you,' she went on, pleased to discover that her voice sounded almost normal. 'Berthe told us that she had let you out. We were all wondering where you had gone.'

'I had to get away, Abbess,' Alba said dramatically, leaning down from her branch. 'Brother Bastian would have me hanged.'

Not allowing herself to turn round and look towards where Bastian stood concealed, Helewise asked, 'Did you kill the young man?'

'I thought he was Jerome!' Alba's voice was indignant. 'I thought I had killed Jerome! I only guessed that I hadn't when I found out Meriel had run away — there was only one person in the world for whom Meriel would have abandoned Berthe, and that was Jerome. They tricked me back in Medely, my sister and her lover, and they made me kill an innocent man! Oh, Abbess, I have prayed and prayed for forgiveness. I didn't mean to kill *Felix* — that was Meriel's fault, Meriel's and Jerome's.'

'But you wanted to kill Jerome,' Helewise said. 'Why was that, Alba?'

'I couldn't let my sister leave me.' Alba

gave a great, dry sob. 'I have to keep them both close, Meriel and Berthe. While Father was alive, I knew they'd stay with him. He'd never have let them go. He only let me enter the convent at Sedgebeck because he had Meriel and Berthe to take my place. I was going to be an Abbess, just like you. I was doing really well, they all liked me. But then they told me Father was dead. I knew what would happen; I knew my little sisters would run away, even before his poor body was cold. And I couldn't allow that. They have to be *close*!' Her voice had turned shrill.

'Why must you keep them close?' Helewise felt a stab of compassion for the woman in the tree. Such a pathetic hiding place . . .

'People leave me,' Alba said. 'My mother left me, and I had to live with Father. Nobody liked Father, and so nobody would be friends with me. You see, Abbess? Meriel and Berthe are *mine*, they're all I have.'

'I do see, Alba,' Helewise replied. Dear God, but there was a weird logic in Alba's argument. 'But you can't keep them with you if the course of their lives takes them away. We're all put here for a purpose. None of us may decide what another's purpose is, no matter how much we love them.'

'I must keep them close,' Alba repeated doggedly. 'Oh, Abbess, it was such a perfect plan to come here! I was to be a Hawkenlye nun straightaway — quite a senior one — and Meriel, then Berthe, would become nuns too. We'd all be together, I could tell them what to do, and they'd never leave me.'

There were so many points to argue with in that little address that Helewise didn't even bother to start. Instead, reverting to something Alba had said earlier, she said, 'Your mother didn't leave you, Alba. She died. When you were born. She couldn't help it, and I'm quite sure it wasn't her choice. She must have wanted more than anything to live, because she had your father and you, and she would have been happy in her new home.'

But Alba was shaking her head; gently at first, the movement quickly became faster and more violent. 'No,' she hissed. 'No, no, no!'

'No?'

'It wasn't like that.' Alba sat rock-still now. 'She was in the whores' home, with the nuns at Denney. They tried to beat her sins out of her. Did you know my mother was a whore, Abbess?' She gave a dreadful laugh. 'God alone knows why they were all so sure I was Wilfrid's child, I could have been anybody's.' She fixed Helewise with a penetrating stare. 'Can you keep a secret, Abbess Helewise?'

'Yes.'

'There was talk,' Alba said quietly, 'that I was begotten on my mother by one of the monks. One of the grand Knights Templar. They keep their pricks, you know, Abbess, when they take their vows. The great and the good, they reckon they are, but let a pretty, compliant whore flash them a bit of leg and they're after her like any other man.'

'Is this true, Alba?' Helewise asked. Dear Lord, but if it were . . .

Alba shrugged. 'Maybe. How should I know?' An expression of craftiness came over her face. 'But if it's not, then why did they work so hard to provide a credible explanation for me? I wasn't the only bastard born in the whores' home, believe me. But I was the only one pushed out and given to its *father*.'

Helewise felt her heart pounding. Was this the truth? She had wondered herself how, out of a whore's many clients, those who had decided Alba's future had settled on Wilfrid as her father. But if they had known who the real father was, known it was a man who could never claim paternity, for whom even a hint at involvement with a whore would be devastating . . .

Suddenly she remembered Abbess Madelina at Sedgebeck. Saying of Alba, 'She arrived with a generous endowment, including both money and goods'.

Wilfrid had been a poor man. *He* surely could not have provided so well for Alba.

Who had, then?

A Templar with a guilty conscience?

But there were far more urgent matters to worry about.

She stared up at the woman straddling the branch high above. 'Alba, you must put all this behind you,' she said firmly. 'It is useless to speculate, and you only torment yourself with these thoughts. Wilfrid is dead, your mother died at your birth, and — '

'That's a lie.' Alba's voice spoke clearly, echoing through the glade.

'A lie? But — '

'They told me that, those warrior monks. It was easier for them if I believed she had gone beyond my reach. But she didn't die.'

'What happened to her?'

'They said she was mad. There's a madhouse run by nuns, close by Denney. In the same place where the whores' hostel is. Whores and mad people, it's all the same to the nuns. They shut her up in there, in the madhouse. I didn't know, Abbess. For years, all the time I was growing up, she was in there. I could have gone to see her, talked to her. But oh, no. They couldn't have that, could they? She might have revealed who my real father was.' Tears were falling down

Alba's white face now. 'So they told me she'd died at my birth, and I never knew her.'

'Alba, I'm so sorry,' Helewise said gently. 'It must have been a terrible blow for you, when you found out.'

Alba nodded. 'I wasn't meant to know, even after she really was dead. Only one of the nuns in the madhouse wasn't aware of the true story. She'd been looking after my mother, and apparently my mother had asked her to come and tell me.'

'Tell you she was dying?'

'No. Tell me after she was dead.'

'Was your mother sick, then? So sick that she knew death was close?'

'She wasn't sick. She hanged herself.' Alba raised the rope belt in one hand. There was a clumsy knot in one end, and she set it swinging gently. To and fro. To and fro.

Helewise watched the knot, hypnotised. Everything was beginning to feel unreal, unnatural. She gave herself a shake. 'Oh, Alba,' she whispered. But she didn't think Alba heard.

'This was hers,' Alba said. 'Her piece of rope. She stole it, and she hanged herself with it. The nuns gave me her poor, ragged robe, and this was wound up in the skirt.' A wail of anguish soared up into the still air. 'There's nothing for me any more, Abbess!

I've killed, I've been tracked down, there's a mighty Templar hunting me to make me confess to my crimes, and they're going to hang me!'

'You will be tried, Alba,' Helewise began, 'and — '

'*They'll hang me!*' Alba screamed. 'Abbess, Abbess, I don't want to die on the gallows, like some wretched thief, with the people all jeering and laughing! Not *me*!'

Suddenly she swung the rope out in a great wide arc. 'I've been trying to hang myself, and save them the bother. I wanted to do it with this, just like Mother' — the wailing had become sobs, loud, heaving sobs — 'but I don't know how to do the noose! Forgive me, oh, *forgive me*!'

She began to lean over, further, further . . .

Helewise rushed forwards, arms outstretched. 'Alba, *no*!'

But Alba ignored her. Leaning further and further over, she went past the point of balance.

And fell, headfirst, thirty feet or more to the forest floor.

Helewise heard Berthe scream, a sound so loud that it hurt her ears.

Slowly she crept towards the body on the ground.

Alba's head was at a sharp angle to her

shoulders; without even touching her, Helewise could see that her neck was broken. Blood was seeping from her ears, staining the starched white coif.

Helewise knelt down, already praying, and felt the wrist. No pulse.

Standing up, she finished her first, urgent prayer for the soul of Alba. Forgive her all her sins, dear Lord; of Thy mercy, show her Thy kindly face . . .

Then, turning to the edge of the glade where, behind the poised figure of Bastian, Josse held Berthe tightly against him, she said, 'I'm afraid she's dead.'

22

It was dusk.

Helewise had remained in the Abbey church after Vespers. The evening prayers had included an impassioned appeal for Alba, and the sisters had put their hearts into praying for the soul of their late companion. Considering that nobody had really liked her — Alba had not been a woman to invite affection — the fervour with which the nuns had pleaded with God to treat her kindly had touched Helewise deeply.

Now she knelt alone beside the trestle table that bore Alba's body. Sister Euphemia had straightened the twisted neck, and one of her nurses had dressed the corpse in a clean coif and brushed the mud and the grass from the black habit. Alba lay with her arms crossed on her breast, her face calm, those troubled, anguished eyes closed forever.

Standing up and leaning over the body, Helewise gave a muffled exclamation. Then, with a quick look to ensure that she really was alone, swiftly she reached down, picked something up and, with some difficulty since it was quite bulky, stowed it away in one of her sleeves.

Then she fell to her knees and resumed her prayers.

She recited the 'Ave Maria'. Then, her mind filled with the love and the mercy of the Virgin Mary, she addressed a special plea to her. Reminding her politely that Alba had cried out for forgiveness, she begged the Holy Mother to intercede on Alba's behalf.

'Sweet Virgin Mother,' Helewise prayed, 'have mercy on one of your daughters who knew no mother of her own. She knew she was a sinner, that she had taken innocent life. But — but — '

Words failing her, Helewise closed her eyes and, trying to fill her heart and her soul with her plea, dropped her face into her hands.

★　★　★

Some time later, she heard the door open and quietly close again.

She stood up, turning to face whoever had just come in.

She was amazed to see that two people were slowly walking towards her: Meriel and Jerome. She waited until they had reached her then, with a small bow, she stood back to let them see Alba's body.

Meriel gave a gasp, and put her hand to her mouth. Her face working, she shook her head. 'Oh,' she whispered, 'oh, I didn't want it to end like this!'

Jerome put his arms round her, holding her close to him, muttering soft endearments. Tactfully, Helewise withdrew; walking with soft footsteps, she let herself out of the church and stood outside to wait.

They were not long.

Jerome said, 'Abbess Helewise, I am very sorry that we ran away. But I saw — '

She put a hand on his arm. 'I know, Jerome. There is no need of explanations, nor of apologies. Indeed, when we set out into the forest earlier, it was my most fervent prayer that you and Meriel would still be in hiding.' She hesitated. 'I feared that Alba would do you harm.'

He was nodding, as if these facts were already known to him. 'Yes. We were not, as you appear to know, fleeing from her.'

'And I *think*,' Helewise went on carefully, 'that her intention was not in fact to hurt you.' She met his eyes; she did not want to spell out, in front of the weeping Meriel, that she thought Alba had run off into the forest only to harm herself.

He said quietly, 'I understand.' He glanced at his wife, huddled against his side in the

336

shelter of his protecting arm. 'Meriel?' he said. 'Are you feeling better, now that we're out in the good fresh air? She felt faint,' he added to the Abbess.

'I am not surprised,' she said.

'I'm all right,' Meriel said, wiping the tears from her face. 'It was just seeing her.'

'And you can only have heard of her death just now, when you returned to the Abbey,' Helewise said.

The young couple exchanged glances. Then Jerome said, 'Actually, we knew much earlier. Soon after it happened.'

'You — how?'

Again, the exchange of glances. Meriel muttered something to Jerome; it sounded like, 'We've *got* to tell her,' and, turning to face Helewise, she said, 'Abbess Helewise, we've been with someone of the Forest People. Er — a woman.'

A shiver went up Helewise's spine. Oh, but she remembered the women of the Forest People! Well, she remembered one of them, and one was quite enough. Trying to sound calm, she said, 'And who was this woman? Did she have a name?'

'She said she was called Lora.' Jerome was still looking uncomfortable, as if having spoken with one of the Forest Folk were somehow a disloyalty to Hawkenlye and its

Abbess. 'She seemed to know all about us, and she was kind. She fed us, gave us a drink. And told us where to find a dry shelter.'

'She'd gone away,' Meriel went on, 'but, this afternoon, she came and sought us out. She said there had been a death. We asked who it was, and she said, 'It is the one who carries a murderer's guilt. The Great Oak has answered her call.' Well, we realised she must mean Alba, but we had no idea what all that about the oak meant. She said we must go. That we could not turn away from those who needed us. Then Jerome — '

'Then I said that I was being hunted by one who wanted to take me away from my wife,' Jerome said, picking up the story. 'And she — Lora — laughed. She laughed quite a lot, Abbess, which we thought was weird considering she'd come to report a death. Then when she stopped, she looked at Meriel and back at me, and she said, 'It is not in the gift of any human being to take an honest, loving husband from his cherished wife. Fear not, he will not succeed.' Then she told us where to go, and she disappeared!'

His voice had risen dramatically on the last few words; with a giggle, Meriel dug him in the ribs and said, 'She didn't *disappear*, Jerome, she slipped away through the trees.'

Helewise's head was spinning. These two

young people had been so lucky! she was thinking. Their love and their honesty seemed to have impressed this Lora of the Forest Folk, and she had looked out for them.

She wondered how the woman had known about the death. Oh, dear Lord, had she been watching?

'Er — Jerome?'

'Abbess?'

'This place where you were, the shelter Lora found for you, was it nearby?'

'No, no, it was miles away. That's why we've only just got here — we've been walking through the forest for ages.'

'Then how did the Forest woman know about Alba?' she whispered. 'There cannot surely have been time for her to witness the death, come to find you, and for you to get back here!'

'She didn't see Alba fall, Abbess,' Meriel said, her voice low. 'But she said they always know when somebody dies in the Great Forest. She said — ' She broke off, her face going quite white. Then, in a whisper, she finished, 'She said the trees tell them.'

The trees. Yes, Helewise reflected, I expect they do.

Then, realising what she had just thought — how readily she had accepted a pagan superstition — she shook herself, and offered a swift, sincere prayer for God's forgiveness.

Really, she thought, still angry with herself, I've lived too long near this Great Forest!

Meriel and Jerome were looking at her in silence, clearly waiting for her to say something. Bringing herself back to the present moment — which was quite difficult — she said briskly, 'Now you must both get some rest. You have had an anxious time, these many days and weeks. You must put it all behind you, and think about the future.'

In a hollow voice, Jerome said, 'I cannot, Abbess. I have to go back to Denney and — '

But she was already shaking her head, smiling as she did so. 'No, Jerome. You do not. Bastian was not searching for you to drag you back to Denney. He needed to find you to tell you that you are free.'

'Free?' Jerome and Meriel spoke in chorus.

'Yes. You had taken no official vows, so there was no need for you to ask for release from them.'

'But I had my hair cropped!' Jerome cried. 'And I'd grown a beard! I only shaved it off to marry Meriel!'

Ah, but he's so young! Helewise thought, her heart melting. 'Those things are but the outer signs,' she said gently. 'They do not alone make a man a monk.'

'Thank the Lord!' Meriel said fervently.

Jerome turned to her and, with a whoop of delight, took his wife in his arms.

Thinking it was time to leave them alone, Helewise slipped away.

★ ★ ★

The Abbey was host to its young guests for almost a fortnight. During this time Alba was buried, and the first desperate grief of her shocked youngest sister began to abate.

Berthe spent much time with Josse. He did not turn the conversation round to Alba, and Berthe rarely mentioned her; for much of the time, they spoke of everyday matters. The weather. The burgeoning spring. The work Berthe was doing in the infirmary.

But once, the girl said, 'Is it for the best, Sir Josse, that she died?'

His mind flying across several possible answers, eventually he just said, 'Aye, child.'

She nodded. As if his word were all she had lacked, straightaway she seemed to be calmer.

And she never spoke of her dead sister again.

★ ★ ★

Bastian, too, stayed on for a while.

He had asked the Abbess to show him

where Brother Bartholomew was buried, which she did. They had put him in the little area, beneath three of the Vale's chestnut trees, that was reserved for pilgrims who died while at Hawkenlye. The graves there were plain and simple, but the grass was kept clipped and sometimes the monks planted flowers.

She stood by his side as he prayed.

'I had thought to take him home to Denney,' Bastian said as they walked back up to the Abbey. 'But I think now that I will not.'

'The decision is, of course, yours,' she murmured.

Bastian was silent for a moment, as if hunting for the right words. Then: 'He is very peaceful where he is, Abbess.'

More peaceful than he would be buried at Denney? he wondered.

But she did not ask.

* * *

Before Meriel and Jerome left Hawkenlye, taking the fast-recovering Berthe with them, Helewise asked the two of them to come to see her.

They stood before her in her room. They were, she noted, holding hands.

It was now ten days since Alba's death, and

the Abbey was still alive with a constant buzz of excited talk. It was understandable, Helewise realised, and probably inevitable.

Still, the sooner they could get back to normal, the better. And a good first step would be to see these two, and the little sister, on their way.

'Thank you for coming to see me,' she said, smiling at Meriel and then at Jerome.

'The thanks are ours,' Meriel said. 'I don't know how we'd have got through this terrible time without you, Abbess.'

'It is my nuns you must thank,' she said gently. 'They have been praying for the three of you. And, with them, prayer also has a practical side — it was a stroke of genius on Sister Euphemia's part, to ask Berthe to help her with the two new babies in the maternity room.'

'I don't suppose for a moment that she really needed Berthe's help,' Jerome said.

'Neither do I,' Helewise agreed. 'How do you think she is? Berthe, I mean?'

Meriel gazed at her for a moment before replying. 'She truly is beginning to get over it, I believe,' she said. 'It was a frightful shock to see Alba fall. It will recur in her dreams for a while, I dare say.'

'Yes, I expect it will,' Helewise agreed.

'But she is beginning to see that there was

343

really no escape for Alba,' Meriel went on. 'Even if you had refused to let Bastian take her back to Denney to answer for the murder of poor Felix — and there was no reason why you *should* refuse, Abbess, we quite understand that — then it was really only postponing the inevitable. Sooner or later, Alba would have had to face up to judgement for her sins.' She paused. Then: 'Is it fairly certain that she killed the monk in the Vale, too?'

'We think so, Meriel, although with both victim and probable murderer dead, there is no way we can be certain. But it seems likely. We surmise that Alba went to the Vale to check that there was nobody there who might have recognised Berthe. And, of course, she found exactly what she was dreading she'd find. Somehow she must have lured him outside, then killed him with his own staff.'

'She'd have recognised a Denney Templar all right,' Jerome said grimly. 'She used to go and spy on their comings and goings — she was obsessed with them. We never knew why.'

Helewise said quietly, 'I believe I do.' Then she told them what Alba had said about her parentage.

Meriel was aghast. 'Did you believe her, Abbess?'

Helewise sighed. 'My reason tells me I

should not,' she said, 'since I knew perfectly well that poor Alba was a liar. But somehow that makes no difference — I *did* believe her, yes.'

'Her father was a Templar!' Jerome breathed. 'No wonder my uncle Bastian was so keen to get her back to Denney. He must have been terrified she'd tell someone!'

Helewise looked at him. 'Your uncle was only doing his duty,' she said. 'He was quite right in wanting to have Alba put on trial for Felix's murder. And as for the other business, he may not even know about the rumour regarding the identity of Alba's father. The warrior knights are, I am quite sure, very discreet.'

Jerome grinned briefly. 'That they are. I've lived around the Templars for much of my life, and I've never heard so much as a whisper of gossip about babies fathered by illustrious monks.'

'And I do not believe it will benefit anybody if such gossip begins now,' Helewise said firmly, looking searchingly at each of the young people. 'Alba is dead, and beyond our help. Even if the truth about her could be uncovered, it would do her no good. And it might do the Denney Templars a great deal of harm.'

'If one of them really did beget Alba, then

don't they deserve having harm done to them?' Meriel said.

But Jerome put his arm round her, hugging her to him. 'The harm would affect all of them,' he said softly. 'And the majority do not deserve it.'

Helewise smiled at him. I couldn't have put it better myself, she thought. 'Brother Bastian is leaving today,' she said. 'I am sure he would want to say goodbye to you both, and to wish you luck.'

'There's no need for farewells,' Jerome said. 'We'll be going back to Denney, too, and there's no reason why we shouldn't ride with him. He's been very good to me.' He gave Meriel a swift glance. 'And he's promised to help us if we decide to settle back near Denney.'

'And will you?' Helewise asked.

Jerome was still looking at Meriel, apparently waiting for her to answer. 'No,' she said. 'We don't think so. Too many memories.'

'I understand,' Helewise said. 'What *will* you do?'

'Jerome has some money, left with the monks in trust for him by his father,' the girl went on. 'That's why we have to go to Denney, to arrange about the legacy. We think we'll use it to set up home somewhere around here. We can both work — Jerome was taught

346

lots of skills by the monks, and I can help him. We won't have much, but we'll manage. We'll have each other. And Berthe can live with us, at first.'

'At first?'

'Abbess Helewise, she wants to be a nurse. She loves working in the infirmary, and she'd like best of all to become a nursing lay nun, if you'll have her.'

'Gladly,' Helewise said warmly. 'But let's wait a while till she's older. She might change her mind.'

'She won't,' Meriel said with a smile.

* * *

Helewise went to the gates to see the three of them, Meriel, Jerome and Berthe, on their way. Brother Bastian was waiting for them, and beside him stood Josse.

She went over to the two men. Josse gave her a smile; Bastian performed his deep bow.

'Abbess, I like your friend Sir Josse d'Acquin,' Bastian said as she approached. 'He is a sound man.' He gave Josse a hearty thump on his arm; fortunately, it was the left one.

'Indeed he is,' Helewise agreed.

'I am full of admiration for your skill in

deduction,' Bastian continued. 'You make a good team.'

'The Abbess is the brains, I am merely the brawn,' Josse said modestly. 'On this occasion, I fear she has had to be both brains *and* brawn.'

'You were sick, Sir Josse,' she said. 'But even from your infirmary bed, you were invaluable.'

Brother Bastian gave a short laugh. 'If ever I have an insoluble problem at Denney, I may send for you,' he said. Glancing at Meriel, Jerome and Berthe, and seeing that they were ready, he swung into the saddle and beckoned to the other three. 'Farewell!'

Helewise and Josse stood watching until the four riders were out of sight. Then, turning to go back inside the Abbey gates, Helewise remarked, 'He said, if *I* have an insoluble problem. As if he were of some importance at Denney.'

Josse chuckled. 'Well deduced, Abbess Helewise,' he said, copying Bastian's tone. 'Our friend Brother Bastian is actually *Master* Bastian. He's in charge at Denney.'

★　★　★

With his wounded arm fully mended and memories of the disturbing presence of Alba and her sisters quickly receding into the past, there was no excuse for Josse to stay at Hawkenlye. He wanted to get home, back to New Winnowlands; Will would have managed in his absence, he knew that, but he missed his home.

Before saying adieu to the Abbess, he went to find Sister Euphemia. Steering her outside into the sunshine for a brief moment, he handed her a purse of coins. 'That is for you to use as you see fit, Sister. It comes with my eternal thanks for saving my arm and probably my life.'

She looked at him. 'I thank you, Sir Josse. I will put your coins to good use, you have my word.'

'I know that.'

'As to saving your life . . . ' She paused, eyeing him. He had the impression she was deciding whether or not to reveal something to him.

'Go on, Sister, you can tell me!' he said with a laugh. 'Whatever it is can't affect me now. Even if you say you almost gave me up for lost, it's over now. And here I am, still alive!'

'It's not that, not exactly.' Again she hesitated. Then she said, 'The wound was not healing. In fact, the infection was getting worse, and everything that I tried seemed to

349

make no difference. Then Sister Tiphaine came up with something, and it worked.'

'So I must thank Sister Tiphaine as well,' he said quietly. 'Which indeed I shall do.'

But Sister Euphemia clearly hadn't finished. 'Sir Josse, whatever it was — and *I've* certainly never seen the like before — she got it from the forest.'

Her eyes fixed to him, she repeated, 'The *forest.*'

And then he understood.

★ ★ ★

He found Sister Tiphaine in her herb garden.

'She told you, then,' she said, hardly looking up from her weeding.

'She did.'

'I've nothing much to add,' Sister Tiphaine said, sitting back on her heels. 'It wasn't Joanna herself that I saw, it was Lora.'

'Lora?'

'One of their elders. Much respected, wise, very skilled in the healing arts. And all the others arts,' she added under her breath. 'Anyhow, it seems Lora's taken a shine to her. To Joanna. Because of old loyalties, so she says. Don't worry about the lassie, she's doing all right.'

'But — does she — '

'No more!' Sister Tiphaine put up a mud-stained hand. 'I can't tell you any more, Sir Knight, because I don't know any more. That was the message, and you're lucky to get even that. They don't like to communicate with Outworlders, them Forest Folk.'

I know, Josse thought. But his heart was singing.

'Thank you, Sister.' He bent down and planted a kiss on her cheek. She gave him a surprised smile, then returned to her weeding.

*   *   *

He had obtained the Abbess's permission to send Brother Saul over to New Winnowlands to fetch his horse. As soon as Horace had been rested and watered, Josse set out for home.

'Take care of yourself,' the Abbess said as she saw him off. 'Come and see us soon.'

'I will,' he promised.

'Which are you answering?' she asked with a laugh.

'Both,' he replied.

Then, with a wave, he kicked Horace into a canter and set off for home. On a dull evening a few weeks later, Helewise slipped out of the Abbey and went into the forest.

She could not rationalise what she was doing. She felt restless, uneasy, and had done so on and off since Alba had died. It ought to have got better as time passed, but it had not.

And, thought the Abbess, I believe I know why.

What she was about to do would, or so she fervently hoped, put an end to her strange feelings once and for all.

She had been informed that Jerome and Meriel were now actually making plans to come back to the area. Which meant that, even though it was unlikely that Helewise and her nuns would see very much of them, one or two visits were not only likely but highly probable.

So this one thing that remained to be done must be done now.

★ ★ ★

Helewise went in under the shadow of the trees. She took the track that she remembered so clearly and, glancing around, followed it. It felt different, walking there alone. She was apprehensive — of course she was — but, she realised, she was not afraid. The forest and its folk would understand, she thought, and probably approve what she was doing.

They would actually understand a lot

better than anybody within Hawkenlye Abbey. Not that it was relevant, since nobody at Hawkenlye Abbey was going to know.

She hurried on.

The trees were now wearing their full summer foliage, and it was quite dark on the narrow path. But Helewise's footsteps were sound and sure; it felt almost as if somebody were guiding her.

She reached the clearing.

There was the oak tree, and the branch where Alba had sat. And there, beneath it, was the place where she had died.

Helewise knelt down and placed the package she had been carrying down on the grass in front of her. She undid the wrapping, which was an old and brittle piece of sacking.

Looking about her, she reached out for some pieces of dry grass, dead leaves, a few twigs. She arranged them carefully around the sacking.

In the midst of the makeshift hearth lay a coil of rope. Knotted at one end, fraying at the other, it was grubby and worn.

This, Helewise thought, this was the rope with which a sad and disturbed woman hanged herself. Her life was a tragedy, and her final sin of despair was to be pitied; even though she probably never asked forgiveness for what she intended to do, we should remember that wrong was done to her. And *I* shall ask forgiveness for her.

And this rope was also the terrible souvenir left to the woman's only child. She wore it all the time, and, in the end, she tried to use it as her mother had done. In her failure, she threw herself from her branch and broke her neck.

Helewise closed her eyes and prayed for some time.

Then, taking a flint from her pocket, she struck a spark against the tinder-dry fuel around the rope. She repeated the action several times, until at last she had a small flame. Bending down to blow it gently, soon the kindling caught hold. The fire was alight.

It took quite a long time for the rope to burn to nothing; Helewise had to get up two or three times to fetch more fuel. But at last it was done.

Helewise sat and watched the last small tendrils of smoke spiral up into the dusk.

And as she watched, she seemed to see figures in the smoke. A woman with wild hair and desperate eyes, clawing at bars in a stout door. Then a young man, laughing as he played his part in a trick that had such dire and unexpected consequences. Then a pilgrim, crop-haired and bearded, rather like Bastian.

And, finally, Alba.

Only this phantom Alba had a smile on her face. Arms up towards the spectral figure of the wild-haired woman, the two shapes seemed to flow together.

Then a sudden puff of wind blew the smoke away.

With a sigh, Helewise stood up, carefully covered the small, dying bonfire with earth, and left the glade.

THE END

We do hope that you have enjoyed reading this large print book.

Did you know that all of our titles are available for purchase?

We publish a wide range of high quality large print books including:
Romances, Mysteries, Classics
General Fiction
Non Fiction and Westerns

Special interest titles available in large print are:
The Little Oxford Dictionary
Music Book
Song Book
Hymn Book
Service Book

Also available from us courtesy of Oxford University Press:
Young Readers' Dictionary
(large print edition)
Young Readers' Thesaurus
(large print edition)

For further information or a free brochure, please contact us at:
Ulverscroft Large Print Books Ltd.,
The Green, Bradgate Road, Anstey,
Leicester, LE7 7FU, England.
Tel: (00 44) **0116 236 4325**
Fax: (00 44) **0116 234 0205**

Other titles in the
Ulverscroft Large Print Series:

STRANGER IN THE PLACE

Anne Doughty

Elizabeth Stewart, a Belfast student and only daughter of hardline Protestant parents, sets out on a study visit to the remote west coast of Ireland. Delighted as she is by the beauty of her new surroundings and the small community which welcomes her, she soon discovers she has more to learn than the details of the old country way of life. She comes to reappraise so much that is slighted and dismissed by her family — not least in regard to herself. But it is her relationship with a much older, Catholic man, Patrick Delargy, which compels her to decide what kind of life she really wants.

PAINTED LADY

Delia Ellis

Miss Eleanor Needwood was about to be married to a most unsuitable suitor when Philip Markham came to her rescue. He arranged for Eleanor to be in London for the Season, a guest of his sister, who decided that everyone would benefit if Markham married Eleanor. And thus the rumour started. The surprised couple decided to play along with the mistaken impression until a scandal-free way to end the betrothal could be found. But when Eleanor agreed to pose for a daring artist, the result was far more scandalous than any broken engagement.